A classic gay mystery available in print again!

Gay bookseller and reluctant amateur sleuth Adrien English's writing career is suddenly taking off. His first novel, Murder Will Out, has been optioned by notorious Hollywood actor Paul Kane.

But when murder makes an appearance at a dinner party, who should be called in but Adrien's former lover, handsome closeted detective Jake Riordan, now a Lieutenant with LAPD – which may just drive Adrien's new boyfriend, sexy UCLA professor Guy Snowden, to commit a murder of his own.

"A tour de force. I think this book is Josh Lanyon's best work to date. To use baseball parlance, he doesn't just hit this one out of the park, he clears the bases."
Wave for *Jessewave Reviews*

DEATH
OF A
PIRATE
KING

THE ADRIEN ENGLISH MYSTERIES
BOOK FOUR

JOSH LANYON

Death of a Pirate King
The Adrien English Mysteries, Book 4
Revised edition, November 2011

Cover by Kanaxa

Book design by Kevin Burton Smith

ISBN: 978-1-937909-26-0

Printed in the United States of America

JustJoshin Publishing, Inc.

3053 Rancho Vista Blvd.

Suite 116

Palmdale, CA 93551

www.joshlanyon.com

This is a work of fiction. Any resemblance to persons living or dead is entirely coincidental.

TABLE OF CONTENTS

Coincidence, if traced far enough back, becomes inevitable.

Hineu

CHAPTER ONE

It was not my kind of party.

Sure, some people might think the dead guy made it my kind of party, but that wouldn't be a fair assessment of my entertainment needs—or my social calendar. I mean, it had been a good two years since I'd last been involved in a murder investigation.

I sell books for a living. I write books too, but not enough to make a living at it. I did happen to sell one book I wrote to the movies, which is what I was doing at a Hollywood party, which, like I said, is not my scene. Or at least, was not my scene until Porter Jones slumped over and fell face first into his bowl of vichyssoise.

I'm sorry to say my initial reaction, as he keeled over, was relief.

I'd been nodding politely as he'd rambled on for the past ten minutes, trying not to wince as he gusted heavy alcoholic sighs my way during his infrequent pauses. My real attention was on screenwriter Al January, who was sitting on the other side of me at the long, crowded luncheon table. January was going to be working on the screen adaptation of my first novel, *Murder Will Out*. I wanted to hear what he had to say.

Instead I heard all about deep-sea fishing for white marlin in St. Lucia.

I pushed back from the table as the milky tide of soup spilled across the linen tablecloth. Someone snickered. The din of voices and silverware on china died.

"For God's sake, Porter!" Mrs. Jones exclaimed from across the table.

Porter's shoulders were twitching and I thought for a moment that he was laughing, although what was funny about breathing soup, I'd no idea—having sort of been through it myself recently.

"Was it something you said, Adrien?" Paul Kane, our host, joked to me. He rose as though to better study Jones. He had one of those British public school accents that make insignificant comments like *Would you pass the butter* sound as interesting as *Fire when ready!*

Soup dripped off the table into my empty seat. I stared at Porter's now motionless form: the folds on the back of his thick tanned neck, the rolls of brown flab peeping out beneath the indigo blue Lacoste polo, his meaty, motionless arm with the gold Rolex watch. Maybe twenty seconds all told, from the moment he toppled over to the moment it finally dawned on me what had actually happened.

"Oh, hell," I said, and hauled Porter out of his plate. He sagged right and crashed down onto the carpet, taking my chair and his own with him.

"Porter!" shrieked his wife, now on her feet, bleached blonde hair spilling over her plump freckled shoulders.

"Bloody hell," exclaimed Paul Kane staring down, his normally unshakable poise deserting him. "Is he—?"

It was hard to say what Porter was exactly. His face was shiny with soup; his silvery mustache glistened with it. His pale eyes bulged as though he were outraged to find himself in this position. His fleshy lips were open but he made no protest. He wasn't breathing.

I knelt down, said, "Does anyone know CPR? I don't think I can manage it."

"Someone ring 911!" Kane ordered, looking and sounding like he did on the bridge of the brigantine in *The Last Corsair.*

"We can trade off," Al January told me, crouching on the other side of Porter's body. He was a slim and elegant sixty-something, despite the cherry-red trousers he wore. I liked his calm air; you don't expect calm from a man wearing cherry-red trousers.

"I'm getting over pneumonia," I told him. I shoved the fallen chairs aside, making room next to Porter.

"Uh-oh," January said and bent over Porter.

* * * * *

By the time the paramedics arrived, it was all over.

We had adjourned by then to the drawing room of the old Laurel Canyon mansion. There were about thirty of us, everyone, with the exception of me, involved one way or the other with movies and moviemaking.

I looked at the ormolu clock on the elegant fireplace mantel and thought I should call Natalie. She had a date that evening and had wanted to close the bookstore early. I needed to give Guy a call too. No way was I going to have the energy for dinner out tonight—even if we did get away in the next hour or so.

Porter's wife, who looked young enough to be his daughter, was sitting over by the piano, crying. A couple of the other women were absently soothing her. I wondered why she wasn't being allowed in there with him. If I was dying I'd sure want someone I loved with me.

Paul Kane had disappeared for a time into the dining room where the paramedics were still doing whatever there was left to do.

He came back in and said, "They've called the police."

There were exclamations of alarm and dismay.

Okay, so it wasn't a natural death. I'd been afraid of that. Not because of any special training or because I had a particular knack for recognizing foul play—no, I just had really, really bad luck.

Porter's wife—Ally, they were calling her—looked up and said, "He's *dead?*" I thought it was pretty clear he was a goner from the moment he landed flat on his back like a harpooned walrus, but maybe she was the optimistic kind. Or maybe I'd just had too much of the wrong kind of experience.

The women with her began doing that automatic shushing thing again.

Kane walked over to me, and said with that charming, practiced smile, "How are you holding up?"

"Me? Fine."

His smile informed me that I wasn't fooling anyone, but actually I felt all right. After nearly a week of hospital, any change of scenery was an improvement, and, unlike most of the people there, I knew what to expect once someone died a public and unexpected death.

Kane sat down on a giant chintz-covered ottoman—the room had clearly been professionally decorated because nothing about Paul Kane suggested cabbage roses or ormolu clocks—fastened those amazing blue eyes on me, and said, "I've got a bad feeling about this."

"Well, yeah," I said. Violent death in the dining room? Generally not a good thing.

"Did Porter say anything to you? I couldn't help noticing that he had you pinned down."

"He mostly talked about saltwater big game fishing."

"Ah. His passion."

"Passion is good," I said.

Kane smiled into my eyes. "It can be."

I smiled back tiredly. I didn't imagine that he was coming on to me; it was more...an actor picking up his cue.

He patted my knee and rose. "It shouldn't take much longer," he said with the optimism of inexperience.

They kept us waiting for probably another forty minutes, and then the doors to the drawing room opened silently on well-oiled hinges, and two cops in suits walked in. One was about thirty, Hispanic, with the tightly coiled energy of the ambitious young dick, and the other was Jake Riordan.

It was a jolt. Jake was a lieutenant now, so I didn't see why he'd be here at a crime scene—except that this was a high-profile crime scene.

As I stared it was like seeing him for the first time—only this time around I had insider knowledge.

He looked older. Still ruggedly good-looking in that big, blond, take-no-prisoners way. But thinner, sharper around the edges. Harder. It had been two years since I'd last seen him. They didn't appear to have been a blissful two years, but he still had that indefinable something. Like a young Steve McQueen or a mature Russell Crowe. Hanging around the movie crowd, you start thinking in cinema terms.

I watched his tawny eyes sweep the room and find Paul Kane. I saw the relief on Kane's face, and I realized that they knew each other: something in the way their gazes met, linked, then broke—not anything anyone else would have caught. I just happened to be in a position to know what that particular look of Jake's meant.

And since I was familiar with the former Detective Riordan's extracurricular activities, I guessed that meant the rumors about Paul Kane were true.

"Folks, can I have your attention?" the younger detective said. "This is Lieutenant Riordan and I'm Detective Alonzo." He proceeded to explain that while the exact cause of Porter Jones's death was as yet undetermined, they were going to ask us a few questions, starting with whoever had been seated next to the victim during the meal.

Paul Kane said, "That would be Valarie and Adrien."

Jake's gaze followed Paul Kane's indication. His eyes lit on me. Just for a second his face seemed to freeze. I was glad I'd had a few seconds' warning. I was able to look right through him, which was a small satisfaction.

"I don't understand," the newly widowed Ally was protesting. "Are you saying…what *are* you saying? That Porter was *murdered*?"

"Ma'am," Detective Alonzo said in a pained way.

Jake said something quietly to Paul Kane, who answered. Jake interrupted Alonzo.

"Mrs. Jones, why don't we move next door?" He guided her toward a side door off the lounge. He nodded for Alonzo to follow him in.

Despite Detective Alonzo's "undetermined causes," it seemed pretty clear to me that if the police were interrogating us, they had pretty much ruled out accidental or natural death.

A uniformed officer took Alonzo's place and asked us to please be patient and refrain from speaking with each other—and immediately everyone started speaking, mostly protesting.

After a few minutes of this, the side door opened again and everyone looked guiltily toward the doorway. Ally Porter was ushered straight out.

"The performance of a lifetime," Al January commented next to me.

I glanced at him, and he smiled.

"Valarie Rose," Detective Alonzo requested.

A trim forty-something brunette stood up. Rose was supposed to direct *Murder Will Out*, assuming we actually got to the filming stage—which at the moment felt unlikely. She wore minimal makeup and a dark pantsuit. She looked perfectly poised as she passed Detective Alonzo and disappeared into the inner chamber.

She was in there for about fifteen minutes and then the door opened; without speaking to anyone, she crossed into the main room. Detective Alonzo announced, "Adrien English?"

Kind of like when your name gets called in the doctor's office: *That's right, Adrien. This won't hurt a bit.* I felt the silent wall of eyes as I went into the side room.

It was a comfortable room, probably Paul Kane's study. He seemed like the kind of guy who would affect a study. Glass-fronted bookcases, a big fireplace, and a lot of leather furniture. There was a table and chairs to one side where they were conducting their questioning. Jake stood at a large bay window that looked down over the back garden. I spared one look at his stony profile before sitting down at the table across from Detective Alonzo.

"Okay..." Alonzo scratched a preliminary note on a pad.

Jake turned. "That's Adrien with an *e*," he informed his junior. His eyes met mine. "Mr. English and I are previously acquainted."

That was one way to put it. I had a sudden, uncomfortably vivid memory of Jake whispering into my hair, "Baby, what you *do* to me..." An ill-timed recollection if there ever was one.

"Yeah?" If Alonzo recognized there was any tension in the air, he gave no sign of it, probably because there's always tension in the air around cops. "So where do you live, Mr. English?"

We got the details of where I lived and what I did for a living out of the way fast. Then Alonzo asked, "So how well did you know Mr. Jones?"

"I met him for the first time this afternoon."

"Ms. Beaton-Jones says you and the deceased had a long, long talk during the meal?"

Beaton-Jones? Oh, right. This was Hollywood. Hyphens were a fashion accessory. Ms. Beaton-Jones would be Porter's wife, I surmised.

I replied, "He talked, I listened." One thing I've learned the hard way is not to volunteer any extra information to the police.

I glanced at Jake. He was staring back out the window. There was a gold wedding band on his left hand. It kept catching the light. Like a sunspot.

"What did he talk about?"

"To be honest, I don't remember the details. It was mostly about deep-sea fishing. For marlin. On his forty-five-foot Hatteras luxury sport-fishing yacht."

Jake's lips twitched as he continued to gaze out the window.

"You're interested in deep-sea fishing, Mr. English?"

"Not particularly."

"So how long did you talk?"

"Maybe ten minutes."

"Can you tell us what happened then?"

"I turned away to take a drink. He—Porter—just…fell forward onto the table."

"And what did you do?"

"When I realized he wasn't moving, I grabbed his shoulder. He slid out of his chair and landed on the floor. Al January started CPR."

"Do you know CPR, sir?"

"Yes."

"Ms. Beaton-Jones said you refused to administer CPR to her husband."

I blinked at him. Looked at Jake. His tawny eyes were zeroed in on mine.

"Any reason for that, sir? Are you HIV-positive by any chance?"

"No." I was a little surprised at how angry I was at the question. I said shortly, "I'm getting over pneumonia. I didn't think I could do an adequate job of resuscitating him. If no one else had volunteered, I'd have tried."

"Pneumonia? That's no fun." This also from the firm's junior partner. "Were you hospitalized by any chance?"

"Yeah. Five fun-filled days and nights at Huntington Hospital. I'll be happy to give you the name and number of my doctor."

"When were you discharged?"

"Tuesday morning."

"And you're already back doing the party scene?" That was Jake with pseudofriendly mockery. "How do you know Paul Kane?"

"We met once before today. He's optioned my first book for a possible film. He thought it would be a good idea for me to meet the director and the screenwriter, and he suggested this party."

"So you're a writer?" Detective Alonzo inquired. He checked his notes as though to emphasize that I'd failed to mention this vital point.

I nodded.

"Among other things," remarked Jake.

I thought maybe he ought to curb it if he didn't want speculation about our former friendship. But maybe marriage and a lieutenancy made him feel bulletproof. He didn't interrupt as Detective Alonzo continued to probe.

I answered his questions, but I was thinking of the first time I'd met Paul Kane. Living in Southern California, you get used to seeing "movie stars." Speaking from experience, they are usually shorter, thinner, more freckled, and more blemished than they appear on the screen. And in real life their hair is almost never as good. Paul Kane was the exception. He was gorgeous in an old-fashioned matinee idol way. An Errol Flynn way. Tall, built like something chiseled out of marble, midnight blue eyes, sun-streaked brown hair. Almost too handsome, really. I prefer them a little rougher around the edges. Like Jake.

"Hey, pretty exciting!" Alonzo offered, just as though it wasn't Hollywood where everyone is writing a script on spec or has a book being optioned. "So what's your book about?"

A little dryly I explained what my book was about.

Alonzo raised his eyebrows at the idea of a gay Shakespearean actor and amateur sleuth making it to the big screen, but kept scribbling away.

Jake came over to the table and sat down across from me. My neck muscles clenched so tight I was afraid my head would start to shake.

"But you also run this Cloak and Dagger mystery bookstore in Pasadena?" Alonzo inquired. "Was Porter Jones a customer?"

"Not that I know of. As far as I'm aware, I never saw him before today." I made myself look at Jake. He was staring down. I looked to see if my body language was communicating homicidal mania. In the light flooding from the bay window my hands looked thin and white, a tracery of blue veins right beneath the surface.

I folded my arms and leaned back in my chair, trying to look nonchalant rather than defensive.

We'd been talking for thirty minutes, which seemed like an unreasonable time to question someone who hadn't even known the victim. They couldn't honestly think I was a suspect. *Jake* couldn't honestly think I'd bumped this guy off. I glanced at the grandfather clock in the corner. Five o'clock.

Alonzo circled back to the general background stuff that is mostly irrelevant but sometimes turns up an unexpected lead.

To his surprise and my relief, Jake said abruptly, "I think that's about it. Thanks for your time, Mr. English. We'll be in touch if we need anything further."

I opened my mouth to say something automatic and polite—but what came out was a laugh. Short and sardonic. It caught us both by surprise.

CHAPTER TWO

"Gosh, you look terrible!" Natalie exclaimed.

I batted my lashes. "You always know the right thing to say." I flipped through the day's sales receipts.

I'd acquired Natalie two years ago when Angus, my former bookstore employee, split for parts unknown. After a string of temps I let my mother— against my better judgment—persuade me into hiring Natalie.

Natalie, at that time, was my brand-new stepsis. After thirty-odd years of widowhood, my mother Lisa had suddenly decided to remarry, and with Councilman Bill Dauten had come three stepsisters, in order of appearance: thirty-something Lauren, twenty-something Natalie, and twelve-year-old Emma.

The Dautens were the nicest family in the world. I kept a watch out for the insidious undercurrents, the clues that all was not as it should be, but nope. Nothing. Okay, maybe Bill overdid the Jägermeister on the holidays and got squirm-makingly sentimental, and I could have done without Lauren and her many crusades—and Natalie had the worst taste in men I'd ever encountered outside of my own—but Emma was a pip.

"Where've you been? I was getting worried."

I replied vaguely, "It took longer than I expected." Anything I told her would hit the familial newswire within the hour, and for now I needed this to be an exclusive.

"Did you have a good time?" She really wanted to know; she really hoped I'd had a good time. This was one of the things that I found hard to get used to in having an extended family. All this friendly interest was nice but it was strange.

After years of it being just Lisa and me—okay, actually being mostly just me—all these interested and involved bystanders made me uneasy.

I glanced without favor at the boyfriend du jour: Warren Something. He lolled in one of the club chairs near the front desk, looking bored. Straggly hair, emaciated body, and one of those wispy goatees that made me yearn for a sharp razor—and not so that I could give him a shave. He wore a T-shirt that read *Chicks Hate Me.* Supposedly he was some kind of musician, but so far all he seemed to play was on my nerves.

Hiring Natalie turned out to be one of my better decisions. My only problem with her was she kept trying to persuade me to hire Warren.

"It was okay," I said. "Aren't you two going to a concert or something?"

Warren showed signs of life. "Yeah, Nat, we're going to be late."

"Lisa called four times. She's really upset you went out so soon after getting discharged. You better call her."

I muttered something, caught Natalie's eye. She chuckled. "You're still her baby."

Warren laughed derisively.

Yep, I was definitely getting tired of old Warren.

"I'll give her a call. Lock up, will you?"

Natalie assented, and I went upstairs to my living quarters. Years ago I bought the building that now houses Cloak and Dagger Books with money I inherited from my paternal grandmother. At the time I thought it would be something to tide me over until my writing career took off.

I turned on the lights. The answering machine light was blinking red. Eight messages. I pressed Play.

"Darling…"

Lisa. I fast forwarded.

"Darling…"

Fast forward.

"Darling…"

Holy moly. Fast forward.

"Darling…"

Jeeeesus. Fast forward.

Fast forward.

Fast forward.

Fast forward.

Guy's taped voice broke the silence of the apartment. "Hello, lover. How'd it go?"

Guy Snowden and I had met a couple of years earlier, and we'd been seeing each other since Jake and I parted ways. I hit Stop on the machine, picked up the phone, but then considered.

If I called Guy now, it wouldn't be a quick call, and I didn't have the energy to deal with what I was feeling, let alone his possible reaction.

I replaced the phone and went into the bathroom, avoiding looking at my hollow-eyed reflection in the mirror. I didn't need a reminder that I looked like something the cat dragged in. I felt like something the cat dragged in— after he chewed on it for a few hours. My chest hurt, my ribs hurt. Coughing really hurt, but suppressing the cough was a no-no because my lungs had to clear. A truly delightful process.

I took my antibiotics and stretched out on the couch. Fifteen minutes and I'd call Lisa, and then if I had strength left, I'd call Guy and tell him about the party and Porter Jones and Jake. Guy wouldn't be happy about any of it, especially the part about Jake. Not that I'd ever really gone much into my relationship with Jake; but Guy, who taught history and occult studies at UCLA, had been a suspect in one of Jake's murder investigations, and it had left him with not very friendly feelings toward cops in general and Jake in particular.

I thought about the party at Paul Kane's. Not that *party* was exactly the word for the afternoon's events. I tried to pinpoint exactly when I'd met Porter Jones. Paul Kane, who had been mixing cocktails behind the bar, had introduced us. He'd handed me a glass that had been sitting on the bar for a few minutes, and said, "This is for Porter. My secret recipe."

I'd handed the glass to Porter.

Of course Porter had had a lot of drinks that afternoon. A lot of glasses had passed his way...

* * * * *

When I woke, the buzzer was ringing downstairs.

I sat up, groggy and a little confused by a series of weird dreams. The corners in the room were deep in shadow. Just for a moment it looked like someplace else, someplace strange, someone else's house. It looked like the home of whoever would live here years after I was gone.

The clock in the VCR informed me that it was eight o'clock. Shit. I'd stood Guy up for dinner.

The buzzer downstairs rang again, loud and impatient.

Not Guy, because he had a key.

No way, I thought. I started coughing like I'd inhaled a mouthful of dust. Dusty memories maybe.

I got up, adrenaline zinging through my system like someone had flipped a switch. Heading downstairs, I turned on the ground level lights. I crossed the silent floor of towering shelves and strategically placed chairs, my eyes on the tall silhouette lurking behind the bars of the security gate.

Somehow I knew—even before he moved into the unhealthy yellow glow of the porch light. I swore under my breath and unlocked the front door. Pushed the security gate aside.

"Can I come in?"

I hesitated, then shrugged. "Sure." I moved out of the way. "More questions?"

"That's right." Jake stepped inside the store and stared around himself.

The previous spring I'd bought the building space next door, and between the bookstore and the gutted rooms was a dividing wall of clear, heavy plastic. Otherwise it didn't look too different: same comfortable chairs, fake fireplace, tall walnut shelves of books, same enigmatic smiles of the kabuki masks on the wall. Everything as it was. Me excluded. I had certainly changed.

I remembered when I'd first met Jake, when he'd been investigating Robert Hersey's murder. He'd scared the hell out of me, and I wondered now why I hadn't paid attention to that first healthy instinct.

His eyes came at last to rest on me. He didn't say anything.

"Déjà vu," I said, and was relieved that my tone was just about right.

It seemed to annoy Jake, though. Or maybe he was annoyed at being forced to remember there had ever been anything between us besides criminal investigation.

He said flatly, "I want to know what you were holding back when we interviewed you this afternoon."

That caught me off guard. "Nothing."

"Bullshit. I know you. You were hiding something."

Now that really was ironic. "You think?"

He just stared, immovable, implacable, impossible. "Yeah."

"I guess some things never change."

"Yeah," he drawled. "Two years later I find you smack in the middle of another homicide investigation. Coincidence?"

"You think not?" I started coughing again, which was aggravating as hell.

He just stood there watching.

When I'd got my breath again, I rasped, "If I were hiding something, I guess it was the realization that you and Paul Kane are also already... acquainted."

He didn't say a word.

"Same club, old chap?"

He raised an eyebrow. "You sound jealous, Adrien. And bitter."

Did I? The thought startled me.

"Nah. Just curious."

"About?"

I shrugged. "Not really my business."

"You've got that right." He was curt. After a moment he said slowly, "So that's all it was? You guessed that Paul and I...knew each other."

"In the Biblical sense?" I mocked. "Yeah."

Silence.

After we'd parted company he'd called twice when I hadn't been there to take his call. Or maybe I had been there, but just hadn't picked up. Anyway, I knew from caller ID who the hang-up calls were from.

And then, eleven months after the whole thing was over, he'd called and actually left a message.

It's Jake.

Like, did he think I'd forgotten his voice along with his number?

Silence.

It'd be nice to talk to you sometime.

As he himself would have said: *Uh-huh.*

Silence.

Dial tone.

What did he think we'd talk about? His marriage? Work? The weather?

"So are we done?" I heard the tension crackle in my voice and knew he heard it too. I didn't have the strength to keep fencing with him. I didn't have the energy to keep standing there pretending this wasn't getting to me, that it wasn't opening up a lot of wounds that weren't as well healed as I'd believed.

He said flatly, "Yeah, we're done."

CHAPTER THREE

"**I** don't believe it," Guy said. "There's something wrong with my karma."

"Check the expiration date," I suggested.

He paused in setting out little white cartons of rice and shrimp in lobster sauce to give me the British two-finger salute.

"Two words," I said. "Sounds like duck flu."

His smile was reluctant. His eyes, green as the curl of a wave, studied my face and narrowed. "You overdid it today, lover."

"I'm out of shape. I find murder tiring."

This reminded him of the thing I kept hoping he'd forget. "And of all the cops in all the world, why the hell would that asshole *Riordan* show up today at Paul Kane's? It's fucking unbelievable. I thought he was a lieutenant or something?"

"He is. I think he knows Paul Kane. It's a high-profile case. There's liable to be a lot of media attention."

"You don't honestly think they—he—thinks you're involved?"

"No."

Guy poured wine for himself and mineral water for me. He sat down at the kitchen table and began to eat, scowling. "You don't plan on…"

"No. I don't."

He relaxed a little.

I said, referring to the murder case where Guy and I first met, "When you talked to the cops about Garibaldi, you kept me out of it, right?"

"As much as was possible."

"What's that mean?"

"It means that Detective Riordan had a pretty good idea of where I got my information." He studied me. "He didn't push it, and neither did I since you'd asked me to keep you out of it. I couldn't help noticing…"

"What?"

"He has this little muscle in his jaw." Guy gestured to his own lean, tanned jaw. "And every time your name came up, the muscle moved."

"It was pretty much a permanent twitch by then."

Guy didn't laugh.

I reached my hand across the table. "Hey. Guy, I'm sorry this is bringing back bad memories for you. I'm not involved. I have no intention of getting involved."

He took my hand, but he was still not smiling.

"You're not the one I'm worried about. I don't trust that bastard Riordan."

* * * * *

Lisa phoned as we were lying in bed watching Michael Palin's *Palin's New Europe*. Actually Guy had been watching, and I had been dozing. Ever chivalrous, Guy took the bullet for me.

Gratefully, I listened to his side of the conversation.

"He's fine, Lisa. He's right here. Just having an early night."

Poor Guy. Nobody expects the Spanish Inquisition. Did my mother think we were in separate rooms? Sleeping in bunk beds? I lowered the TV volume with the remote control. The TV in the bedroom was Guy's idea. He found watching TV together more companionable than reading—not that we spent a lot of sheet time in intellectual pursuits.

"Yep, he's taking all his meds."

"Oh my God," I said.

Guy's eyes laughed at me.

"He's eating. He's resting. He'll give you a call tomorrow. I give you my word."

I raised my brows at this. Guy raised his own in reply.

Folding my arms behind my head, I stared at the streetlamp shining behind the lace drapes over the window. Not that I would have admitted this to anyone, but my lack of energy scared me. I knew it was normal after pneumonia, like the sore ribs and the ugly cough, but the fatigue and shortness of breath brought back unpleasant memories. As had the hospital stay.

When my number came up, I wanted it to be lightning-bolt fast. I sure as hell didn't want to end things struggling for breath in a hospital bed, hooked up to machines and stuck full of needles.

"Sweet dreams," Guy cooed and leaned over to replace the handset on its hook.

"I owe you, man."

"She's a doll, really."

"Mm. Bride of Chucky."

He chuckled and bent over me, his breath light and cool as his mouth touched mine. "Say the word and I'll make running interference a permanent part of my job description."

I kissed him back lightly.

"No?" He raised an eyebrow.

I sighed.

"What's it take to convince you I'm here for the long haul?"

"Maybe I'm just too set in my ways," I said. "I've been living on my own a long time."

"You're thirty-five, Adrien. It's not like your best years are behind you."

They felt behind me, I thought, with my heartbeat fluttering in my throat as it did more often now. But I couldn't tell Guy that. I couldn't tell anyone that.

"You know I love you," Guy said. "Right? So what's the problem?"

"I don't know. I guess I'm the problem."

"No. You just need time." He kissed me again. "That's okay, lover. You take all the time you need."

* * * * *

The next morning, Monday, Natalie and I were having a little debate about inventory loss control—Natalie taking the view that stealing books was not really a crime so much as a cry for help—when Detective Alonzo showed up with Jake in tow.

"Can we talk to you for a few minutes, Mr. English?" Alonzo asked over the din of power tools from behind the plastic curtain.

I looked at Jake. His face gave nothing away.

We went back to my office. Jake leaned against the wall as though he were strictly there in some official capacity as observer in a training exercise for Alonzo.

Alonzo said, "We were wondering if you'd had a chance to remember anything else after you made your statement yesterday."

"You mean like, did I remember I killed Porter Jones?"

He smiled, a genial cat to a smart-ass mouse. "Something like that."

"Not that I know of."

He looked interested. "What's that mean?"

I'd been debating since the evening before whether to mention the thing about handing Porter his drink before we went into lunch, and I concluded that it would be easier—safer—to have it out now. I said, "It means that if he was poisoned, then I think there's a possibility I handed him the drink that killed him."

"You think he was poisoned, Mr. English?"

"I think I'd have noticed if he'd been shot or stabbed."

Alonzo looked toward Jake as though seeking confirmation. "You got a little bit of an attitude, Mr. English, if you don't mind my saying so."

"I don't mind."

His black brows drew together.

"I guess you won't be surprised to hear that the coroner's preliminary findings indicate that Mr. Jones *was* poisoned."

"I see." And I thought I did.

"We've found the glass that was probably used to administer the poison. It was broken in a bag of trash, but there was enough to lift fingerprints."

"Let me guess. Mine."

"Jackpot," said Detective Alonzo. He did seem to enjoy his work.

I reminded myself I'd been through police questioning before and that I had nothing to hide. "I did say I might have inadvertently given him the poison. I passed him his glass right before we went into lunch. There should be other prints on the glass as well."

"The vic's."

"Paul Kane's fingerprints should also be on the glass."

"Well, it's his house," Alonzo pointed out.

Jake said, "The interesting thing is the poison."

I had avoided looking his way till now. His gaze was impassive.

Alonzo asked, "Do you have a heart condition, sir?"

Jake's gaze shifted pointedly to Alonzo.

I nodded.

"What medications do you take?"

"Digoxin and aspirin."

"Digoxin. That's a form of digitalis, right?"

"Right. It slows and strengthens the heartbeat."

"You take tablets or injections or what?"

"I take tablets."

I waited. I knew what was coming.

"You'll find this interesting. The autopsy results indicate that Mr. Jones died of a massive heart attack brought on by a fatal dose of some form of digitalis."

They both stared at me.

Two or three murder investigations ago I might have panicked. As it was, I studied Detective Alonzo, perplexed.

"The glass was sitting on the bar for a few minutes. It was crowded, especially by the bar. Any number of people could have slipped something into that drink."

"How would they know whose drink it was?"

"How would I? Paul Kane picked it up and said it was Porter's drink. I handed it to Porter."

"You need a prescription for digitalis, right?"

"No. That is, it's a cardiac glycoside found in the foxglove plant, which is pretty common." I thought of Lisa's house in Porter Ranch surrounded by a classic English cottage garden full of graceful spires of foxglove. "The entire plant is toxic, but the leaves especially so."

"You seem to know a lot about it."

"I watch a lot of TV."

"And you're a mystery writer. I bet you know a lot about poisons."

"Enough. I'm also a heart patient, so if I was going to poison someone I'd choose something that wouldn't immediately make me a suspect."

Detective Alonzo gave Jake another one of those looks as if seeking guidance. None was forthcoming.

"You know, I've got to say, Mr. English, I've interviewed a lot of suspects, and usually people react a lot differently when they're questioned in a homicide investigation. Innocent people, I mean."

"It's not my first homicide investigation." I replied. I turned to Jake. "Maybe you should fill him in on how we know each other."

He didn't move a muscle. "He knows."

"Really?" I smiled crookedly. *"Everything?"*

Not a bat of an eyelash. "Everything relevant."

He waited for me to say it. My heart sped up as I pictured myself speaking the words, betraying the secret he had protected for forty-two years. I could hurt him every bit as badly as he had hurt me—and the hurt would be lasting, permanent—devastating everything he cared about, from his career to his marriage. I could wreck him with a couple of sentences, and he knew it. He could see I was considering it.

He expected me to say it. His eyes never left mine, but there was no asking for quarter. He just...waited. Not breathing.

I said to Alonzo, "Then you know that I understand how this works and that I have confidence in the process."

Alonzo, who had been looking from Jake to me, put his hand to his jaw like I had sucker punched him.

Jake straightened from the wall and said, his voice unexpectedly husky, "Thanks. I think that's about it." He looked to Detective Alonzo who said, "Uh, yeah. I guess that's it for now. Thanks for your time, Mr. English."

"What was *that* about?" Natalie demanded as soon as the front door closed behind Jake and Alonzo. "Were they *police?*"

"Yeah. It's just routine," I told her. "Someone died at the party I was at yesterday, so they're just checking with people to see if anyone noticed anything suspicious."

"Oh, *wow*! You mean, like a murder?"

"Maybe." I was purposely vague. Natalie is a mystery buff, and she's often lamented that she wasn't around to "assist" me the last few times I was involved in a homicide investigation.

"Are you going to investigate?"

"You're joking, right?"

She seemed slightly puzzled. "No. Oh, hey, a bunch of calls came in for you. Lisa *really* needs you to call her." Here she gave me the look that managed to indicate sympathy while still spelling disapproval of me dodging my filial responsibilities. "Your doctor appointment is confirmed for three o'clock. And *Paul Kane* phoned."

"What did Paul Kane want?"

Natalie gave a disbelieving laugh. "Adrien, you never said you knew *the* Paul Kane!"

"I don't. He's sort of interested in one of my books."

"Interested? You mean in the *film* rights?" Her voice rose on the magic word "film." I winced.

"He's just expressed interest," I said hastily—and not totally truthfully. "It probably won't go any further than this." Her expression was disbelieving. "Did he say what he wanted?" I asked again.

"He didn't say. But he wants you to call him right away."

I nodded, returned to my office, and dialed Kane's number.

I expected to have to go through at least one personal assistant, but Kane himself answered on the third ring. "Adrien, how are you?" He had a great voice. Smooth and sexy. I wondered if he had ever considered recording audiobooks. "I can't apologize enough for yesterday."

"Is that a confession?"

"Is that a—?" He laughed. "You've been chatting with the coppers. Apparently I'm their number one suspect."

"I didn't get that impression."

"No? I did. Look, are you free for lunch? I've got something I want to discuss with you."

All I wanted was to lie down and sleep for an hour or two. I was so damn tired all the time. But I wanted this film to be made. The bookstore expansion was costing a fair bit, and I was still five years away from inheriting the balance of the money left to me by my grandmother.

"I'm free," I said. "Where would you like to meet?"

"I'm working on the lot today. What about the Formosa Café? Shall we say one o'clock? I've a proposition I think you'll find rather intriguing."

CHAPTER FOUR

Walking into the Formosa Café is like stepping into Old Hollywood: red bricks, black and white awning, and a neon sign. It looks like the kind of place where Raymond Chandler would have knocked back a few highballs while he was writing for the studios; maybe he did. The Formosa has been around since 1939 and still bills itself "where the stars dine."

Over two hundred and fifty of those stars are plastered on the walls in black and white stills, including Humphrey Bogart, Elizabeth Taylor, James Dean, and Elvis. Even New Hollywood dines at the Formosa—or at least stops in for drinks. The mai tais are legendary, and Paul Kane was enjoying one when I found my way through the gloom to his table.

"You made it," he said in relief, as though there had been some doubt about my showing up. He beckoned to the waitress, indicating a mai tai for me. I quickly signaled *no thanks* as I slid into the red leather booth.

"Don't tell me you're afraid I'll poison your drink," Kane said, pulling a rueful face.

"What would be your motive?"

He laughed delightedly. "You really *are* a mystery writer!"

"Tell it to the critics." I smiled at the waitress and ordered an orange juice. "So what makes you think the police suspect you more than anyone else?"

He sighed and reshaped his mobile features into another of those charming expressions. "It's been tactfully pointed out to me that I mixed the fatal cocktail."

I considered him objectively—tried to, anyway: he was distractingly good-looking, and this was the perfect setting for his old-fashioned handsomeness. I seriously doubted that Jake considered him a real suspect. Jake's sense of self-preservation would have ensured he steered clear of Paul Kane's sphere if he suspected Kane was really involved.

Wow. Maybe Jake was right. I *was* getting cynical in my old age. After all, even if Jake knew Kane was innocent, eager beaver Detective Alonzo would—should at least—consider the possibility that Kane was guilty. And, unless Jake had changed a lot in two years, he would allow the investigation to proceed unimpeded.

"Let's order," Kane said.

I had the chopped cucumber salad which offered carrots, cilantro, daikon radishes, bean sprouts, and Napa cabbage with crisp won ton strips. Kane had the rack of lamb. While we ate he chatted amusingly, cattily, about various celebrities—including a couple seated within earshot of us.

He was on his third mai tai—and I was seriously considering giving in and having one too—when he said, "I assume Jake mentioned that we know each other...socially."

I managed not to snort at the delicate pause before that "socially" comment. Because nothing said social occasion like butt plugs and paddles. I'd heard a few rumors that Kane, who was openly bisexual, was into the BDSM scene. It wasn't a world I knew much about, but it was Jake's playground—or had been before his marriage.

"I gathered," I said. I also gathered that he must know something of my own former relationship with Jake, although—Jake being Jake—no way would he know a lot beyond the fact that there had been a relationship.

Kane smiled as though amused by everything I wasn't saying. "He happened to mention that in addition to writing mysteries, you're something of an amateur sleuth—and not a bad one."

I choked on my orange juice—which triggered one of my coughing spells. When I had regained my composure, and the worried-looking waiters had retreated once more, I said, "No way did Jake tell you I was an amateur sleuth—let alone a good one."

"He didn't say you were a good one," Kane admitted with a little bit of a twinkle—yeah, a twinkle, and if that wasn't stagecraft, I don't know what is. "But he did say you had a real knack for it."

Was that what he'd said? Interesting. Because I distinctly remembered...

Yeah, misty watercolor memories. There must have been something grim about my expression because Kane said quickly, "It wouldn't be a formal arrangement or anything."

"What wouldn't?"

"I was thinking that you might—unofficially—ask a few questions."

"About?" I blinked. "You're not asking me to...what *are* you asking?"

He reached across and squeezed my hand in a lightly reassuring gesture. "It probably sounds mad, but I think someone like you would have greater luck getting to the bottom of this tragedy than Jake and his storm troopers. And I say this as someone who adores Jake, with or without his storm troopers."

I was still trying to make sense of the words "Jake" and "adore" in the same sentence. "I'm not sure I'm following," I said slowly. I already knew that Jake and Kane were playmates—but former playmates? Or was Jake back doing the club scene? And they were apparently friends? Like, did they go to each other's birthday parties? It seemed unlikely, given how skittish Jake had been about our own friendship. I said, "I feel like I need to ask: what exactly *is* your relationship to Jake?"

Kane's brows drew together. "I thought you knew. Jake and I have been lovers for about five years."

I didn't say a word.

Apparently I didn't need to.

He said awkwardly, "I don't know why I thought you realized." His sensual mouth pulled into a little grimace. "I knew about you."

There was a grinning Buddha statue sitting a few feet from us; I could see it peering right over Paul Kane's shoulder, and I felt like I had been staring at that knowing stone face for years, and that years from now I would be able to close my eyes and still see those crinkled laughing eyes and the wide gleeful mouth and the delicate folds of jowls frozen in sidesplitting merriment. And I thought maybe I didn't need to worry about my heart anymore because it had stopped beating a couple of seconds earlier, and I was still sitting there living and breathing—though admittedly I wasn't feeling much of anything.

"No," I said, "I didn't know." And I was startled to hear that level, cool voice come out of my face.

"Anyway," Kane continued, "It occurred to me when that ape, Detective Alonzo, was grilling me for the third time that people are far more likely to talk to someone like you than the police. Someone with a little tact. A little sensitivity. A little discretion. I could ask people to cooperate with you, and they would. Of course any information you uncovered would be immediately turned over to Jake. I'm not asking you to solve a murder or anything, just to...informally support the efforts of our boys in blue."

I laughed—and that was a surprise too because I didn't really find much funny about this. "You can't have discussed this with Jake. He would never have agreed to it."

"Er...no," admitted Kane. "But I don't tell Jake everything." His eyes met mine. "And Jake doesn't tell me everything."

Which I suppose was intended to restore confidence that my boyish secrets were still my own.

I said, "I don't think you realize how badly Jake reacts to interference in a police investigation. Believe me, it wouldn't be pleasant—for either of us."

I had a sudden memory of myself flat on my back, blinking up at the decorative molding of my entrance hall, and Jake, his face dark with fury, looming over me.

"Let me handle Jake," Kane said, and he spoke with easy confidence. Hey, and why not? He'd survived five years and Jake's marriage. Safe to say he knew Jake a great deal better than I ever had.

He smiled at me, waiting for my answer. It was petty, but it was a pleasure to deny him something. I said with false regret, "I don't think so, Paul. I don't think it would be a wise move on my part."

It seemed to catch him by surprise, though he recovered fast, hiding his disappointment. "Bollocks! Is there a way I can convince you to change your mind?"

I was shaking my head, still regretful but firm. I sipped my orange juice, and I was pleased that my hand was perfectly steady. Maybe it was because I felt numb. Or maybe it was because it had all been a long time ago, and none of it really mattered now.

He eyed me speculatively. "You know, mate, it's going to be very difficult for me to concentrate on getting this film of yours made while I'm under a cloud of suspicion."

He did it beautifully—charming and rueful and mostly joking. Not for one instant did it seem a serious threat. And it's not like I was a stranger to the gentle art of blackmail; my mother would have put Charles Augustus Milverton to shame. And in Kane's favor, I understood very well how it felt to be the prime suspect in a murder investigation. He had my sympathy there, even if I thought he was wrong about being the prime suspect; I happened to know that I was a popular contestant in the suspect sweepstakes too.

Which, come to think of it, did give me an incentive in seeing this investigation wrapped up as quickly and quietly as possible.

He must have caught my hesitation because he coaxed, "What about this? Suppose you simply start out by asking a few informal questions, and if you decide you don't want to continue, then it ends right there. I won't say another word."

I sighed.

"Please?" he said.

He really was a very good-looking man, and he really did have an engaging smile. All the same, I'd have read his obituary without a flicker of regret. And how unfair was that? He'd done nothing to hurt me. It wasn't Paul Kane I should be angry with—assuming I should be angry with anyone.

So I said slowly, reluctantly, "I guess it wouldn't kill me to ask a few questions."

You'd think by then I'd have known better.

* * * * *

Dr. Cardigan draped the stethoscope around his neck. "Your lungs appear to be clearing nicely. How are you feeling?"

"Tired," I said.

I know it isn't logical, but I don't trust a doctor who is younger than I am. Dr. Cardigan was a comfortable sixty-something with shrewd, black-cherry eyes and a brisk but attentive manner. I liked him about as well as I was ever going to like a doctor, and I trusted him. Which didn't mean I looked forward to seeing him, and if my stepsister wasn't apparently in the employ of my mother and faithfully reporting back to HQ on my every movement, I might have blown off my appointment at Huntington Hospital.

Especially after lunching with Paul Kane. About three minutes after I agreed to ask a few informal questions on Kane's behalf, I was having second thoughts. Anything liable to put me in Jake's path was a bad idea. And the very thought of poking around in Porter Jones's death was...wearying.

The black gaze met mine. "How tired?"

I shrugged. "Still short of breath, still coughing a lot."

"That's to be expected. Are you using oxygen at night?"

I shook my head.

"Adrien..."

"I'm not *that* short of breath. It's okay with a couple of pillows."

He gave me a disapproving look. "It's very important that you get plenty of rest and that you do not push yourself."

I nodded.

He studied me, and I tried not to shift uncomfortably. I hated this part. Actually, I hated all the parts of being a young guy with a funky heart. He said, "Because of your history it's probably a good idea if we run a couple of tests, do another ECG."

I kept myself from sighing again. He was liable to think I needed on-the-spot oxygenating. "Okay," I said.

He raised his brows at my tone and started scribbling out prescriptions. "Meantime, get plenty of rest, drink lots of fluids, and continue taking your antibiotics."

"Okeydokey."

He glanced up. "And cheer up, Adrien."

* * * * *

It had taken some doing, but I had finally persuaded Lisa to agree to riding lessons for my youngest stepsis, Emma. Mondays, Wednesdays, and Fridays, I drove Em down to Griffith Park and the Paddock Riding Club to watch her go through her paces. The kid was a natural—even more of a horse nut than I'd been at her age—which was why I had been determined to win that particular battle with Lisa. Next, I planned on getting Em her own horse, but I knew I'd have to wait for the right psychological opportunity to spring that one. I figured I could start small and suggest a hamster.

Usually Em and I would ride together after the lessons—Griffith Park has something like fifty riding trails—but a little less than one week out of hospital I still didn't feel up to it. Instead I watched her sailing over her jumps in one of the six sandy arenas—cute as a button in her riding apparel—and tried to think about how best to approach Porter Jones's widow. Significant others are always the first suspects in a murder investigation—which doesn't say much for the course of true love.

Anyway, thinking about how to approach the widow Jones was a lot better than thinking—brooding—about the fact that all the things I had believed about Jake Riordan were pretty much a lie. And now that I thought back, I wasn't sure why I'd believed he'd given up his S/M activities while he'd been seeing me. He had never specifically said so; I guess I had just assumed it. Because I wanted it to be so.

If I was honest, Jake continuing his S/M activities wasn't even the part that gnawed my guts. It was the idea that he'd been seeing Paul Kane steadily during that time—because I really had flattered myself that I was his first genuine relationship with another man. He'd said so. But whatever he called his encounters with old English Leather, five years was a relationship to my mind.

So, yes, it bothered me. And it bothered me that it bothered me because... Jesus Christ, it was over. It was two years over. I was involved with someone else myself, so why the hell was I standing there with the smell of manure and horse in my nostrils and my stomach in knots over something that didn't matter anymore?

It made murder seem like a cheerful change of subject.

According to Paul Kane, the only person at the party with motive to kill Porter Jones was his much younger and soon to be ex-wife, actress Ally Beaton-Jones. If Paul's intelligence was correct, Porter had been planning to divorce Ally, and he'd had a PI following her.

"Let me guess," I'd said. "There's a prenup?"

"Common sense in this day and age," Paul had replied.

And maybe it was. I'd never reached the stage of negotiations in my *affaires de coeur,* as my old friend Claude would have put it.

"Adrien, watch me!"

I looked up out of my thoughts, catching Emma's grin as she cantered toward the next jump. I gave her a thumbs-up and wondered if Lisa and Bill Dauten had drawn up a prenup, and what the odds were of my getting Em in any possible settlement.

Not that my mother's second marriage looked shaky. Far from it. Which just went to prove how little I understood about these things. I thought of Guy and my thoughts shied as though faced with their own unexpected triple bar.

As fond of Guy as I was, I wasn't ready to make any commitments—and hearing from Paul Kane that he and Jake had been carrying on the whole time I'd been seeing Jake didn't do much to improve my attitude. Why was it such a shock? After all, I'd known Jake was seeing Kate Keegan during that time—engaging in unprotected sex that resulted in a pregnancy—and I'd been able to deal with it. I'd even accepted it on one level. It was a little late to be angry now. Posttraumatic Sex Syndrome?

And why the hell was I once again thinking about this? Once more—with feeling—I redirected my thoughts.

My own impression of Ally and Porter was vague at best. If I'd realized he was going to get himself bumped off, I'd have paid closer attention. He had seemed too old for her—and way too obsessed with deep-sea fishing. She had seemed very...blonde.

Blonde or not, I couldn't see why she'd have to resort to murder. Granted, I was no judge, but she seemed like a girl who wouldn't have a lot of trouble landing another meal ticket—assuming her acting skills weren't breadwinner caliber.

Maybe Porter had told her one too many deep-sea fishing stories. In that case, she had my sympathy. There had been a moment or two at luncheon when I wouldn't have regretted seeing Porter impaled on a swordfish's bill and disappearing into the sunset à la Captain Ahab in the last act of *Moby Dick.*

Anyway, it wasn't like I had any theories, so Ally Beaton-Jones was as good a place to start as any. I just couldn't imagine her willingly opening up to me—even if she hadn't knocked her old man off—regardless of how sensitive and tactful Paul thought I was.

"Look, Adrien!" cried Emma.

I looked and smiled. Her cheeks were pink, her blue eyes sparkled, the dark ponytail bobbed perkily beneath her safety helmet as she cantered past, the gelding's hooves thudding rhythmically on the sand. I never saw myself as the paternal type, but even I had to admit I was pretty damned fond of Emma.

"Heels down," I ordered.

She giggled.

Paul had promised to phone Ally and set up my visit. That was fine as far as it went. I wondered if there was some way of my finding out the name of the PI that Jones had hired.

Jake probably knew. Jake was a methodical and relentless investigator. By now he'd be deeply immersed in Porter Jones's public and private lives, sifting and sorting through the kinds of things most of us would prefer to have buried with us. But cops can't afford to be tactful—not in the ordinary course of things. In a homicide investigation every minute counts; most murders are solved within forty-eight hours. Of course, that's because most murders are committed by morons.

Yeah, if Porter Jones had really hired a PI, Jake probably knew all about it. But there was no way I could ask him. I wasn't going anywhere near Jake. Of course, I could always ask Paul Kane to talk to Jake, but—funny thing—I didn't like that idea any better than the idea of me talking to Jake.

In fact, I liked it less.

CHAPTER FIVE

The Joneses were keeping up with everyone else in Bel Air.

The house sat at the end of a long, hedge-lined drive behind tall and ornate gates reminiscent of those guarding Paramount Studios. It looked like a small-scale replica of the Palace of Fontainebleau—and probably cost more. Just one of any number of the lushly landscaped multimillion-dollar mansions dotting the winding hillside of Chalon Road in the Platinum Triangle of Los Angeles's Westside.

A maid with a German accent opened the door to me, and I was escorted upstairs to an enormous bedroom suite. It looked like it had been decorated for Barbara Cartland—or Emma. I've never seen so many shades of pink in one room. The grieving widow greeted me in her red satin slip. By greeting, I mean she spotted me and said, "I don't have time to talk to you."

"Would you prefer that I come back later?"

"I'd prefer you not to come back at all." She held up two black dresses on hangers. "Which do you think?"

Did I look like Mr. Blackwell? "The one on the right," I said, which is what I always say on the rare occasions a lady asks for my sartorial guidance.

"That's what I thought," she said, and tossed both dresses over the winged back of a rose-colored Queen Anne chair. Then, propping her hands on her hips, she stared at me.

I estimated her age as a little younger than mine. She was very tanned and very blonde. I'd assumed because her hair was such a brassy color that she—unlike my stepsisters—dyed it, but the startling absence of eyelashes and eyebrows indicated otherwise.

"I just have a couple of questions. I won't take long," I assured her. The flimsy slip and bedroom setting pretty much guaranteed that. Nothing against Ally, who was built like a Valkyrie, because I wouldn't have been happy interviewing any half-naked stranger in his chamber.

"Hmph," she said with a little toss of her head. I didn't know women really did that. *Hmph!* Just like a cartoon character. Like Betty Rubble when Barney was more of a bonehead than usual. She turned away, rifling through one of those tall jewelry boxes that could have doubled for a walk-in closet, and muttered, "This is the dumbest plan. I don't know what Paul is thinking."

I was with her on that one. I said, "I guess he's hoping to circumvent a lot of unpleasantness with the police by having people talk to me." Yeah, hand me my monocle and top hat because I can babble this stuff on cue.

While she pawed through the crown jewels, I took a look around the bedroom. Either she'd had every trace of Porter removed or she was sleeping single. There wasn't so much as a stray slipper or tie pin. Nor was Porter featured in any of the numerous gold-framed photographs.

Of course, some married people did sleep separately. Or she might have gotten rid of all the painful reminders.

"Well, I don't see how talking to you is going to save me any unpleasantness with the police. I've already had to talk to them once, and I'm sure I'll have to talk to them again," Ally said. Which just goes to prove that a woman may be foolish enough to receive you in her boudoir wearing nothing but her slip, and yet not be a total idiot.

So I changed the subject. "How are you holding up? I never got a chance to tell you how sorry I was about Porter."

She raised her head and gave me a wide-eyed stare. "Can you fasten this for me?"

Where were the sleaze horns when I needed them?

She sauntered over to me and turned her back, indicating that I should fasten the necklace around her throat. I obliged. For all the obvious care and pampering that had been bestowed on Ally, there was something sort of coarse about her, but I couldn't pin it down. Her neck was a little on the thick side. She smelled of Chanel, which my mother occasionally wears, but somehow Ally made it smell cheap. Her back to me, she said, "I know what

Paul thinks. Everyone thinks I didn't love Porter, that I just married him for the money, but Porter and I—" She shrugged.

As avowals of lasting love go, I've sat through more professional presentations.

But I said, "No outsider can understand a relationship between two people." Hell, sometimes even the people *in* the relationship couldn't understand it.

"That's right," she said, turning to me in surprise. "People on the outside never understand. They always want to give you advice or tell you off or... something."

I said, "Maybe everyone hadn't heard the divorce was off."

"What divorce?" Her expression changed. "I know where you heard *that*," she spat. "That's totally Paul. I don't know why, but he has *always* had it in for me. Maybe he had a thing for Porter."

I tried to picture that, but the picture wouldn't come—thankfully.

She went on, "Yes, Porter and I did discuss divorce, and we realized we loved each other too much to do anything so silly."

"That's got to be a comfort to you now," I said. "I can imagine how painful it would be to have someone you care for die with a lot of unresolved—"

"Yes!" she exclaimed. "That is *exactly* right!" She gave me an approving lashless gaze. "See, gay guys always understand these things!"

"We're born with that understanding gene," I said. "Do you and Porter have kids?"

She swallowed hard at the idea. "No."

"How long were you married?"

"Four years."

"Was it your first marriage?"

She smiled at this bit of whimsy. "It was my first *real* marriage." She shot me a speculative glance. "You know, if I had to pick someone who I thought might have wanted Porter out of the way—which I wouldn't do because that would be *totally* crass—I'd suggest you talk to Al January."

"You're kidding." If I'd had a monocle it would have popped right out at that point.

She shook her head. "Paul didn't tell you *that*, did he? No. Because he likes Al. And because he needs Al for this movie. Al's like his Bosley."

"His what?" I had a sudden vision of Jill, Kelly, and Sabrina gathered around the loudspeaker to receive orders from Charlie.

"Oh, you know. His biographer. Al's like his personal screenwriter. Paul's happy to throw *me* to the wolves, but he doesn't want anyone looking too closely at Al January."

I deciphered this as best I could. "What would there be to see if someone looked closely?"

Ally got a mulish expression. "Well, for one thing, Porter and Al have never been that close even though they were all part of that whole Langley Hawthorne clique, and for another thing, they've all been arguing a lot recently. Porter and Al were arguing at the party. Plenty of people heard them, including Paul."

"I don't remember that," I said.

"I don't think you were there yet. You arrived pretty late." She smiled. "I noticed you right away." She gave me an approving look. "I like quiet, polite men. And men who wear Hugo Boss. I was hoping you weren't gay. Or that you were only half-gay. Like Paul."

"Uh…sorry," I said. "It's pretty much full-time now. The pay's not great, but the perks…"

She squealed with laughter. "I *scared* you!" Then she turned grave and dignified. "You know, I *am* a widow."

"I know," I said. And God help the unsuspecting Southland with Ally on the loose once more. I thought Kane had it right: Mrs. Jones wasn't all that broken up over her older husband's death. That didn't mean she'd knocked him off, though. Frankly, the poisoned cocktail seemed a little complicated for Ally. I figured she was more the type to run him over with the Jaguar or clunk him with a marble finial and toss him into the pool out back. "Do you have any idea what your husband and Al January were arguing about?"

She had moved over to the dressing table where she proceeded to put mascara on, tilting her head at an unnatural angle and ogling herself open-mouthed in the three mirrors. Framed there in gilt, she reminded me of a split-image Picasso.

"No." She formed the word carefully, still combing her lashes out. "Business, I suppose."

"Was business bad enough to kill?"

She shrugged another plump shoulder. "I never listened to Porter when he got going."

Ah. At last. The secret to a successful marriage.

"January tried to save Porter," I pointed out. "He was the one who administered CPR."

"You'll notice he *didn't* save Porter, though," she pointed right back.

"From the little the police have said, I don't think anyone could have saved him. It sounds like he got a massive dose of whatever killed him."

"Heart medication," she said.

"Did Porter have a heart condition?"

She pumped the mascara wand in the tube. "Nope."

"Do you?"

I smiled in answer to her indignant look. "See, I do," I said.

"Oh." She unbent a fraction. "Really?"

I said, "Can you think of anyone else who might have had a reason to get your husband out of the way?"

She blinked, creating an effect reminiscent of Malcolm McDowell in *A Clockwork Orange*. "Fuck!" She grabbed tissues and began dabbing away the black dots. When she had wiped away the smears, she recapped the mascara, and placed it neatly back on the tray of cosmetics. "No," she said flatly, and it took me a second to remember exactly what I had asked her.

"Did Porter have any enemies? Or any problems with anyone besides Al January?"

She shook her head, staring down at the collection of cosmetics.

"Was this a second marriage for Porter? Does he have an ex? Or maybe kids by another marriage?"

She brightened. "Yes. He was married to Marla Vicenza. But they didn't have any children." She slanted me a look. "Porter was sterile."

Too much information. See, this is why I really wasn't cut out for the amateur sleuth gig. I really didn't want to know that much about my fellow man.

"How did Porter get on with his first wife?"

"Fine." She shrugged. "Listen, if Marla was going to kill Porter she'd have done it twenty years ago." She waved a makeup brush at me and little specks of powder flew through the air. "Now is that it? Because I have to get dressed."

I noted that she had decided I needed to leave once she was putting her clothes *on*. I said, "Yeah, that's it. Is it okay if I call you if I have any other questions?"

She sighed. "I guess. I just want to make sure you understand that Porter and I were *very* happy. Our marriage had *never* been stronger."

"Sure. And thank you for talking to me so openly," I told her.

"I just want this all to go away," she said, and while I sympathized, I could have told her from personal experience that murder took a long time to go away.

I found my own way downstairs through all the marble and tile and priceless art. I'd rarely seen a place that looked less lived-in, unless it *was* the Palace of Fontainebleau. Casa Jones had the chill feel of an after-hours museum. Maybe it was the décor or maybe it was just the domestic vibe.

Not that I was convinced Ally was a murderess. I thought she had been telling the truth right up until the end of our interview. And she might still have been telling the truth when I asked her about other people with a motive for wanting Porter out of the way, but she had definitely got cagey. Of course everyone got cagey in a murder investigation—including me.

She didn't have any qualms about putting Al January under the bus, so it wasn't like she was resisting the idea that Porter had been murdered. She seemed to have accepted that. So who had she suddenly realized had a motive for murder—and why did it bother her?

I crossed the brick courtyard, climbed into my Forester and started down the long drive through what looked like a private park. Positioned outside the gates at the bottom of the driveway was a silver unmarked police car, prickling with antennae. Jake Riordan leaned against the side of the car, arms folded, clearly waiting.

I pulled through the gates and parked beside his car, rolling down my window.

"Well, well," he said. "This can't be a coincidence."

"It could," I said. "The odds aren't high, but they do exist."

"Uh-huh." His face was impassive as he stared at me, and I felt a flare of nerves. I think it was nerves; certainly I knew firsthand just how unpleasant he could make himself. "So you're trying to tell me that this is just a sympathy call, and you're not thinking of sticking your nose into this investigation?"

I didn't say anything. According to Paul Kane, my asking a few questions wasn't supposed to be a problem, but here Jake was, and that generally spelled p-r-o-b-l-e-m in my book.

Into my silence, he said, "You mean like you kept your nose out of the Garibaldi investigation?"

"Sure," I said warily.

He snorted. "You'd think with all the practice you'd be better at lying."

"*My* lies?" I said, forgetting caution in an irrational surge of anger as I remembered Paul Kane admitting that Jake had been fucking him all the time he had been fucking me. He straightened up at whatever he read in my face. I hoped we weren't in for another wrestling match because, really, what would the neighbors think? Even in Bel Air, where they say celebrities get away with murder, there were standards.

I said, "Maybe I was invited over here."

"Maybe you were," he agreed—and it dawned on me that despite the hard appraisal of his eyes, he wasn't angry. He should have been. The old Jake would have been. This Jake seemed...watchful? Guarded? The truth was, I didn't know what he seemed. I couldn't read him. And that, more than anything, confirmed for me how much time had passed since we were together. *Together* being relative.

It was painful and it was freeing at the same time.

"Maybe me and Mrs. Jones, we got a thing going on," I said.

His mouth twitched into that reluctant, wry half smile I remembered so well. "I hope not," he said. "That would make you a prime suspect in Mr. Jones's murder."

"I thought I already was."

Astonishingly, he said, "Yeah. Well. Maybe we should talk."

"Is that why you're waiting here?"

"I'm waiting for Alonzo," he said. "He's late." He checked his watch, and I found myself staring at his wedding ring again. Not that it was particularly flashy, but it kept catching my eye. "It's nearly lunchtime. Let's go grab something to eat."

I didn't want to have lunch with him. I didn't want to ever see him again, but I needed to hear what he had to say, so I nodded and rolled up my window.

I followed him to the Beverly Glen Deli at the top of Beverly Glen Boulevard just below Mulholland Drive.

We got a table on the patio. The sun was already warm on this late June morning, which was fine with me; I felt like I'd been cold ever since I got out of the hospital. Jake sat back in his chair, studying me, and I studied him right back.

What was his secret? Did he get vitamin B shots? How the hell did he keep up with all the men and women and barnyard animals in his life? And if he'd intended to continue playing dangerous liaisons with Paul Kane, what about all that bullshit about breaking off with me because he wanted a real marriage? It didn't make sense—even from Jake's admittedly screwy point of view.

Or maybe he hadn't intended to continue with Kane. Maybe nine-to-five normal had just proven harder than Jake anticipated. Two years ago, desperate for a family and a "normal" life, he'd broken off his relationship with me in order to marry policewoman Kate Keegan. End of story. A few months later I'd learned from his partner, Paul Chan, a member of the writing group I ran at the bookstore, that Kate had miscarried and returned to duty. I guess there was still a chance of the family Jake always wanted, but the fact that he had resumed his old extracurricular activities—had, apparently, never broken them completely off—seemed to limit his chances of success.

I wondered if I'd have still managed to restrain myself from outing him to Detective Alonzo if I'd known then about the five years with Paul Kane. I wanted to think I was that chivalrous, but I wasn't sure.

The waitress appeared and handed us menus. I ordered orange juice. Jake ordered coffee. His cell phone rang. "Alonzo," he said, and he excused himself.

I watched the locals come and go in their Mercedes and Maseratis, picking up their take-out orders of lox and cream cheese or corned beef sandwiches. Even the car exhaust smelled more expensive in Bel Air.

Jake returned a few minutes later and sat down again.

Neither of us said anything. It was the strangest moment. I thought of all the times I had longed for something as simple as going to eat with him that he didn't spend the entire time worrying about somebody he knew seeing us together, and I thought of how we had never run out of things to say to each other until today.

The waitress brought our beverages and prepared to take our orders. Jake nodded for me to go first.

I said, "No, that's okay. I'm not hungry."

He scowled. "You need to eat something. You look like a goddamn skeleton."

I sighed. "I know, I know. I look like the skeleton of that guy who was in *Red River*."

It was an old joke. I didn't think he'd remember, but his mouth tugged and he uttered a brief, harsh laugh. He shook his head like *I* was the nut at the table, and said to the waitress, "We'll both have the chicken pot pie."

She raised her eyebrows at this highhandedness, but I've learned to pick my battles. "Yeah, that's fine," I confirmed indifferently.

She went away and Jake drummed his fingers restlessly on the table. His eyes rested on the cars in the parking lot—probably mentally running wants and warrants. He asked abruptly, "So, how did you get pneumonia?"

Dear God. We were going to make conversation.

"How does anybody get it?" I finished my orange juice. I wasn't in the mood for chitchat—and I didn't remember it being Jake's style either. At this rate he'd be asking about my mother and I'd bounce my juice glass off his head. "I caught the flu and it went into pneumonia." Two weeks' worth. I was relatively young and reasonably healthy, but my heart complicated things.

"You didn't get a flu shot?"

We'd had an argument on this very subject about a million years ago. Jake, being a public servant, was obsessed with the notion that the right people had their fair share of flu shots. People like me. People technically at risk.

I gave him a long look. "No, Lieutenant Riordan. I took a chance. Now I've learned my lesson."

There was another one of those bizarre pauses. The waitress brought our pot pies, refilled Jake's coffee and asked if I wanted another juice. I declined.

Jake mashed the top crust of his pot pie, letting the heat escape in a spurt of lava-hot gravy and steam. It seemed so him: blunt and efficient. His lashes threw dark crescents on his cheekbones. I'd forgotten how long his eyelashes were. He raised his gaze to my face, and I realized I'd been staring. He said, "Did you know Calamity Jane died of pneumonia?"

"No kidding."

His tongue appeared to be probing his back molar. I had a sudden unsettling memory of other things it had probed. "I saw it on the History Channel." His light, restless eyes tilted in a sudden smile. "That's the kind of useless knowledge you always had handy."

I snorted, looked away, watched a blue jay stealing crust from beneath another table. When I looked back Jake was contemplating me with an expression I couldn't, for the life of me, fathom.

He said in that brusque way, "Let's stop fencing. Paul told me his idea of having you go around quizzing people."

"And you think it's a lousy idea," I said. "And so do I."

"I didn't say that."

At my expression, he shrugged. "I'm not averse to using outside resources when circumstances warrant it."

"Who are you and what have you done with that asshole Riordan?" I asked.

His mouth curved again in one of those grimaces that was not exactly a smile. "Hey, special circumstances call for special measures."

"Sure, but since when do you not think me asking questions of suspects is a really bad idea?"

He said, "I told you a long time ago you had a knack for investigation."

"That's funny," I said. "I do not remember that. I remember being told to butt out on pain of death."

He flushed. "I never—" A muscle moved in his jaw and he said, "You're good at talking to people. You like people and they like you. You're easy to talk to—and they end up telling you things. So here's the deal: so long as you let me know who you plan on talking to—and turn over to me anything you learn—I don't see a problem. It might even be helpful."

"Turn over to *you* anything I learn," I repeated. "Not Detective Alonzo?"

"I'll brief Detective Alonzo on anything relevant."

My smile must have been sardonic because he said irritably, "Whatever you're thinking, you're off base. This is a very close-knit community, and we—the police—have to tread carefully. If Paul can convince these people to open up to you, it's a win-win for all of us."

Unbelievable. I picked up my fork and started eating. I wouldn't have believed it if I hadn't heard it myself. Jake was trying to intercede behind the scenes on behalf of his lover. And he was willing to use me to do it. I felt disgusted and disappointed, but really, what the hell did it matter? Whatever his motives were, they didn't concern me, and I should be grateful that he was giving me the opportunity to clear myself of suspicion as well. Which reminded me.

"Does Alonzo really think I'm a suspect?"

"He finds your attitude...suspicious."

Feeling his gaze, I raised my eyes, and sure enough he was staring at me—at my mouth. I licked my bottom lip suspecting errant pastry crumbs. His gaze flickered.

I needled, "And did you vouch for me?"

"I told him not to waste his time."

I said, "But I could have changed, you know. Maybe I'm not the guy you thought I was. Maybe I never was."

He met my gaze levelly. "I don't think you killed Porter Jones," he said.

I let it go. "Who do you like for it?" I asked.

"I think the wife's as good a place to start as any. What did she have to say?"

"That she and Porter had their problems but that was all in the past. She said Paul has it in for her, although she didn't make it clear on why that would be. She tapped Al January."

"The screenwriter?"

I nodded, forcing myself to take another bite of pot pie—the food was good. I just wasn't hungry these days.

"Did she offer any reason why she thought January might want her husband out of the way?"

"She said they never got along and that they were arguing the afternoon of the party."

"That shouldn't be hard to verify," Jake said. "Did you have a chance to form any opinion of the Joneses at the party?"

"Not really. They didn't seem to spend much time together, but married people don't always hang out at parties." I said consideringly, "There didn't seem to be any sign of him in her bedroom, and she isn't exactly prostrate with grief." I pushed my plate away.

"Is that all you're eating?" he questioned, disapproval clear.

I glanced down. "Yeah." And then unkindly, "You want the rest? You always did have quite an appetite—although you haven't done a bad job of keeping the weight off."

He stopped midchew. There was a hint of color in his face. He swallowed and said mildly, "You have changed."

I felt petty and mean-spirited—especially since he was the leanest I'd ever known him. All hard muscle and bone. All sharp edges and bite—except he wasn't biting.

When I couldn't come up with a reply, he said, as though that exchange hadn't happened, "The wife seems to inherit the bulk of Jones's estate—that's several million motives right there."

"Except I don't think she has the brains to poison someone without taking herself out as well."

"You'd be surprised."

"Yeah, I can still be surprised," I agreed. His eyes met mine, and I realized I needed to knock it off if I didn't want a confrontation—and I didn't. It was over. And it's not like I had been some virginal youth seduced off the streets of Paris by the wicked comte. I'd known what I was getting into. I amended, "Well, they say poison is a woman's weapon."

"Yeah, but not always," Jake said, "so don't make any assumptions. Since our killer used heart medication to trigger a fatal attack, I'd say it wouldn't hurt you to be especially careful about eating or drinking anything anyone offers you. Someone might argue that you accidentally overmedicated yourself."

It had occurred to me that what I was doing was potentially dangerous. Even so, what Jake said gave me pause. I didn't plan on pushing anyone too hard or too far, but who knew how a guilty conscience might interpret a few casual questions?

I asked, "Would you happen to know the name of the PI that Porter used?"

His face went blank. "What PI?"

Hell. My mistake. I said cautiously, "I had the impression Porter had hired a PI to follow Ally."

"Did she tell you that or did it come from Paul?"

I said reluctantly, "Paul mentioned it, yeah."

How well I remembered that old flash of anger—and how happy I was that this time it wasn't directed at me. Jake said curtly, "Leave the PI to me. That's a different thing."

He didn't say anything else but I could see that he was not happy. We finished our meal—rather, he finished his and I watched people go in and out of the pet shop next door. I thought about what Lisa would do if I showed up with a puppy for Emma. What she would do was call my bluff, and as I didn't really have a place to keep a dog, I let the idea go.

Jake paid the bill—and since as far as I was concerned this was a business lunch, I let him pick up the tab without comment. We parted ways as soon as we were through the glass door, Jake heading for the back parking lot, I walking toward the front. As I unlocked the Forester, he called, "Hey."

I turned inquiringly, and Jake was striding back toward me.

"I'm dead serious about this: I want you to call before and after each interview. Understood?"

Understood? Wow. Was there an echo out here? Like from two years ago?

I sketched a salute and he said as though I had objected—which I wouldn't, since it made perfect sense to me to have some kind of safety net, "Call me *before* you talk to anyone else."

And for one stupid moment, I was actually touched, thinking he might be concerned for me—except that his concern would be that I didn't screw up his investigation or that a civilian didn't get injured poking around. Either scenario would not go over well with the brass, and no way would Jake want to endanger those all-important stripes he wore to funerals and award ceremonies.

"And here I thought you didn't care anymore." I was smiling, mocking him a bit—and myself.

He said evenly, "You're the one who cut all ties, Adrien. That wasn't my choice."

I don't know why his words hit me so hard. To start with, it wasn't true—but that was sure as hell not a discussion I planned on ever having with him. My smiled faded. I said, "Ancient history."

He didn't say anything.

I got into my car, started the engine, and reversed under his hard gaze. As I pulled out of the parking lot, I could see him in my rearview, standing there straight as a soldier, the afternoon sun shining on his blond hair.

CHAPTER SIX

*D*ear Adrien,

I hope you are well and that business is great. I have been thinking of coming home. Do I still have my job at Cloak and Dagger Books?

Yours sincerely,
Angus Gordon

"Did you forget to meet Lisa for lunch?" Natalie asked over the din of power tools and construction workers shouting to each other behind the plastic wall that separated Cloak and Dagger books from the adjoining space.

I looked up blankly from the postcard offering four scenic shots of the pyramids at Chichen Itza. "Huh?"

She said, "Isn't today your day for lunch with Lisa?"

"Jesus!" I yelped, dropping the card—and knocking over the stack of mail that had accumulated while I was ill and that I'd been sorting through.

"Adrien! What's the matter with you?"

"It totally skipped my mind."

Her blue eyes widened. "Yeeowch," she said, which was the understatement of the year.

By then I was on my cell phone dialing.

Before my mother remarried, we had a long-standing tradition of Saturday brunch. She wanted to keep up this tradition after her marriage—and include her new family and Guy in the mix. I'd declined on the basis of not being able to afford getting genteelly snockered with the stepfamily every weekend, and had managed to move our weekly session to lunch on the first Tuesday of the month. I told myself that this way it kept the innocent bystander casualties to a minimum.

I got her on the first ring.

"Adrien!" Lisa said, and lucky for me the blend was ninety percent relief and only ten percent caustic acid.

"Lisa, I can't apologize enough," I said—although I was well aware I was going to have to. I couldn't believe I'd forgotten, and put it down to the fact that my schedule was still whacked after nearly a week in hospital.

"Why weren't you answering your cell phone? I've been so worried. Darling, *where* in the world have you been?"

I wasn't about to tell her where I'd been. Jake Riordan had never been on Lisa's A-list, and she'd been even less keen on him after he and I had parted ways—not that I'd ever discussed my relationship with her. Before or after.

"I know, I'm sorry. I just got caught up in some things." The story of my life, actually.

She protested, "But Natalie says you haven't been at the shop all day."

If only they hadn't outlawed corporal punishment for bookstore employees with big mouths. "No, I've been running errands," I admitted, glaring at Natalie.

She spread her hands in a *What? What'd I do?*

"Darling, you're not well enough to do all this racing around. Horseback riding lessons for Emma last night and these mysterious errands today. You're just out of hospital. You mustn't tax yourself."

I managed to swallow my impatience. "Lisa, I'm fine. Really. And I've been out of the hospital for a week."

"You're not strong, darling. I wish—"

"I know you do," I said. "So what's the plan now?"

There was a pause while she registered my tone. Then she sighed. "Well, we've missed lunch. I suppose we could meet for drinks."

My heart sank. There was nothing I wanted more than to lie down for half an hour, but I could hardly insist on naptime, having stood her up and then made a point of how terrific I felt.

We arranged to meet at Villa Piacere on Ventura Boulevard in forty minutes.

I took my meds, checked my wallet, grabbed a jacket despite the warmth of the afternoon. The phone was ringing as I headed out the side door. I stopped when Natalie called to me.

Handing over the mouthpiece, she hissed, "It's *Paul Kane* again."

"I'll take it in the office." Back in the storeroom that doubled as my office, I picked up, waited to hear Natalie clicked off, and said, "Hi. I was going to call you later."

He chuckled—a lazy, vaguely seductive sound. I wondered if he and Jake laughed a lot together. Not that Jake was exactly Comedy Hour material...but, yeah, there had been some good times. We had found a lot of the same things funny.

"I'm not expecting an hourly report," he assured me. "Just wanted to make sure you hadn't had second thoughts. I'm afraid Jake was rather... hacked off with our arrangement." He added. "I do apologize. Was he particularly obnoxious?"

"Not for Jake," I said. And in fact Jake had been uncharacteristically agreeable to my poking around, so Paul's apology caught me off guard.

"He did give in, in the end," Paul said ruefully, "but he said he was going to have a word with you. Establishing the parameters, I suppose." He chuckled. "He tore a strip off me for not telling him that Porter had hired a PI."

"*That* he didn't seem pleased about," I admitted. Although I hadn't realized that Jake didn't know about the PI, just that he was annoyed at the possibility I might trespass too far with my interviewing.

"The thing is," Paul said—and I wished suddenly that I could see his face because his tone was...not quite right—"I had thought it might be more pleasant for all concerned if you spoke to this bloke first. And then, depending on what you learned, we could decide whether to bring Jake in or not."

We?

I said, "Yeah, well. Too late now. I've got orders from the top to call in before and after I interview anyone."

There was a pause. I heard the echo of my words: *Orders from the top?* I had to bite my lip to contain an inappropriate laugh. This was followed by even more inappropriate speculation as to who *was* the top in that relationship? I didn't see Paul Kane as the submissive type, but picturing Jake on his knees to anyone was pretty much...although there had been one astounding night, one transcendent night.

I remembered the soft drift of his mouth on my naked skin, the delicate rasp of tongue as he licked and nibbled the point of my chin, the thin skin of my throat where the jugular vein pounded in crazy hot excitement...taking a sweetly torturous lifetime to kiss his way down the length of my body—a seductive game of connect the dots: collar bone, breast bone, belly, the sensitive joining of groin and inner thigh until at last his wet, hot mouth closed around me...

Heat washed through my body. I made myself focus as Paul said carefully, "But you see, I didn't tell Jake the name of the PI. I told him I didn't know it. In fact, I told him I wasn't absolutely certain Porter had gone ahead and hired anyone. That it might have been nothing more than bluff."

"But you do know the name of the PI?"

"Er...yes."

I said, equally careful, "Why wouldn't you tell Jake?"

He made a little sound of impatience as though I were being disappointingly slow. "In addition to being a very dear friend of mine, Porter was my business partner. I'm not in any way suggesting we would or should keep information from the *politzia*, but I should like to hear firsthand anything that's liable to prove damaging—rather than wait for the police to inform me."

I was silent.

"I've shocked you, haven't I?" He laughed but I could hear the unease.

"No," I answered. "But if this investigator was hired to follow Jones's wife, what potentially damaging information do you think he might have?"

"I don't know, do I?" Kane said. "That's why I'd like to hear whatever it is first."

It's not that I didn't understand or sympathize, but no way was I going to be placed in that position.

"Look, Paul. I appreciate what you're telling me, but I gave Jake my word. Not to mention the fact, he'd throw my ass in jail if he found out I tried to go around him."

"He wouldn't, you know," he said. "Jake's a pussycat."

Yeah, just a big old saber-toothed tiger.

"Then you go talk to this PI," I said shortly.

"I'm afraid that really would put a strain on our relationship," Paul said, and I was pretty sure he didn't mean his and mine. "Look, the bloke's name is Roscoe Markopoulos. Markopoulos Investigations. He's in the book. Just think about it. I won't tell Jake for a day or two."

Safe to say, few people ever told Paul Kane no. I said, "You might as well tell Jake now because I'm not going behind his back. Also, since we're sort of on this topic, I don't think Ally is your murderer. She admits she and Porter were having some problems, but she says that was all in the past."

"Of course the stupid slag says that," Paul said without any particular venom. "She married Porter for his money, and when she realized he wouldn't put up with being cuckolded, she decided to play the devoted wife in hopes of keeping him from changing his will. She's an actress, Adrien. Not a very good one, I admit, and I didn't expect you to fall for the act. I tell you, that woman is evil."

Cuckolded? Will?

I said, "Right, did you want me to focus on Ally to the exclusion of everyone else? Because, personally, I don't see why she didn't knock Porter off at home and in private where there was less chance of the poisoned cocktail going astray."

He said quickly, "No, no. I'm not trying to railroad the woman. I trust your instinct. You're the expert here, after all. By all means, you must keep talking to people—with my blessing. Besides, perhaps someone will have seen something to prove Ally is guilty."

He was so sure. What was it he hadn't told me? And why wasn't he telling me?

Into my silence, he said, "Why don't you speak to Valarie?"

I was totally blanking on the name. "Valarie?"

"Valarie Rose?" He gave that attractive laugh. "She's going to be directing *Murder Will Out.*"

"Oh God," I said. "I remember. I do remember. Any particular reason you think I should talk to Valarie? I was thinking maybe I'd talk to Al January next."

"Al?" Kane sounded wary. "Why?"

"He was a longtime friend of Porter's, right?"

"Er...yes. But Al tries to stay removed from all of our little personal dramas."

"Is there any reason I shouldn't talk to Al?"

"No, of course not." His amusement sounded perfectly natural—but then he was an actor. "I'll call Al and arrange a meeting."

And I was apparently paranoid.

I said, "And if you could also set something up with Valarie, that would be terrific."

"I'll see what I can arrange," Kane said—still sounding amused.

* * * * *

Lisa was sipping a G&T in the brick courtyard behind the Villa Piacere restaurant. The broad pepper and willow trees shading the patio threw lacy shadows over the white canvas umbrellas, and the fountain in the rear alcove splashed soothingly.

"Sorry about lunch," I told her, slipping into the chair opposite.

She fastened those wide Siamese blue eyes on me and gave me the maternal once-over. "Oh, darling," she said in gentle dismay. "You look so *tired.*"

I beckoned to the waitress.

"You're not drinking, are you?" Lisa protested.

"Not so far. The afternoon is young."

She tittered. "*Darling.* I just get frightened with everything you've been through. And it's not like you to forget our lunch date."

"I know. I am sorry. I'm a little distracted right now."

She waved this off as if it were of no consequence. The waitress appeared and I ordered apple juice for a change of pace.

"How's Guy?" Lisa asked.

"He's fine." I pushed my sleeves up, and reflected I did need to get out in the sun more often. I've seen polar bears with more color.

Lisa seemed to be following my train of thought; she said, "What did the doctor say, darling?"

I hadn't really thought she didn't know the exact day and hour of my doctor appointment, had I?

"He says my lungs are clearing nicely," I said. "But it's not a pretty process, so I'm limiting my social engagements."

"And you *are* feeling better?"

"Than I was a couple of weeks ago?" I laughed. "For starters, not having an oxygen tube rammed up my nose is a big improvement."

She made a little moue of distaste at this reminder.

"You would tell me if you weren't all right, wouldn't you, Adrien?"

"Of course." Would I? I'd have to. But in all honesty, I'd probably wait to the last possible moment.

Dark head bent, she nodded distractedly and traced a little circle in the white linen tablecloth with one pearl-colored nail. A pose I recognized only too well. Granted, she had always been overprotective, but something else was going on here. I said gently, "Come on, Lisa. What's up?"

She looked at me. "You've changed your will."

I stiffened. *How the hell—?*

Her mouth quivered, and there was a sheen in her eyes that might have been actual tears—unlikely though that was. "You've made Em your sole beneficiary."

As shocked as I was, I almost laughed. "Is that a problem? It's not a secret that I don't plan on getting married anytime soon."

"You know what I'm talking about, Adrien. You've never given your will a thought in a dec—"

"How the hell did you find out I'd changed my will?" I interrupted.

For a split second she looked discomfited. "Mr. Gracen."

What a pity Mr. Gracen was about a hundred and eighty years old and fragile as cracked porcelain because it would have done my nerves a world of good to be able to holler at someone without inflicting permanent damage. As it was, I wasn't sure he'd even survive my firing him—which I planned on doing before the afternoon was over.

I said, "Yes, I changed my will after the pneumonia. I'm fond of Em and I've got to leave the money to someone. I did it because it seemed like a practical thing to do, not because I'm not planning to be around for much longer."

She looked unconvinced.

I said, "I'm okay, Lisa. Really. And even if I wasn't...it's my life. Understood?"

Understood?

Her jaw dropped. Just for a moment. She pulled herself together and said, "You never used to be like this, Adrien. So...hard."

"Hard?" I blinked. Was I hard? In the space of a couple of days I'd been accused of being bitter, jealous, and hard. Funny, I still felt like me. Just... tireder.

"Jake Riordan did this to you," Lisa said, and there was genuine anger in her face. "He hurt you so—"

"God, *don't!*"

She broke off, looking shocked.

"I'm sorry," I said, more calmly, "but please don't bring Jake into this."

After a moment she wiped her eyes and picked up her glass, and I picked up mine.

* * * * *

I was lying down that evening when Guy let himself in. I got up quickly and went to greet him. The savory scent of chicken curry filled the flat. I found Guy in the kitchen, unpacking foil-wrapped containers of Thai food from Saladang Song. The same place Jake used to pick up dinner sometimes—and I really, *really* needed to stop thinking about Jake.

I kissed Guy and he smiled and said, "Grabbing a kip, were you? Why don't you go lie down and I'll call you when it's ready?"

I pulled out a chair and sat down backward, folding my arm along the back. "It's takeout," I said. "It's ready. How was your day?"

"The takeaway will wait. Go have your lie down."

"I don't need a lie down," I said pleasantly. "I'm hungry. Let's eat."

For the first time, Guy's vaguely British accent and those little affectations of speech were irritating me—and so was that Father-Knows-Best attitude. The realization dismayed me.

He had turned to get plates from the cupboard. I rose, slipped my arms around him and rested my face against his hair, which was pulled back in a long ponytail. The silvery strands were soft as silk, smelling of the apple shampoo he used and more faintly of pipe tobacco; it smelled familiar and comforting. He put his hands over mine, raising one to his mouth and kissing my palm.

The feel of his mouth nuzzling my skin was pleasant too, and when he turned to take me in his arms, I was glad. He kissed me, and I knew his taste and liked it. I kissed him back and opened my mouth for his tongue, and it slipped in wet and slick. His kiss deepened; his hands stroked my back, warm through my T-shirt, pulled me closer—and I wondered why I wasn't getting hard like Guy was.

It had to be because I still wasn't feeling one hundred percent.

After a few seconds he pulled back, kissed my lips lightly, and said, "You sure you're feeling all right?"

"I'm fine. I wish people would stop asking."

Guy was smiling. He ran his hands lightly down my arms, caught my fingers briefly, and let me go. He turned once more to lift the plates down. "It's the beautiful but frail shtick," he said over his shoulder. "You bring out my maternal instincts."

He was joking, but I knew he worried about me. The fact that I'd waited until we were seeing each other fairly steadily to confess I had a heart condition hadn't helped—nor did the fact that I currently looked like I was related to those big-eyed waifs that Margaret Keane paints.

I said, "Appearances are deceptive. I'm more than capable of taking care of myself."

Guy said, "Don't I know it. I've never met a more self-sufficient little prick."

"Hey, watch the adjectives."

He grinned, handing the plates to me. "You have a problem with *self-sufficient*?"

* * * * *

We ate our meal on the sofa, watching a History Channel special on the Salem witch trials—and I remembered Jake's comment about Calamity Jane.

I was doing it again. In fact, I was brooding over Jake's reentry into my life more than I was worried about being suspected of murder. All I could figure was that my ego had taken a bruising with the knowledge that Jake had continued his S/M pursuits during the time we'd been seeing each other—well, and that it had been with one steady partner.

Because I *knew* he cared about me. Maybe I wasn't the most experienced guy in the world, but I wasn't inexperienced either. I remembered...

But if I had any brains, I *wouldn't* remember. Because that was painful and pointless.

What I needed to be thinking about was how the hell did I break it to Guy that I was getting involved in the Porter Jones murder investigation despite having assured him I had no such intention. I knew he was going to be upset. He'd have been upset even if Jake hadn't been part of the equation. And the fact that Jake *was* part of the equation was definitely not going to go over well.

Maybe I could wait another day or two to fill him in.

I glanced at his profile, and Guy glanced back and smiled. "That tom yum goong soup has put some color in your face."

"It's very good," I said. It could have been warm water for all the attention I'd paid. I was stalling out of sheer cowardice. I needed to tell him.

I'd finally wound myself up to it when Guy glanced at the clock on the bookshelf and said, "Damn and blast. I promised I'd go to Margo's signing tonight. I didn't think—did you want to come? It's not like you don't get enough of book signings."

I said, "I've got the Partners in Crime group tonight. But give Margo my love."

His brows drew together. "I thought you were going to cancel Partners in Crime?"

"They're meeting in my bookstore. How am I going to cancel them?"

"Simple. Tell them you don't want to host the group here anymore. Last week you said you were fed up with it and wanted out."

"I'd just got out of the hospital last Tuesday," I said. "I was tired and irritable."

Like now—only then I'd had a good reason. I could hear Guy thinking it, but he didn't say it. Already in motion, he carried his plate into the kitchen, dumped it into the sink. Pausing by the hall table, he gathered his keys and sunglasses.

"Shall I come back later?" he asked, and I wasn't sure if there was a hesitation in his voice or not.

I said, suddenly awkward—it was untypical for Guy to ask permission—"I think I'm going to make it an early night after the writing group."

He came and kissed me, lingering a little, combing a strand of hair behind my ear as he studied my face. "That's a good idea, lover. You're still looking awfully peaked."

I smiled politely, unfairly annoyed with him again.

Guy kissed the bridge of my nose and departed.

A minute or two after the door shut behind him, I noticed that he'd left his tweed jacket. I grabbed it and started downstairs, but I had to take it slowly and I reached the side door in time to see the taillights of his red Miata disappearing down the street.

Closing the door, I started back upstairs. An envelope dropped out of Guy's jacket pocket and landed on a step. I picked it up, glanced at it, then glanced again as I took in the return address.

As I stuffed the opened letter into his jacket pocket, I wondered who was writing Guy from Tehachapi California Correctional Institution.

CHAPTER SEVEN

Wednesday morning was wasted at Huntington Hospital on the battery of tests Dr. Cardigan had ordered.

It was nearly eleven when I got back to Cloak and Dagger Books. I parked, let myself in the side door in time to hear Natalie saying indignantly, "I don't think it's such a strange coincidence. Adrien used to date a cop. If it's anyone's fault he keeps getting involved in murders, it's—"

"Natalie!" I said sharply.

She jumped guiltily, breaking off midsentence. Detective Alonzo turned from the counter where he had cornered her. He held a Starbucks cup, which he raised in greeting.

"Hey there, Mr. English. I've got a few follow-up questions, if you don't mind."

"What if I do mind?"

He smiled a smile I'd have loved to wipe off his face.

"This way," I said, leading him to the back and my office. I shut the door behind us and leaned against the wall. No way was I sitting down while this asshole towered over me.

He said, "So you used to...uh...*date* a cop?"

"No," I said. "She got that wrong. I used to 'uh date' a guy who was in the police academy. He washed out."

"With you and with the academy, is that right?"

"That's right."

He continued to smile that broad smile.

Lout. I glanced at my watch.

He said, "We got the toxicology report on Porter Jones back."

"That was fast."

"These are important people."

Maybe in Southern California. I couldn't see the rest of the world unduly shaken by the passing of a Hollywood financier—although marlin everywhere might be dancing on the waves.

"Apparently the poison was administered in a special cocktail mixture Paul Kane made up." He checked his notepad. "A Henley Skullfarquar."

"A Skull…" I trailed off. "Right."

Alonzo began reading, "One bottle of Smirnoff Ice, a quarter of a liter of Strongbow Cider, fifty milliliters of Pip's Cup—"

"Pimm's Cup," I said.

He smiled as though I had walked right into his trap.

I said, "There's no such thing as Pip's Cup. My mother drinks Pimm's in the summer. It's some kind of gin-based liqueur."

He was still grinning that "gotcha" grin. "I think it's very interesting you would happen to know about this particular drink."

"It's not that unusual. A lot of Brits like Pimm's."

"But you're not British, and *I've* never heard of it."

"My mother is English," I said. "And *I'm* not surprised."

"About what?" he asked warily.

"That you've never heard of Pimm's Cup."

He stared at me, unable to pinpoint the insult, then returned to his notes. "Maybe you'll be surprised to hear what substance actually killed Mr. Jones." He fastened his gaze on me again.

I waited, guessing what was coming.

"Digitoxin." He pulled it out like he was playing his trump card.

I said more calmly than I felt, "Digitoxin is not digoxin."

"Close enough."

"Not really. Both require a prescription, and digitoxin isn't used as much these days. I think it would be harder to get. It's also not as toxic as digoxin."

"So?"

"So why would I bother to use digitoxin which would be harder to get hold of and less lethal than my own medication?"

"Because you were hoping to avoid drawing attention to yourself."

I laughed. Granted, it wasn't much of a laugh. "Really? Then why did I use heart medication which would immediately bring attention to me?"

"Because it was convenient."

"But we've just established that I used a heart medication that would be harder to get hold of."

He shrugged. "It doesn't have to make sense to me."

I assumed it had to make sense to someone, though. I had to wonder about Jake assigning someone like Alonzo to this high-profile case. The guy was a moron. So did that mean Jake put him in charge because Alonzo would be easy to control if the evidence pointed in a direction Jake didn't like? It was a cynical thought, but apparently I was a lot more cynical these days.

I said, "Okay, well, let me ask you *why*, if I didn't want to bring attention to myself, would I break the glass I used and throw it in the trash? I can't think of a better way to draw police attention to the fact that Jones was murdered than that."

"You were trying to destroy evidence."

"But if you hadn't found the broken glass, you would probably never have suspected Jones's death wasn't natural. Given his age and weight, you'd probably have accepted that he died of a heart attack. Wasn't finding the broken glass the first tip-off?"

"No way. We suspected homicide right off the bat."

I didn't know if that was true or not. I said, trying to keep my patience, "But why wouldn't I just wipe my fingerprints off the glass? Why go to the trouble of breaking it and throwing it outside—and *leave my fingerprints* on it? It brought attention to the crime."

His tone and expression were patronizing. "You're thinking of all this after the fact. At the time of the murder you panicked and tried to destroy the evidence."

"I panicked? I thought I premeditated this crime?"

He eyed me without favor.

"According to you, I'm an old pro at murder investigations."

He said, "Yeah, and I'll tell you straight up, I don't care what the lieutenant says, there's something hinky about a guy like you involved in three separate homicide cases."

My heart was starting to lose its rhythm, that uncomfortable fluttering filling up my chest, closing off my throat. I took a deep breath. Then another. I needed Alonzo to go away.

"I didn't know Porter Jones," I said, sitting on the edge of my desk. "What the hell is my motive?"

"We put these other pieces together, the motive will fall into line."

I'd heard Jake say similar things often enough, so I sort of understood where he was coming from. Taking into account that Alonzo was an idiot.

"Yeah, well, good luck with that because none of those pieces fit," I got out. "Are you arresting me? Because I've said everything I have to say, and I'm calling my lawyer."

He looked suddenly alert, and I wondered if I had been taking him a little too seriously. "It's my experience, Mr. English, that innocent people don't start yelling for their lawyers immediately."

"Have you been watching *The Closer* again?" I inquired nastily. It was all I could do to keep my voice and hands steady. "This isn't *immediately*. You obviously think I had something to do with Jones's death, and I'll be frank. I don't have time or energy for this bullshit."

He stared at me for a long moment, then snapped his notebook shut. "I'll be in touch, Mr. English."

After the door closed, I dialed a number I had never thought to dial again.

* * * * *

"Are you thinking of hiring someone for the bookstore?" Natalie asked me later that afternoon.

I was on my laptop finding out what I could about Porter Jones. Not that I'm an expert—regardless of what Detective Alonzo thought—but in my experience, the more thoroughly you understood the victim, the better the chances of narrowing down the suspects. All I knew about Porter Jones was that he had bankrolled a number of successful movies—several of them starring Paul Kane—and that he liked deep-sea fishing for marlin. And that going on *The Newlywed Game* with Ally would not have been a moneymaker for him.

I looked up from a couple of blurry photos of Porter at Hollywood functions and concentrated on Natalie. Her voice had that high, slightly shaky top note I associate with impending disaster of the feminine variety.

"Sorry?"

"I saw that postcard," she said. Her chin was raised—I guess at the idea she had been reading my mail—and, yes, her voice was definitely wobbling.

"Which postcard?" I asked warily.

"The postcard from That Boy."

Ah. *That Boy* was how Lisa referred to Angus. I said, "Well, we need more help, right? That's what you've been telling me."

"I've been telling you that you should hire *Warren*."

"Nat, I'm not going to hire Warren."

"Why not?"

I opened my mouth to tell her exactly why not, but as I stared at her too-bright blue eyes and the way her chin was quivering, I chickened out.

"Because...because I promised Angus when he left that he could have his job back."

"Adrien, he was involved in a *murder*."

"But he was very good at alphabetizing."

"Adrien! It's not funny."

I bit my lip. "I know. Angus fell in with the wrong crowd, but he's not one of the bad guys. And I think he deserves—needs—a second chance."

She stared at me, her breasts rising and falling in agitation. "You're too trusting, Adrien. Of all the wrong people."

My cell phone rang.

"I have to take this," I said. I didn't care if it was the *Los Angeles Times* with a Very Special Offer. I intended to take it.

"Fine," she clipped, and stalked out.

I checked the number on my cell phone. Guy.

"Hey," I said.

"Why don't we go away this weekend?" Guy said. "Just you and me. Los Cabos is only a two-hour flight. I could book a hotel at one of the resorts. Somewhere on the beach. Somewhere romantic."

"I…" The call waiting beeps went off. I glanced at the caller ID display and my heart skipped a beat—but I was pretty sure that had to do with the various strains of the day.

I clicked the incoming call. "Hang on," I said. I clicked back to Guy. "Can I put you on hold for a sec?" I asked.

"I've got class in five minutes," he said. "We'll talk tonight, lover. Take it easy this afternoon, right?"

"Right," I said, and clicked off.

"I'm back," I told Jake.

"You sure are," he said. "What the hell did you say to Alonzo? He's now convinced you're our perp."

I'd had time to cool down from the morning, but the sound of Jake's voice sent my heart into that jittery and unpredictable rhythm. I was beginning to think he was hazardous to my health. Certainly to my mental health.

I said shortly, "I threatened to call my lawyer."

Silence. Jake said, "What did he say that rattled you?"

"You mean besides implying I'm a serial killer?"

I had the mixed pleasure of knowing he was struck speechless.

"I just…lost my temper," I admitted. "I'm tired of being suspected of murder. This is the second—no, third—time."

Even I could hear the tension in my voice. Jake said slowly, "I see." Then he threw me entirely by asking, "Has something else happened? Because this doesn't sound like you."

"How the hell would you know what sounds like me?"

"I know you don't panic easily. If you did, I wouldn't have agreed to this plan of Paul's."

"Yeah, well that's a mystery in itself, isn't it?"

Aggravatingly, he didn't answer. What was with him? If this was what marriage had done to him, he might as well have got a lobotomy.

I said, "He told me the toxicology report identified digitoxin as the poison used to trigger Jones's coronary, and he told me that traces of it were found on the broken glass with my fingerprints."

"Which we were expecting."

We? Him and me or LAPD? I wasn't sure.

"I seem to be his only suspect."

"Listen," Jake said. "You know how this works. He's giving Paul and the Beaton-Jones broad the same star treatment. You didn't kill Jones, right?"

"No. Jake—"

"Right?"

"Right."

"So relax."

"That's easy for you to say."

He laughed. "It is?"

Well, maybe he had a point there. For the first time it occurred to me how precarious Jake's own position was—or at least, given his paranoia, how precarious it might feel to him. I asked, "Why does Alonzo suspect Paul Kane?"

"He doesn't like fags. He doesn't like Hollywood types. And he hated Paul's last movie. Oh, and Paul mixed the fatal cocktail."

"I feel much better."

He asked, "Who are you planning on talking to next?"

I said, and I wasn't exactly sure why, "I'm not sure. I need to talk to Guy. He doesn't know I'm deliberately involving myself in this investigation. I don't think he's going to be too thrilled when he finds out."

"Oh, yeah," Jake said drily. "How is Captain Crunch?"

"He's fine. He's back teaching at UCLA."

"So I heard. Because no college education is complete without a course in Applied Hokum."

"It can't be all Police Science and SS Interrogation Techniques."

"Speaking of which, remember to let me know before you talk to anyone—assuming you decide to continue."

"Roger wilco."

He sighed and rang off.

* * * * *

"Maybe one of us should learn to cook," I said as Guy dished out teriyaki salmon, vegetable rolls, and tofu salad from Japon Bistro.

"You don't eat enough to make it worth either of our time." He opened the fridge. "Mineral water?"

I sighed. "I guess."

His smile was sympathetic as he poured lemon-flavored mineral water into a goblet. "How'd your tests go, luv?"

"I've no idea. I don't see Dr. Cardigan until next week."

He sat down across from me and said, "Did you think about going away for the weekend?"

"Er...yeah." I sipped my mineral water. "The thing is—"

"I was thinking of Palmilla Resort," he said. "It's right on the ocean. Right between San Jose del Cabo and Cabo San Lucas. Every room has a patio and an ocean view. They've got two infinity edge swimming pools, a spa, restaurants—and a wedding chapel."

I dropped one of my chopsticks. "Guy..."

"All right." His smile was rueful. "Don't panic. I'm not going to push you into anything, but we need this time together, Adrien. You need this time. We can lie in the sun and swim and sleep late and fuck like minks..."

"I'd...like to," I said, constrained. "But this isn't a good time."

He kept smiling, but I could see the effort. "I know exactly what you're going to say. You're going to say you can't leave when you've already been out of commission for a couple of weeks, and with the renovations going on next door. But we're only talking about a weekend. I think Natalie can handle things for two—two and a half—days."

I said, "I'm a suspect in a murder investigation. How's it going to look if I suddenly pull an O.J. and run for the border?"

"No one could seriously believe you're a suspect in this bloke's death. You didn't even know the man."

"But I *am* a suspect, and that's why..."

"Why what?" he inquired, when I paused.

"Paul Kane asked if I would—just informally—talk to a few people."

I met Guy's gaze. His eyes were just the color of green when surf hits rock. "What exactly does that mean: 'informally talk to a few people'? You mean he's asked you to...*investigate*?"

"Nothing that formal," I assured him hastily. "I'm just going to ask a few casual questions. This is apparently a very close-knit and closemouthed group, and the idea is that they might open up more readily with someone like me."

"Someone like you? A complete outsider?"

"But Kane is sort of vouching for me."

Guy put his chopsticks down and folded his arms. "That asshole Riordan would never go for that."

I said very carefully, "Well, surprisingly, he seems open to the idea, provided I keep him updated on anything I learn."

Guy stared at me as though I'd offered him a bite of my blowfish. "You're joking."

I shook my head.

"There's no way that sonofabitch would be okay with that."

"Guy!"

He waited, brows knitted, still angry.

I swallowed my first response, made an effort to relax my grip on the stem of my glass. Of course Guy hated Jake—and my instinctive desire to defend him was just an old bad habit I hadn't quite managed to break myself of.

"Nothing. Look, I don't know. I don't know if this is just Jake's way of pacifying a media darling like Paul Kane or if he really thinks I might be of help." I shrugged. "Maybe he's learned a few things."

"Maybe he has. I'm surprised you haven't."

He seemed to be pushing me toward confrontation, and that was unlike him. "Come on, Guy," I protested.

"Even if you were well enough to take something like this on—"

"Oh, for chrissake!"

He was staring at me with a look I hadn't seen on his face for a long time—two years, to be exact. "You *enjoy* this, don't you? I never understood that before."

"I don't enjoy it. I'm a suspect, Guy. I can't just sit here and—"

"Why not? That's what normal people do. They let the police and the trained investigators deal with this kind of thing."

He was perfectly right. That *was* what normal people did.

"I don't want to argue with you," I said at last.

"Well, we can add that to the list of all the other things you don't want to do with me. Like getting married—or even going away for the weekend."

"Guy..." I didn't know what to say to him. This outburst was so out of character, and I knew I was at least partly to blame. He already felt that I kept him at a distance, and my unwillingness to commit, to take our relationship to the next level exacerbated the situation—and now this: the return of Jake and everything he represented—probably the things Guy liked least about me.

He shook his head, closing the discussion, and resumed eating. We finished our meal in silence.

We recovered a little amicability during the course of the evening. Guy was grading essays and I was watching some cheesy flick on the Sci Fi Channel—nothing like a little CGI horror to put your own problems into perspective—but eventually he was lured over to the sofa by my commentary. Before long he was playing Siskel to my Ebert.

That was one of the nicer things about Guy: he didn't hold grudges. My first adult lover, Mel, had been a gold medal winner in the long-distance silent treatment. And even Jake had a tendency to revert to terse monosyllables when he was *really* irritated with me. Guy fought like a civilized person. He didn't shut me out, and he didn't try to thrash me into submission.

When we finally went into bed, Guy leaned over me, his mouth finding mine. He tasted like toothpaste with a hint of the plum wine he'd had for dessert. His mouth moved over mine with more insistence than he'd shown recently.

I kissed him back. His long hair feathered lightly across my face and chest. It tickled a bit.

"What do you want?"

What I wanted was to go to sleep—but I knew how that would go over after our earlier argument. I kissed him back, and tried to put a little energy into it.

His mouth delved mine, his tongue slipped inside, and he murmured something soft and urgent. I murmured in return, stroked his back. His cock pressed into my abdomen, and I reached down to fondle his balls. I could practically feel the rush of heat beneath his skin, and I began to consider strategies for bringing him off fast.

He thrust against me. His hand stroked my hip and groin—and he'd have had to be fairly oblivious not to notice I wasn't as interested as I ought to be. One thing Guy was not was oblivious.

His hand slowed. Stopped. He leaned back from me, staring at my face, trying to read my expression in the lamplight. He said, "We haven't made love since you got out of the hospital."

"I know. I'm sorry." I felt his erection wilting against me, and felt worse. "I'm just tired."

He said wearily, "I don't want you to be sorry, I want you to want me the way I want you."

"I do."

He stared intently down at my face. I turned my head and coughed. "I do," I said, turning back to him. "I'm just not back to normal yet."

He raised his brows.

"Normal for me," I clarified.

Finally he sighed, reached behind himself, and turned off the lamp.

We lay there side by side not speaking.

CHAPTER EIGHT

Supposedly, the elegant entrance gates to Forest Lawn in Glendale are the largest wrought iron gates in the world. I'm not sure. I think the gates at Porter Jones's Bel Air mansion might have given Forest Lawn a run for their money, but the cemetery entrance was admittedly impressive.

And brought back a number of memories. My father is buried at Forest Lawn; I actually remember childhood trips to the cemetery better than I remember him. Lisa tells me I'm a lot like him, although there were presumably a few crucial differences. In any case, when I attended Porter's funeral on Thursday, I decided to visit my father's gravesite.

The grave was on a hillside with a number of other graves marked "English," and I realized—belatedly—that I had quite a bit of family interred in these stately green parklands. It was an odd feeling. So was staring down at the bronze memorial tablet and realizing my father had been younger than me when he died.

It occurred to me I should have brought flowers or something. I hadn't been to his gravesite since I was small enough to play on the bronze statuary by the lake with the Heron Fountain—Lisa strangely indifferent to decorum on those long-ago field trips.

I wondered if my old man and I would've got along—if he'd have been all right with the fact that I was gay. I wondered in what ways I'd have been different if he had lived—besides my sexuality. Jake had been convinced my pop's premature departure from the mortal coil during my formative years was responsible for my inverted orientation, but I'd known I was different before I was an adolescent. Nor did I consider my orientation inverted. But that was just one of many areas in which Jake and I disagreed.

* * * * *

I couldn't help but think of Evelyn Waugh's *The Loved One* as I stood near the back of the Wee Kirk o' the Heather and listened to Porter Jones's nearest and dearest send him off with fond recollections and anecdotes.

From the jolly time everyone was having, it sounded like Porter was headed for that grand Opening Night in the Sky, and although he was not precisely a celebrity, he drew a reasonably full house. I recognized more than one familiar face—not including those cast and crew members I'd already met.

Paul Kane was there, naturally, and he spoke eloquently and amusingly about Porter and their long association. They had apparently met through a mutual friendship with Langley Hawthorne. I recalled Ally mentioning something about Langley Hawthorne, and I made a note to see what I could find out about him. He sounded like another Hollywood mogul.

I had to admit—grudgingly—that I learned more about Porter Jones from Paul Kane's eulogy than I did from anyone else's reminiscences. Kane managed to cover the fact that Porter donated to numerous charities, gambled on small, noncommercial but deserving indie projects, and served on many industry committees and scholarship boards—while poking gentle fun at Porter's passion for deep-sea fishing, modern art, and gourmet cooking. According to Kane, Porter had his sensitive side: he had always wanted to write, and penned terrible screenplays in addition to several attempts at writing his memoirs—but he had also been loud and crude and more than capable of drinking anyone or anything under the table. But most tellingly, in Paul Kane's opinion, was the fact that Porter stayed friends with everyone.

Porter's first wife, Marla Vicenza, was a well-preserved sixty-something. She looked like a bargain-brand Sophia Loren; I recognized her from too many late nights spent watching TV. She confirmed that Porter was a hard man not to like. Even when he had broken it to her that he was ending their thirty-year marriage and replacing her with a blonde trophy wife, he had apparently done it in the most charming way possible. By which, I gathered, he'd given Marla one hell of a generous settlement.

Marla seemed pretty easygoing herself. She sat next to Ally in the front pew of the chapel, and they seemed—from where I stood—to be on friendly terms.

Ally was apparently too overcome with grief—or guilt—to speak. She wore one of those flimsy black dresses that looked like it was designed for use while consuming apple martinis and bacon-wrapped scallops, and she leaned heavily on the arm of a short, brawny, and very good-looking young man. Maybe he was her brother. Because showing up on the arm of someone who wasn't her brother was surely flying right in the teeth of LAPD—and the teeth were very much in attendance.

Both Alonzo and Jake stood in the back of the Wee Kirk o' the Heather—on the opposite side of the door from me. Alonzo kept grimacing and tugging at his tie. Jake looked grave and distant in a well-cut dark suit, although I knew he was observing closely and taking mental notes on the mourners and homicide suspects. Even so, I couldn't help but notice he smiled frequently during Paul Kane's eulogy.

Not that I was watching him or anything.

I nodded hello to Al January, who also did not choose to reminisce in public about the good times with Porter. He paused long enough to invite me to lunch the following day, so Kane had been as good as his word.

I recognized a few other faces from Kane's party—or from television and film roles. Valarie Rose didn't recognize me when I said hello after the service finished and we all filed out into the little courtyard. Paul reintroduced us; she was friendly, if preoccupied.

"I've told Valarie you'll want to talk to her," he said.

"Oh. Right." I smiled at Valarie and she smiled politely back. I could see she thought this idea of Paul's was lunacy. I was beginning to think she was right, though not for the same reasons.

Paul made one of those rueful, charming faces. "You're not going to bail on me, are you?"

"No," I replied.

"Paul, you're putting Mr. English in a really awkward position," Valarie said.

Something in the way she stood brushing shoulders and arms with Paul told me that they were—or perhaps had been—lovers. Kane had a reputation for playing the field, and certainly Jake was not in a position to complain about double-dipping, but I wondered as I saw him approaching us.

"Not at all," Paul said. "Adrien and I are very much alike. We both enjoy puzzles." He added, eyes on Jake, "And other things."

My gaze met Jake's—locked—and I felt a flush of heat. Then again, I was standing in a stone courtyard with the bright June sun beating down on my head. I deliberately moved my gaze to Alonzo, who was staring at me with that amorphous hostility. His suit was dark olive and the finish looked shiny in the bright sunlight; for some reason I found that comforting.

As Jake and Alonzo drew within earshot, Paul said conversationally, "Has anyone ever told you your eyes are just the color of the Mediterranean?"

I noticed, tardily, that he was speaking to me. I could feel Valarie, Jake, and Alonzo all gazing at me, and I realized that while Paul Kane and I might both enjoy puzzles, we did not share a love of all the same games.

"Yeah, I get that a lot," I said, and I squeezed his arm in friendly farewell, moving away into the crowd.

"That *dress*. Oh my *God*. What was she *thinking*...?"

"He must have paid for his plot back in the seventies..."

"Please. Memorial Property..."

I stepped around the snickers and whispers, keeping an eye out for Ally and her stalwart escort as I listened in on the conversations floating around me.

"Sudoku? The *New York Times* provides all the mentalrobics I need..."

"Funny no one mentioned how he had no problem pulling financing when the mood suited him..."

As I joined the line of mourners straggling down the shady road to Porter's gravesite, I zeroed in on the dialog behind me.

"I'm surprised Valarie would work with him after the way he torpedoed her last project."

"If Paul Kane told Valarie to jump, she'd be the first one on the ledge."

I missed the next comment or two as a black limousine rolled slowly past and we all moved to the side of the road.

"It's ironic, really. He had so little time left."

That was the woman walking ahead of me. I considered the elegant line of her black-clad back, the glossy brown bob, and I recognized Marla

Vicenza, the first Mrs. Jones. From behind she could have been a woman half her age. Like so many actors, she spoke in a slightly louder than normal voice.

I unobtrusively picked up my pace.

"Do the police know that he was ill? Maybe it *was* an accident?" Her companion was an older woman in a dark pantsuit.

"Apparently not. It was some kind of heart medication. Not the kind of thing someone takes accidentally. Anyway, Jonesy was always careful about things like that."

"That alone should tell the gestapo that it couldn't have been anyone who really knew Porter—as if anyone who knew Porter would want to hurt him."

"The whole thing is ridiculous," the Vicenza woman said. "No one would want to hurt Jonesy. Jonesy was a lamb."

"What about that slut?"

"What would the hurry be? She'd have had everything in a few months anyway."

They nattered on, but after a bit I stopped paying attention. It was obvious neither of them had any idea who would want to kill Porter Jones. Just as it was obvious that there had been no need to kill him. He had already been dying.

So the question was: who couldn't wait for Porter to die?

* * * * *

"How was your funeral?" Natalie asked when I got back to the bookstore later that afternoon.

"Well, when you put it like that, I was hoping for better music." I popped open a can of Tab from the office fridge.

She laughed. "It can't all be Verdi's 'Requiem.' You should let Warren pick the music."

Over my dead body. I took a swallow of Tab. Caffeine. Ah, yes. I remembered it well.

She asked suddenly, "Hey, what are you wearing tonight?"

"Is this a trick question?"

She gave me a look of sisterly exasperation. "The family portrait? The one Lisa's been talking about for over a month?" She burst out laughing. "Oh my God, your expression, Adrien!"

Too bad the cameras weren't clicking right then. I asked, "What time and where?"

"At the house. Seven o'clock—but I think Lisa is expecting you to come for dinner."

"I don't know about dinner," I said.

"We noticed! That's why she wants you to eat with us."

"Funny."

Natalie seemed to think so. I left her chortling and went upstairs to change out of my funeral wear. I donned Levi's and a black T-shirt from the Santa Barbara winery, which Guy and I had visited last year. For a moment I studied myself in the mirror behind the bedroom door. I looked all right. Thinner than usual—okay, maybe my Levi's hung loosely off my hips in disconcertingly gangbanger fashion—and I definitely needed some sun. A haircut wouldn't be a bad idea either. I'd totally forgotten about the damned family portrait.

I went downstairs and, for a change, it was halfway quiet while the construction crew knocked off for lunch. Natalie was special ordering some small press titles for a customer; I grabbed the phone book and settled down in the office flipping through, searching for Markopoulos Investigations.

They weren't hard to find. The half page ad proclaimed *Lying spouses? Spying Louses? We are discreet and diligent!* There was a cartoon of a man who looked disturbingly like Luigi from *Super Mario Brothers* smiling through a spyglass at his prospective clients.

Me, if I was reduced to setting a shamus on my straying spouse, I'd go for a company that looked less…fun. I noted the website address and looked them up on my laptop. No goofy logo. Just a picture of a generic Los Angeles skyline and the information that Markopoulos Investigations was bonded, licensed, and insured—with an "eleven-year track record."

I phoned and asked for Roscoe. The secretary came back and asked who she should say was calling. I told her. She put me on hold—treating me to some fuzzy local radio—and then returned to ask what it was in regards to.

I told her. Back on hold in time to hear Miley Cyrus—a big favorite with Emma—singing about having the best of both worlds.

Miley disappeared and a brusque male voice said, "Markopoulos. Can I help you?"

I reintroduced myself. "I understand you were working for Porter Jones, the film producer."

Silence. At last, the voice said grudgingly, "Maybe."

"Then you're probably aware that he was the victim of a homicide a couple of days ago."

Another silence. Either Mr. Markopoulos didn't read the newspaper or he was processing very slowly.

"Maybe," he said finally.

I said, "Would it be possible to meet and go over a few things?"

"Are you with the media?" he asked suspiciously.

"No. Absolutely not. I've been asked to look into a few things."

"You another investigator?"

"Something like that."

Silence.

"I'm going out of town this afternoon," Markopoulos announced at last. "I'll be gone for nine days. Call me in nine days."

"If I could just have half an hour," I said quickly. I glanced at the astronaut clock hanging above the desk. "I could be there within the hour."

Silence.

"If you can get here before three o'clock," he said grudgingly.

I hung up and told Natalie I was going out.

"This is why we need help!" she called as I started up the stairs. I nodded distractedly, already dialing Jake.

My call went straight to message. I dialed again. Straight to message. I changed out my jeans and T-shirt into trousers and a tailored white shirt. I called Jake again. It went to message.

I opened my mouth, then rethought. If I was doing this—and I obviously was—maybe it would be a better idea to talk to Jake when my meeting with

Markopoulos was a fait accompli. I settled for asking him to call when he had a chance—and then I turned my phone off.

"Where are you going?" Natalie asked as I returned downstairs. "Are you working a case?"

The queen's spies—that would be the other queen—were everywhere. "Don't worry," I assured her. "I'll be back in plenty of time for my close-up."

"Adrien!"

I closed the door firmly on her protest.

CHAPTER NINE

"**M**r. Markopoulos will see you now," recited the receptionist at Markopoulos Investigations. I tossed aside the copy of *SC Magazine* I'd been browsing, and she buzzed me into the hallway leading to the inner offices.

It wasn't Pinkerton's, but Markopoulos Investigations—or MI as they now called themselves—was more than a grubby guy in an office with a bimbo secretary and a bottle of rye in the right-hand drawer. In fact, the receptionist didn't look old enough to drink. Come to think of it, I'm not sure she looked old enough to work. Maybe it was the Elly May pigtails. Or the Tootsie Pop. Were there intern positions for receptionists?

She led me down a starkly lit hallway past three other empty offices. The nameplate beside each door bore the last name Markopoulos. Roscoe had the corner office overlooking Wilshire Boulevard.

He rose from behind his desk, a small, energetic man with an enormous mustache. He bore a disconcerting resemblance to the Luigi character of the phone book ad.

We shook hands and sat down. I declined an offer of coffee.

"I've been out of town," Markopoulos told me. "That's how come I hadn't heard about Mr. Jones. You say you're working with the police?"

I sidestepped that one. "Not on Jones's murder, no."

"The cops!" He shook his head like, what could you do with pesky law enforcement underfoot all the time? "So what are you working on?"

I'd been giving this some thought on the drive over, and I said, "There are some questions regarding Jones's will. You know the kind of thing: what his mental and emotional state might have been at the time of his death." I shrugged. "I think the fact that he had considered divorcing his wife—"

"He wasn't just considering it," Markopoulos interrupted. "He was just getting his ducks in a row."

"And were his ducks in a row?"

Markopoulos grinned toothily. "His ducks were lined up like they were in a shooting gallery."

I said, "So the wife was having an affair?"

He nodded his head up and down like one of those oil derricks along Santa Barbara. "Oh yeah."

"And you handed that proof over to Jones?"

"Yep. Every last photograph."

"Can I ask—?"

He contemplated me with his dark, alert eyes. "Well, let me ask you this, Mr. English. What's it worth to your client?"

I had to think about that one. "The going rate?" I suggested.

He startled me by laughing. "It's the first wife, isn't it? Your client is Marla Vicenza?"

I smiled and spread my hands.

He pointed at me and laughed harder. I laughed too—a little giddily.

He considered. "Okay," he said. "Professional courtesy. Five hundred bucks and you get it all."

I decided Paul Kane could afford it. "Done."

He swiveled his chair around, did some typing at the computer, and then buzzed his secretary and requested the file for JON398.

I wrote out a check while we waited for the secretary to bring the file in. She bounced in. Markopoulos handed her the check and me the file.

There were photos—lots of photos—of Ally with a stocky, good-looking man I recognized as her funeral escort.

"Does he have a name?" I inquired, flipping through the photos.

"Duncan Roe," Markopoulos said with satisfaction. "He's her personal trainer."

"What's he training her to do?"

He laughed.

I shuffled through the log of times and dates and locations. I tried to think of innocent reasons why Ally and Duncan Roe needed to meet at the Luxe Hotel once a week for two and three hours at a time. Ally already had her own tennis courts, pool, and exercise room. True, I'd heard nice things about the Zen-inspired spa at the Luxe.

"Kelly will make you copies of anything you need."

"Thanks." I held up a picture of Ally and Duncan lunching on the bougainvillea-covered terrace of Hotel Bel-Air. They sure as hell didn't appear to be concerned with covering their tracks. "You followed her for six weeks. Any idea of how long it was going on?" I asked.

"Three or four months, as far as I could make out."

I thanked him and asked for copies of everything in the file. Roscoe left while Kelly was still Xeroxing.

"You like the PI business?" I asked her.

She shifted her Tootsie Pop to reply. "It's a living."

* * * * *

Checking my messages when I climbed in the Forester, I saw that Jake had called.

I clicked on the message and listened to him politely ask me to call him back, and I thought again how odd it was to be on formal terms with someone you had once permitted to lick your ears.

I called him back—prepared for another round of phone tag—but he picked up, catching me off guard.

"Uh, hey," I said. "It's Adrien. English."

There was a pause and he said, "I haven't forgotten your voice. Let alone your last name."

A funny little tingle rippled down my spine—infuriating, considering everything that I knew.

"Right. Well, I tried to get you earlier but—anyway, Kane came up with the name of the PI Jones hired."

Silence. But I thought I knew that silence. Knew that undertone of anger. And I assumed Paul Kane knew it as well, but apparently he was immune to it. That must have been some inoculation period.

"Which is what?"

His tone was neutral—his beef was with Kane, not me—but I knew he was wondering why Kane had handed me that information instead of giving it to him. Or maybe he knew Kane well enough to know how his brain worked. It wasn't my problem.

I gave up Markopoulos's name and address, and then steeled myself to tell him the rest of it. Not like I didn't know how this went, but I also knew there was a good chance he would kick me off the case. And to be honest, I wasn't sure if I minded or not. In a way I didn't want to examine too carefully, it would be a relief.

"Look, Jake," I said. "You're not going to be happy. Markopoulos agreed to see me. He was on his way out of town and there wasn't time to talk to you first."

There was an astonished pause. "Are you telling me you went to see Markopoulos after I asked you not to?"

I took a deep breath. "Pretty much. Yeah."

I closed my eyes and waited for the sky to fall.

His tone was flat. "Why would you do that after I asked you not to? After you told me you wouldn't."

"He was going out of town. I thought—"

"No, you didn't think," he cut in. "There was no good reason for you to bypass me. I don't give a shit if he was going out of town. I don't give a shit if he was going to Mars. We have recourse—"

He bit off the rest of it. There was a sharp silence. I wondered if he heard the same echo I did. Remembered the last time we'd argued a similar situation—remembered the way it had ended.

He said into that resounding silence, "I'm disappointed in you, Adrien."

He was in the right all the way—no question, really. I'd wanted to hear firsthand what Markopoulos had to say. I didn't want to wait for Jake to filter it for me—assuming he bothered—but that particular choice of word was... unfortunate.

"Really?" I said. "I disappointed you? I can't imagine what that feels like—to be disappointed in someone you trusted. How's it feel?"

He said tightly, "All right—"

"Does it? Feel all right? Terrific! Then I have something to look forward to—"

"God damn it!" he said, and that quiet fury shut me up like no amount of yelling could have.

I could hear him breathing hard. He said, "Listen, I know you think I'm an asshole—I *am* an asshole—but this is for your protection. I don't—" He broke off whatever he was about to say.

I snarled, "This isn't for my protection. Who are you kidding? You're worried about me screwing up your case. Same thing you've always been worried about. So don't feed me some line of bullshit about giving a fuck about what happens to me." Some people developed acid reflux. I had developed acid *reflex*—and it was becoming chronic.

"You don't have a clue what I think," he shot back. "And you don't have a clue what I feel. I'm not going to waste time with empty threats. We both know I'm not going to throw you in jail. But I can—and I will—make it impossible for you to be involved in this goddamned mess. I don't want to go that route, and believe me, you don't want me to go that route—"

I waited for him to finish it.

He inhaled and exhaled. I had driven him to deep breathing exercises. With an obvious attempt at control, he said, "So will you just, for *once* in your bullheaded life, do the reasonable thing and touch base with me—like you gave me your word you would—before you interview anyone else?"

In the pause that followed his words I realized that he wasn't kicking me off the case. It took me a bewildered moment to register it.

"Yes," I bit out. "I can do that."

"Thank you," he bit back. "I'll talk to you later."

"I can't wait."

He disconnected.

* * * * *

"Darling, that blue is just *wonderful* with your eyes," my mother said as the photographer busied himself setting up his equipment in the Dautens' formal living room in their Chatsworth Hills home.

"This old thing?" I inquired, glancing down at the silk Tommy Bahama camp shirt she'd bought me for my last birthday.

Natalie snorted, and Lauren—who I rarely saw these days—bit her lip trying not to laugh. I found it entertaining that my mother never bought me a garment in any color but blue. Different shades of blue—and occasionally a pattern—but always and without fail, blue. I'd pointed this out at the last Christmas extravaganza, and it had become a little family joke—that Lisa did not acknowledge.

"He even got a haircut for the occasion," Natalie offered.

Narrowly eyeing the photographer's shapely assistant who was positioning Bill Dauten on the end of the sofa, Lisa replied absently, "That's nice. Are you sure you don't want Guy to be part of this portrait?"

"I'm sure," I said, and my three stepsisters gazed at me with interest.

"It's too late for that, darling," Bill Dauten remonstrated gently.

"You're a bit shiny," the assistant told him, and Dauten grunted.

Dauten was a big man with the L.A. City Council. A big man in general—a little soft around the middle—bald and tanned. He had that aura of wealth and power that makes up for lack of looks and charm—but he was unexpectedly both shrewd and kind.

And he'd managed to spawn three darling daughters.

They *were* darlings, too. Dolls. All three of them. Lovely, charming, intelligent girls bearing no physical resemblance to Dauten—except they all had those blazing bright blue eyes. Maybe they took after Rebecca or Eleanor or whatever her name was: the first Mrs. Dauten. Or maybe Dauten was cranking them out of a factory somewhere.

"They aren't married, Lisa," Lauren said. Lauren was married—for now—to a handsome dolt who was wed to his upper management job; the spouse had apparently popped in for dinner, but couldn't stay for the photo shoot. I wondered if Lauren sensed her days as Mrs. Corporate Clone were numbered. She was the toughest of my stepsisters to read.

"No, I suppose not," Lisa said, meeting my eyes thoughtfully.

"That's funny," Natalie piped up. "Nobody has a problem with Warren not being part of the family picture."

"Come on, Nat," Lauren murmured.

"It's hardly the same thing, darling," Lisa put in. "Adrien has been seeing Guy for two years. You and Warren have only been dating a few weeks."

"We've been dating for three months," Natalie said.

No one responded to that.

Emma, sitting next to me, fidgeted in her frilly pink dress, and said, "I hate taking pictures."

"Emma, don't encourage Adrien," my mother remonstrated, and Emma giggled. I met my mother's gaze and she flicked her eyelid.

The photographer's assistant began positioning us around the sofa, moving lights.

"What a lovely family," she said, and Lisa preened as though she had responsibility for the whole kit and caboodle.

Eventually everyone stopped blinking and sweating and complaining about their bad sides—and assuring each other they didn't have bad sides—and the photographer got down to it, clicking and snapping away while his assistant continued to flatter and instruct.

Finally it was over. The photographer packed up his gear and his assistant and left. Lauren and Natalie immediately fled to the nether regions of the house to "get comfortable." Emma, who had complained several times about her scratchy, uncomfortable dress, apparently forgot all about it and settled on the floor with the box for Worst Case Scenario—and a hopeful expression.

"Em…" I said.

"Adrien, you couldn't take the time for dinner," Lisa said. "At least you can visit for a bit."

By which, I understood, that she planned on having a *word* with me.

I said, "In that case, I need a drink."

"Darling, you mustn't have alcohol while you're on antibiotics."

"I'm joking," I said, although I wasn't really. I missed alcohol. I missed it a lot at times like these.

She poured me mineral water, cut a wedge of lime, said way too casually, "Natalie said that your book is going to be made into a movie."

"It's been optioned. But lots of books get optioned, and almost none of them get made into movies."

"You should have had Bill look at any contract before you signed it, darling."

I nodded, sipped my mineral water, glanced at the clock.

"I've seen some of Paul Kane's movies," Lisa said. "He's very good. Very handsome. He makes a very good pirate."

I shifted my eyes her way. "So does Bill," I remarked.

"But Bill has kind eyes," my mother returned equably. "Were you at Paul Kane's house when that terrible tragedy on the news happened?"

By which, I assumed, she meant Porter Jones's murder.

"Yes," I said. "But you don't need to worry about me getting involved in some murder mystery."

She grimaced. "I notice you say I don't need to worry about it, not that you're not involved."

"Adrien!" Emma called impatiently from the front room.

I bussed Lisa's cheek. "Don't fuss," I said and went to join Emma.

* * * * *

Emma read, "'How to get skin out of a zipper. Do you, A - Rub peanut butter or margarine on the zipper and gently jiggle it—'"

"Wait, I already know this one," I said. "Give me something about recognizing bubonic plague. I always forget that one."

"Ad-ri-en!"

"What?"

She tucked the card away, read the next one. "'How to soothe a wound in the wilderness. A - Rub tree sap between your hands, then apply it to the wound as a soothing sealant. B - Wrap the wound in wet dark green leaves. C - Wrap a warm rock in a piece of cloth, then press it against the wound.'"

"I'm going to go with the warm tree sap," I said.

She gave a throaty Ming the Merciless chuckle. "*Wrong.* 'Wrap a warm rock in a piece of cloth, then press it—'"

Lauren appeared in the doorway. "Guy's on the phone, Adrien." She studied her sister. "Emma, you should change that dress. And you're monopolizing Adrien."

"Not yet. Monopoly is next," I told her, going into the kitchen to pick up the phone.

"Where are you?" Guy asked.

The question was clearly rhetorical since he was calling on the Dautens' land line. Just one of those subconscious little guilt inducers, I guess. "At Lisa's," I said. "I told you. It's the photo thing tonight."

"You didn't tell me that was tonight."

"Yes, I did. Didn't I?"

"No." He sounded put out, which was not normal for him. "I'm over at your place but you're not here. It's beginning to feel eerily familiar."

I started to answer, then lowered my voice, aware I had an audience although the adults in the family room appeared to be mesmerized by some reality show on the television. "What are you talking about?"

Guy said, "Paul Kane left a message for you, apologizing for landing you in deep shit with Riordan again. What was that about?"

"It's not a big deal—"

"Really? Because it sounded like it was a big deal to Paul Kane."

"Really." I glanced over at the family room again—the Dautens looked like a magazine layout for fine living—their taste in television notwithstanding. "It was—look, we'll talk about it when I get home." I hesitated. "I mean, if you're going to be there?"

"Of course I'll be here." His tone changed again—flattened. "Or would you prefer that I wasn't?"

"No, I wouldn't prefer that." I caught a look exchanged between Lauren and Natalie and broke off the rest of what I had been about to say. "I'll be home in an hour or so, all right?"

"I'll see you then," he said.

I hung up.

"There's Tab in the fridge, Adrien," my mother said brightly.

"Thanks. I've got to get going," I said.

I returned to the living room to break it to Emma. "Just one more game!" she pleaded.

"I can't, sweetie."

"Please!"

"Emma," Lisa said sharply from the doorway. "Adrien's tired. He's played with you for over an hour. We didn't get to visit with him at all."

Emma directed a mutinous face at Lisa. I ruffled her hair, and said, "Next time for sure, Em."

She gave a sort of droopy, unappeased nod.

I followed Lisa back to the family room to make my good-byes. There was the usual ring of kisses and then a handshake with Bill.

"We don't see enough of you, Adrien," he said, clearly cued by Lisa.

I watched her stage-managing the Dautens, and I thought how perfectly she fit in here. She had successfully managed to build a new life, a new family for herself—and I was happy for her. But yet tonight I felt distant, detached from it all. Or maybe it was just the knowledge that Guy was sitting at home waiting for me—seething.

"You know Guy is always welcome here," Lisa said, walking me to the front door.

"I know."

She opened the door to the scent of smog and jasmine. Crickets chirped loudly.

"Good night," I said.

But she said, as though she had been thinking it over all evening, "It's a pity you can't make up your mind to settle down with Guy. He's very good for you. But you're still not quite over Jake, are you?"

I stiffened. "*Jake*? Where the hell did you get that idea?"

"Watching you," my mother said with unexpected dryness, and kissed my cheek.

CHAPTER TEN

Coward that I am, I was half-hoping that Guy would have gone to bed by the time I reached home, but he was still up, drinking cognac and waiting for me when I unlocked the door to my living quarters.

"So Riordan is back in your life," he said by way of greeting.

I dropped my keys and wallet on the hall table. "Jesus, Guy. He's not 'back in my life,' whatever that's supposed to mean. He's overseeing this investigation. Which you already knew."

"I sure as hell did. I knew *this* was going to happen."

"I have no idea what you're on about."

He said wearily, "Oh, for God's sake, Adrien. Do you think I don't know about you and Riordan? You think I can't put two and two together? You obviously had some kind of relationship. It was very obvious from the way you used to clam up every time his name was mentioned—and you still do it, for your information. Same with him. Every time your name came up, he froze."

I felt a great resentment that this long-held secret was being pried out of me; but then I realized how unreasonable I was being. Regardless of what Lisa thought, of course I wanted a real relationship with Guy. Of course I did. He was smart and funny and caring and sexy as hell. And I wanted the trust and intimacy of a committed relationship. I wanted the real thing.

And besides all that, this long-held secret really wasn't much of a secret anymore.

"Yes, I had a thing with him," I said. "It was sex. That's all it was. And it was over a long time ago."

"It was a hell of a lot more than sex," Guy said. "For Christ's sake. You couldn't talk about it for two years. Not to mention the fact he used to park across the street and watch this place."

"What are you talking about?"

"Your Lieutenant Riordan used to park across the street from the bookstore and watch for you."

I laughed. "There's no way." I mean, it was ridiculous, but ridiculing the idea didn't do a lot to calm Guy down.

"You think I couldn't recognize that asshole behind a pair of mirror sunglasses? He used to wait out there for you. And now he's got an excuse to come back into our lives."

I went to the sideboard and poured myself a cognac. One drink wouldn't kill me, and I needed a drink or I was going to say a lot of stupid shit I would regret in the morning. Guy watched me slop cognac in the balloon glass, watched me swallow a mouthful.

I said, striving to modulate my tone, "Guy, where is this coming from? Jake didn't arrange for Porter Jones to be murdered, and he didn't arrange for me to get dragged into the investigation. It just happened."

"Nothing just *happens*," Guy said. "There are no accidents. There are no coincidences. Everything happens for a reason, for a purpose."

The Metaphysical Mystical Tour was waiting to take me away!

I swallowed the rest of my cognac and said, "Believe me, this just happened. There is no higher—or lower—power at work here."

"*You're* at work here," Guy said. "Riordan is at work here. Hell, Paul Kane is at work here. You all have and are choosing to exercise your freedom of will, of choice. You're *choosing* to get involved in another murder case. And Riordan is choosing to let you. Why do you think that is?"

"I think he wants to keep Paul Kane happy. And I think he wants, needs, for this to be wrapped up quietly and quickly."

"The only person you're fooling is *you*," Guy said with great—and infuriating—finality.

This was my fault. I was making Guy insecure. I was making him crazy. My inability to commit was going to bring about the very things I feared. I put my glass aside. "Guy, I'm tired. And this is crazy. Can we just...go to bed, please?"

He stared. "You mean, can we go to *sleep*, right?"

The surge of anger I felt took me by surprise. With something less than my usual finesse, I returned, "You want to fuck? Fine. Let's go fuck."

* * * * *

Easier said than done. And after about a half hour of what felt like manual labor with tongues, Guy dropped back in the sheets and stared up at the ceiling.

"Have you mentioned this to the doctor?" he asked shortly.

I was equally short. "No."

"Maybe you should."

After a moment, I got up and went into the living room. I poured another cognac and sat down on the sofa to watch the moonlight travel slowly across the room, limning each item on the bookshelf in pallid light.

* * * * *

Al January lived high on a hillside on the northwest side of Elysian Heights. The house was one of those modern designs: clean, geometric lines and angles.

January met me at the door wearing peacock-blue trousers and a gold-and-blue Hawaiian shirt, two of those wrinkly, Chinese shar-pei dogs at his heels. He led the way into the front room, chatting about the problems he was having keeping the local raccoons out of the house.

"Don't the dogs scare them off?" I asked.

"You'd think so," January replied. "They're good watchdogs, too."

I didn't catch the rest of what he said, distracted by the gorgeous view. Who needed artwork with windows that offered the incredible vista of the canyon, the mountains, and the city lights at night? Even so, January did have an impressive collection of South American art—including two huge mural segments—adorning the spacious, stark white room with its towering vaulted ceiling.

"We'll have lunch in a bit. What will you have to drink?" he asked.

I requested fruit juice and got a bottle of noni juice. January poured himself Bushmills.

"So Paul tells me you don't just write murder mysteries, you also solve them?"

We had settled on the long deck that looked out over about seven thousand square feet of wooded hillside. The air was sweet with the scent of sun-warmed earth and wild mustard. Bees hummed drowsily.

"Well...one way or the other I've probably been involved in more than my fair share of homicide investigations," I admitted.

What I was thinking, though, was that I hadn't solved those other crimes on my own. I had certainly played a part in helping solve them—maybe I had even been instrumental—but Jake had played every bit as vital a role in closing those cases. It had been teamwork all the way—even if Jake hadn't wanted me on his team.

If Jake didn't want Porter Jones's murder solved, it wouldn't be solved.

I'm not sure where the thought came from, but once it occurred to me, it was hard to shake.

"Porter wasn't the kind of person that gets murdered," January said. I opened my mouth, and he waved me off. "Oh, I know what you're going to say—that there is no particular type of person who gets murdered, but Porter was..." He shook his head.

"I got the impression at the funeral that he was well liked," I agreed. "But murder isn't always about the victim. Sometimes it's more about the perpetrator."

"I see what you mean," he said. He sipped his whiskey. "Porter was a big old teddy bear, but...if you crossed him..."

"Had anyone crossed him lately?"

January's eyes were that very pale blue that looks gray in a certain light. He gazed out over the treetops. "I guess he had his share of conflicts," he commented.

I realized that January, while not hostile, was not going to be hugely helpful at the expense of his old friend's good name. And I liked that about him. In fact, I liked January, period—and not just because he was adapting my book for a screenplay and had said nice things about it. Though that didn't hurt.

I said, "Well, I know he was having some marital problems."

"Who isn't?"

The bitterness of that caught my attention. I was pretty sure January was gay. There was no sign of a Mrs. January—actually, there was no sign of any other person beyond a maid—in January's life.

He added, "Ally doesn't have the brains to kill a fly."

"Paul Kane seems to think otherwise. He's pretty sure Ally wanted Porter out of the way."

"She might have wanted him out of the way, but I don't buy for one moment the idea that Ally killed Porter."

We chatted for a bit—mostly about Ally. While January didn't seem to bear the hostility toward her that Kane did, I got the impression he thought Ally had the brains and morals of a ground squirrel. He mentioned that Porter met her on the set of some film Ally had a part in; he didn't go so far as to say she was an actress, and whatever Ally's career ambitions had been, she seemed content to abandon them in favor of becoming a full-time Hollywood wife. But maybe Hollywood widow was an easier gig. Especially with a studly personal trainer waiting in the wings.

The maid brought out a platter of tortilla wraps: grilled chicken and cheese and avocado wrapped in flour tortillas slathered with herb mayonnaise. January and I helped ourselves.

Swallowing a bite, I said, "Had any of Porter's recent business deals gone wrong?"

He washed down a mouthful of wrap with whiskey. "As a matter of fact, Porter had withdrawn financing for a project Valarie Rose and I were involved in—and neither of us was too happy about it."

"Why did he withdraw financing?"

He smiled. "You're being very diplomatic. Why don't you just come out and ask me if I killed Porter?"

"I'm assuming your answer would be no."

"It would, but in this case it happens to be true."

"For the record, I don't think you killed Jones," I said, "but his wife suggested that there was bad blood between you."

"Oh, Ally." He waved another dismissing hand. "What can I say? From the start Ally was jealous of the friendship between Paul, Porter, and me." He shook his head very definitely. "No. Porter and I bickered over scripts and finances and the usual things, but we'd been friends a long time. A very long time."

"Did you argue at Paul Kane's party?"

He wrinkled his forehead like he was trying to remember. "I don't think so. Maybe there was some good-natured ribbing."

"No shouting, no gunplay?" I was trying to keep it light. "No songs and switchblades at thirty paces?"

"No shouting," January said. "Maybe we got a little...pointed with each other, but anyone who knew us knew it wasn't anything."

"Was Porter always the money man on Paul's projects?"

"God, no. Porter financed Paul's indie projects, but most of Paul's work is through the studios. *The Last Corsair*—his pirate movie—that was through Paramount. Everyone wanted to do pirate movies after the success of that Johnny Depp thing. Although I think the last one probably killed swashbucklers for the next decade or so."

I brooded for a moment on the likelihood of that. Even I had been relieved to see the Pirates of the Caribbean franchise shipwreck with *At Wits' End* or whatever it had been called.

January said, "Now on these indie projects—take your own *Murder Will Out*—Paul picks the projects, Porter financed, and I write the screenplays. We've been very successful. I mean, given that most indie projects are lucky to break even."

"Where did you first meet Paul Kane?" I asked. Porter and Al had been of the same age, but Paul Kane was quite a bit younger. I wondered about that.

"Hold that thought," he said, rising. He pointed to my glass. "Did you want another?"

"Sure."

He disappeared inside the house, and I wondered if he had deliberately called for a time-out. He didn't seem unduly troubled by any of my questions.

In fact, Al was about the most relaxed I'd ever seen someone in a murder investigation—taking into account that I wasn't the police and we both knew it.

He came back with a second bottle of noni juice for me and another whiskey for himself. He stretched his long legs out and tilted his face to the warm afternoon sun.

"I met Paul through Langley Hawthorne. You probably never heard of Langley."

"Paul mentioned him during his eulogy."

"That's right," he said vaguely. "Langley was the brains behind Associated Talent, which is now Paul's production company. It started out as me, Langley, and Porter. Langley came from old money. A son of the South." He winked at me. "He was raised on Stephen Foster and mint juleps."

"Doesn't sound like much of a background for going into the moving pictures business?"

"Everyone loves the flickers," January said. "Anyway, Paul was a friend of Langley's. That's how we originally met."

"What happened to Langley?"

"He drowned off Catalina." A funny expression crossed his face.

He picked up his glass, and I said, "What? You just thought of something."

"It's a crazy idea, really, but you were wondering if anyone had a motive to get rid of Porter. Langley's daughter Nina sort of had a motive. This is years ago, mind, but Nina and Porter had an affair. It didn't end well. Porter was married at the time—not to Ally. He was married to an actress by the name of Marla Vicenza."

"She was at the funeral yesterday," I said. "In fact, I heard her mention something about Porter not being in good health."

"I don't know about that. His doctors were after him for years to cut back on his drinking and to give up cigars. Anyway, Langley insisted that the affair end."

"How young was Nina?"

"Very young. Just eighteen, I think."

"I can see why Langley had a problem."

He stroked his mustache, smiling. "You don't have children, obviously."

"Obviously."

"Nina was furious with Langley—and Porter. She felt doubly betrayed."

"This was back when? The eighties? Could she still be holding a grudge after all this time?"

"Nina is a world-class grudge holder," Al said, "but in fairness to her, I don't think she killed Porter. She's not the...lie in wait type. If she killed anyone, it would probably be three and a half minutes after they pissed her off. Especially back then."

"Why especially back then?"

"Nina was not always...in control in those days. Well, it was the eighties. I don't know anyone who was in control."

"Was she at the party last weekend?"

"No." January got that evasive look again. "Not exactly. Her company catered the party."

CHAPTER ELEVEN

Friday afternoon traffic was a bitch—as usual—and I got back to Pasadena in a less than jolly mood. Shelling out over fifty bucks on gasoline and the same again on a few staples like tilapia, Tab, and the magical elixir known as orange-pineapple juice did little to improve my mood.

When I reached Cloak and Dagger I saw that—predictably—the construction crew had knocked off work early again, and that the store was empty of customers barring one: a slim young man who looked like a sexy Harry Potter. He wore artfully ripped jeans and a fitted bronze mesh T-shirt, and he was contemplating Natalie over the top of his Windsor-style specs.

"Oh, here's Adrien," she said as I approached the counter. "He can probably tell you when the best time to drop by is." To me, she said, "Hey, Adrien, this is...uh...one of Guy's former students."

I nodded hi, setting the bag of groceries down, and then I took another look. There was something very familiar about Guy's former student. Something familiar about the cool, slightly challenging way he stared back at me. But it took a minute to place the pale pointed face and cropped dark hair.

Peter Verlane.

Last time I'd seen him, he had been doing his level best to help kill me. Well, no. To be fair, the very last time I'd seen him, he'd been fleeing into the night trying to avoid arrest for kidnapping, extortion, and murder. And suddenly I had a clear memory of the envelope that had fallen from Guy's pocket the night I'd tried to catch him before he left for Margo's book signing—the letter that had borne the return address of the men's prison in Tehachapi.

"Peter Verlane," I said. "Who left your cage open?"

He reddened, glanced at Natalie, and said stiffly, "I did my time. I've got as much right to be here as anyone."

"Not exactly," I said. "She works here, and I own the place. Remind me why you're here again?"

Natalie looked from me to Verlane and said uncertainly, "He was asking for Guy."

"Why?" I asked him.

"Not that it concerns you," he said, "but he told me to contact him when I got out. We're friends."

"There's no accounting for taste," I admitted. "But why are you *here*?"

He said evenly, "I know he's seeing you now."

"I'm relieved he thought to mention it," I said. "Didn't he also mention that he still keeps an office at UCLA? Or that he still has his townhouse?"

The glasses gave Verlane an unfairly vulnerable look; scorpions have offspring too, after all.

He said, "I wanted to see you."

"Uh-huh. Well, you came, you saw, you confounded. Now how about you skedaddle? I'll let Guy know you called."

"Guy *wants* to see me," he said with complete and quiet conviction.

Against my best effort I was getting mad, and my heart was starting to race. I said, "I'm betting he wants to see you *else*where. And *I* sure as hell want to see you elsewhere. So leave a number where he can reach you, and go."

I wasn't being magnanimous there. I thought it might be a good idea if I knew where Verlane could be found—just in case.

Bewildered, looking from me to Verlane, Natalie pushed a notepad at him and he scribbled something down.

He raised his bespectacled gaze to my face. "Guy wants to see me," he said again with certainty.

"I don't," I said. "And if you show up here again, I'll have a restraining order slapped on you."

He gave me a final assessing look, turned and walked unhurriedly up the aisle, pushing out through the glass doors. As they jingled shut behind him, Natalie let out a long breath.

"What an arrogant little prick!" she said indignantly. "He seemed fine until you walked in."

"It's all right," I said. "Don't worry about it." I started for my office. My heart was starting that uncomfortable tripping beat, signaling trouble. Aggravatingly, she followed me, still talking.

"I've never heard you talk to anyone like that. You were kind of an arrogant prick too." She sounded like she found it entertaining. If only I did.

I sat down at my desk, pulled open a drawer, and pulled out my pills.

"Are you okay?"

I looked at her. "I just need a minute or two."

She nodded but didn't go away. Wouldn't the normal thing be to give me a few moments? Controlling myself with an effort, I popped my pills, took a swallow from the bottle of tepid water on my desk. I drew a couple of experimental breaths. I seemed to be okay. My heart was already slowing back to its normal rhythm, so maybe I'd just mistaken reasonable agitation for something else.

"I really am okay," I told her. "Do I have any messages?"

"Hmm? Oh. Paul Kane called again. A couple of authors want to set up signings. It was a pretty quiet day. Only three people came in searching for books with red covers and the word 'murder' in the title."

Guy would have called my cell phone or left a message on the upstairs phone. Assuming Guy had anything to say to me. He'd left without waking me that morning.

"Are you sure you're okay?" Natalie said.

"I'm fine," I said, and despite my efforts, it snapped out. I glanced at the clock over the desk. "Shit. And I'm late picking Em up."

"Adrien, Emma can do without her horse riding lessons! You need to—"

"There's no need for her to do without." I rose, and she asked, "Aren't you going to call Guy?"

"No." And that was much curter than I intended. I glanced at her. "Sorry. Listen, Nat, can you do me a favor?"

"Of course."

"Please don't…discuss what's happening here with anyone."

She said honestly, "I don't know what's happening, Adrien. I know you and Guy are having a rough patch and that some parolee came to see Guy. Where would that guy even know him from? That writing program Guy runs at the prison? Do you think maybe this Verlane is stalking him?"

"No," I sighed. "I don't."

As I went out the side door, she called, "Are you *sure* you're okay?"

* * * * *

A deer crashed through the manzanita and underbrush beside the wide trail, springing away to vanish into the dusky evening. As Emma's horse shied, I leaned across, grabbed his bridle, and yanked him down hard on the packed earth. The gelding tossed his head, blew out nervously, but settled fast, falling back into stride with my own mount.

Emma sat up very straight in the saddle. Her eyes were huge, but she said bravely, "I could do it!"

"I know you can."

"I wasn't afraid."

"There's nothing wrong with being afraid," I told her. "It's how you handle it."

Like, don't ever kill anyone because they scared you.

Emma's chatter, the creak of saddle leather and jingle of bridles, the thud of the horses' hooves on the trail faded out and my thoughts turned inward once more.

The reasons people killed each other were as varied as the people themselves. Porter Jones, for instance, appeared to me to have been taken out mostly because he stood between someone and what they wanted. Well, that made sense. Most homicides seemed to be motivated by greed, and one thing I'd learned from Jake was that, mostly, murder wasn't complicated. The most obvious suspect usually was guilty. Even in the unsolved cases that went cold, the police generally had a pretty good idea of who the culprit was; they just couldn't successfully take them to trial. Or if they went to trial, they weren't able to secure a conviction.

I thought there was a pretty good chance that Ally Beaton-Porter had offed her old man. She had the best possible motive: several million dollars and an illicit affair with a handsome young stud.

Although if Porter really hadn't been in good health, it would have made good sense to wait—except that Porter had hired a PI, presumably with some purpose in mind. Paul Kane had insisted that Porter planned on divorcing Ally, and that had seemed to be reinforced by Roscoe Markopoulos.

And while Ally didn't strike me as having the brains to pull off poisoning her husband without killing half the other people in the room, I'd be the first to admit my instincts—crime solving and otherwise—weren't always infallible.

It just bugged me that everyone—barring Al January and myself—seemed to take it for granted that Ally was guilty. She probably *was* guilty—she didn't exactly seem grief stricken at Porter's demise, and there was good reason that wives were the first suspects in a husband's suspicious death.

So what about Marla Vicenza? Had Porter left her any million-dollar behests? Because some people committed murder over twenty bucks in change. I wondered what Marla's finances were like. She was certainly past her prime as far as Hollywood box office went, but if she had invested—or remarried—wisely, maybe money wasn't an issue for her. But maybe getting dumped for a blonde bimbo was.

This is why I had a problem with the idea of this Nina Hawthorne as murderess du jour. Yes, she did own Truly Scrumptious Catering, but if she hadn't been on the scene, I didn't see how she could have orchestrated getting poison into the right glass by remote control. Besides, having the patience to wait nearly twenty years to destroy Porter didn't seem to mesh with being motivated by that whole passionate woman-scorned thing.

I glanced at Em as she prattled on, and I tried to picture her at eighteen. Tried to picture her having an affair with some married asshole a couple of decades her senior. Now, had Langley Hawthorne killed Porter, I could more easily understand it. But Langley Hawthorne had been dead for years.

Still…if Nina's company had done the catering, then there was a very good chance that Nina had been on the premises at some point—maybe the day before or earlier in the day of the party? That would have given her access to…but there again was the problem. How could she anticipate what Porter would drink or what glass would be used?

She would have to be very familiar with Porter and with Paul Kane's bar setup.

Maybe Paul Kane used her catering company a lot. Maybe she was familiar with his bar setup, and maybe she knew that he always made these Henley Skullfarquars, but again, how could she control administering the fatal dose? I doubted the mixture was made ahead of time, and she couldn't poison one of the ingredient bottles because no one else had died or even gotten ill from the cocktails.

I kept coming back to the problem of Porter's glass. Of course the simplest explanation was that Porter had taken the stuff himself. This mysterious ill health of his that—assuming I'd heard correctly and wasn't jumping to conclusions—his ex-wife had referred to at the funeral: what if it was heart trouble?

But no. That would have been determined right away—the rest of his prescription would have been found on his body, for one thing.

Could he have taken the stuff thinking it was something else?

Like what?

Emma said thoughtfully, "You know what doesn't make sense? Why does an X stand for a kiss? I think an O should be a kiss because it's like your mouth." She demonstrated with an O that made her look very young and very surprised.

"Who are you sending love letters to?" I asked.

She giggled. "No one."

I looked skeptical and she laughed again. "I'm *not!*"

* * * * *

I dropped Emma off at her home—managing to avoid any meaningful discussion with Lisa, who tried to insist that I stay for dinner—and headed back to the bookstore.

By then Natalie had closed up for the night and gone home. It was very quiet as I locked the door behind me. The forest of bookshelves stood motionless and silent in the gloom. Outside the front windows the streetlamps were coming on, the traffic thinning in this mostly retail part of town.

I stared through the paint- and plaster-spattered plastic wall separating the store from the gutted rooms next door. Remembering Peter Verlane's earlier visit, I hoped the construction crew had locked up properly before leaving for the day.

Not that I was unduly worried about Verlane. Not about him killing me, anyway. I believed that, like Angus, he had been caught up in something larger than himself, swept along by a more powerful and unscrupulous personality. That didn't mean I had forgiven him—or was likely to any time soon—but I wasn't afraid of him. Which didn't make his showing up at the bookstore any less of a shock. Nor did it mitigate my anger at Guy—although maybe that wasn't fair.

I went upstairs and checked the phone machine, but there were no messages. I recalled Natalie saying that Paul Kane had called earlier, but I really didn't have the energy to talk to Paul Kane right then.

And it's not like I had anything to tell him. My efforts at sleuthing seemed pretty ineffectual so far, if I did say so myself.

I poured myself a glass of orange-pineapple juice—and I realized that Natalie must have put my groceries away for me. I was grateful, but it gave me a strange feeling to think of her—to think of anyone—wandering through these rooms. Guy and Lisa had double-teamed me on that one, insisting after I'd developed pneumonia that my family needed access to my home in case of emergency. Guy had a key, of course, but now so did Lisa—and Natalie.

I drank my juice and stared down at the empty street. It was a warm, dry June evening. The summer night smelled of smog and distant dinners cooked in restaurants on the other side of town. A kid with a guitar sat on the stoop of the closed boutique across the street singing—practicing, apparently—an old Beatles song. The bald and featureless mannequins in the brightly illuminated boutique windows modeled their finery and gestured elegantly into space.

"*...of lovers and friends I still can recall, some are dead and some are living...*"

I thought about the league of extraordinary gentlemen I'd dated through the years. There was a lot to be said for being single; you couldn't go by Friday nights.

I wondered what Paul Kane did on Friday nights.

I wondered what the hell Guy was doing tonight. Had Peter managed to track him down?

I wondered what Jake and his wife did on Friday nights.

Anyway, I could always call Guy. Ask him directly what the fuck was up with him and Harry Potter. Put him on the defense for a change. Because in my humble opinion there was a significant difference between working with an ex-lover, and continuing a friendship with someone who had tried to TWEP your current lover.

Yes, I could call Guy, but I wasn't sure I was ready to hear what he might have to say.

* * * * *

Nina Hawthorne was something of a celebrity. She had inherited a bundle from her father when he fell off his yacht and drowned off the coast of Catalina, but she was a successful businesswoman in her own right. Truly Scrumptious Catering boasted an impressive roster of A-list clients, but it didn't take a lot of Googling to figure out that Nina was a woman with a past—and it wasn't all lemongrass chicken meatballs.

Before discovering her future was in food services, Nina—who, from her photos, looked small and dark and rather chic despite the crew cut—had tried acting, painting, and bounty hunting. Reading various interviews and reviews, I reflected what an excruciating thing it must be to grow up in the public eye. Every mistake was captured for posterity—and reviewed by the pundits. And Nina had made many mistakes—Porter Jones was the least of it.

There had been rock stars, movie stars—and even an astronaut. There had been car accidents, drug busts, alcoholic outbursts, and a Playboy centerfold.

And there had been Paul Kane.

Yes, about six pages back in my Internet searching I found a passing reference to a court case between Nina and Paul Kane. And before long I had the whole sad and sordid tale—and it was sad.

Not long after her father's death, Nina—who was about nineteen at the time—had had a fleeting—very fleeting—affair with Paul Kane, which resulted in an illegitimate child: a little girl by the name of Hazel Honeybelle. The name alone proved pretty conclusively that Nina was probably not a fit parent. In any case, because of Nina's much-publicized history of drugs, drinking, and promiscuity, Kane was able to win custody of the child—whose name he promptly changed to Charlotte Victoria.

This was the first salvo in a series of mildly comical skirmishes—legal and personal—between Kane and Nina as they fought for custody and control of their child, and it probably would have gone on for years, endlessly entertaining the readers of *Us* magazine. But farce turned to tragedy when Hazel/Charlotte drowned at age three in Paul Kane's swimming pool at his villa in Sardinia.

I stared at the grim photos of a black-clad Nina and an equally somber-looking Paul Kane at the child's funeral.

Now there, in my opinion, was a motive that age could not wither nor custom stale.

I picked up the phone and dialed Jake's cell before I remembered that it was Friday night, and he was probably off duty—or at least not taking my calls.

The phone rang, I got ready to leave my message, and Jake said crisply, "Riordan."

It startled me into one of my coughing fits. When I got my breath back, I said huskily, "Believe it or not, I think I have something for you."

There was a peculiar pause. I heard the echo of my own words—and my tone—and considered how I might conceivably be misinterpreted. I said hastily, "I mean, I think we may be approaching this from the wrong angle."

"What are we talking about here?" he asked neutrally.

"Porter Jones's murder. I don't think he was the intended victim. I think someone was trying to kill Paul Kane."

CHAPTER TWELVE

"Where are you?" Jake asked.

"At home."

He hesitated. Said, "You want to meet for a drink, and you can tell me what you've found?"

I hesitated too. Glanced at the clock. Five after nine. But it's not like I had anywhere to be—nor was I apparently going to have any company that night. "Sure," I said colorlessly. "Where?"

"Do you know where Brits Restaurant and Pub is?"

"East Colorado Boulevard?"

"I'll see you there in about thirty minutes."

I hung up and went to change my T-shirt and sweats for jeans and a long-sleeved shirt in a charcoal multistripe. I wasn't about to shave for a drink with Jake, but I did drag a comb through my hair and brush my teeth.

I didn't have as far to go and I got to the pub before Jake, and—remembering that I hadn't had dinner—ordered a roast beef sandwich while I waited.

He arrived a few minutes after my food. The *Veronica Mars* theme song was playing as I watched him—tall and sort of compelling in black jeans, black T-shirt, and black leather jacket—threading his way through the tables to the beat of the music. I smiled sourly as the lyrics to "We Used to be Friends" registered.

A long time ago. Yeah. Only it didn't feel as long ago as it probably should have.

He spotted me at the bar, pulled out a stool next to me, and sat down. "Something funny?" His eyes—I'd forgotten how light they were: almost whiskey-colored—met mine warily.

"Not really. I'm surprised you could make it on such short notice."

"Why's that?"

"Friday night." I shrugged. "I figured you'd be home with the little woman doing whatever it is little women like to do on Friday nights."

"Kate's working tonight." The bartender approached us, drying a glass with a Scottish tea towel featuring Queen Elizabeth's somewhat damp face. "What are you drinking?"

I considered it. "A Henley Skullfarquar," I requested.

The bartender and Jake exchanged a look; the bartender nodded as though conceding a point to me. "But you usually don't get it by the glass, mate."

"How does it usually come?"

"Usually make 'em up by the jug. They serve it during the Henley Royal Regatta. Not to worry. I'll do it for you. You want soda water?"

"Do I? What's in it?"

"Smirnoff Ice, Strongbow Cider, Pimm's Cup, gin, grenadine, a slice of orange or lemon. You can add lemonade or soda water if you like."

"Jesus," Jake said. "Are you on antibiotics?"

"I won't need them after this. No germ could survive that amount of alcohol."

"At least it's got vitamin C." He asked the bartender what he had on tap and requested Bass ale.

I realized something that had been subconsciously bothering me. He had changed his aftershave. Not that I didn't like this one. It was nice: a sharp, oriental, woody fragrance. But it made him smell...different. Alien. A stranger.

Of course, he *was* a stranger. That was the point.

Jake got his ale, took a long pull on it, and turned on his stool to face me. "So what makes you think Paul was the target last Sunday?"

I ignored the fact that our knees were brushing—denim had never seemed like such a flimsy barrier—that he was close enough for me to see that there was a little more silver at his temples than I'd realized. I told him about my lunch with Al January, and January's belief—which coincided with my own—that the crime just didn't seem to fit Ally's profile. I said, "She just strikes me as the type to try to fake a burglary—and do something like knock the windowpane glass out the wrong way. Or anonymously report the break-in from her own cell phone."

"Maybe she didn't come up with the idea," Jake said. "Maybe the boyfriend did. He works as a personal trainer to a lot of people. He might have picked up heart meds from a client. It will take a little time, but we can check that out. It's just a process of elimination."

"Fair enough," I said. "But after I left January's, I did some checking on Nina Hawthorne."

"Hawthorne." I watched him run it through the old memory banks. "The caterer?"

"Right." I told him what January had told me about Nina's youthful affair with Porter. "Except it turns out she had a lot of youthful affairs—and one of them was with Paul Kane." This was the difficult bit—for a lot of reasons. I told him about the child who had played the role of Briseis to Kane and Hawthorne's Achilles and Agamemnon.

He was silent as the bartender set my drink before me and departed.

"I know about Paul's daughter," Jake said quietly. "He was devastated."

"That's not the point though, is it?" I said. "The point is, does Nina blame him? And if she does, is she capable of committing murder in revenge for the death of her daughter?"

At one time, there would have been no question. Wild child Nina would have dispatched Paul without a moment's qualm—although she might not have remembered it a few hours later. The old Nina clearly had the imagination and recklessness for this kind of crime. But Nina had been a solid citizen for nearly a decade.

I sipped my drink—choked on what appeared to be pure alcohol—and managed to set the glass on the bar before I started coughing. It hurt like hell, my ribs still very painful.

"Are you okay?" Jake rose, moving behind me, but was apparently reluctant to thump me on the back—and that was fine by me. The last thing I wanted was his hands on me. I waved him away, and he ordered, "Put your hands up."

Which—don't ask me why—struck me as funny. For a spluttering, spiraling moment, I thought my last vision would be of Jake's scowling alarm.

But he rested a steadying hand on my back, and that warm weight between my shoulder blades drained all the laughter out of me. He smoothed his hand up and down my spine, and I got control, drew in a long, wavering breath.

"I'm okay," I said, shrugging him off.

"What the hell is in that?" He picked up my glass, sipped from it. His eyebrows rose. "You're not drinking that," he said.

"Drink okay?" asked the barman, coming up.

"He'll have a Harp," Jake told him, and the man sighed at this disrespect to his creation and stepped away.

I sat back and examined Jake derisively. "Have you ever heard the phrase 'arrogant asshole'?" I inquired—the effect slightly spoiled by my hoarseness.

"Once or twice." He sat down again and grinned crookedly. "Come on, you didn't want to drink that. Who are you kidding?"

"Not you apparently." It was like I could still feel his hand lightly smoothing up and down my back—cell memory or something.

He didn't seem to have an answer.

The bartender slid a pint of Harp in front of me. I took a sip. Big improvement, I had to admit—not that I would.

Jake said—as though we had not been so rudely interrupted—"I don't think Paul would have used the Hawthorne woman to cater his company if there was still bad blood between them. I'll check on that, obviously, but even so, I can't see how she would have introduced the poison to the vic. She wasn't there—unless she was there in disguise, which seems unlikely."

"That's the problem I keep running into," I admitted. "How did the poison get into Porter's glass? Especially if these Henley Skullfarquars are made by the gallon." I gave him a questioning look.

He said matter-of-factly, "I wouldn't know. I don't attend parties at Paul's."

"But you're friends."

"We're friends."

"*Old* friends."

He gave me a funny look. He said, "Let's just say we travel in different social circles."

No exchange of Christmas cards with naked Santa whipping naughty elves?

I said, "There were a lot of us grouped around the bar. Me, Porter, Valarie Rose, Al January. I don't remember if Ally was standing next to us or not, but there were a lot of drinks lined up—half-empties, that kind of thing. I mean, barring someone reaching over and dumping poison out of his pinky ring's secret compartment, I don't think anyone would have paid much attention."

Jake snorted. "I assume you didn't notice any pinky rings in play?"

"No."

He drank his pint in thoughtful silence, then said, "It's not a bad theory. A little too Sherlock Holmesy maybe, but we'll talk to the Hawthorne woman." His eyes slanted to mine. "That was clever, making that connection."

"I learned from the master," I mocked. I actually hadn't intended the double meaning, but it worked well.

He reddened. Turned a stony profile to me.

"The thing is," he said curtly, after a moment or two, "the Beaton-Jones chick still has a better motive, and she was on the scene."

"I'm the last guy to underestimate the power of the almighty dollar, but I think blaming someone for the death of your child—"

"But that's *my* point," he interrupted. "After I talked to the PI, Markopoulos, I went to see Ally's boyfriend." His eyes met mine again. "According to Duncan Roe, he got Ally pregnant. Jones forced her to have an abortion."

Out of the blue I remembered that little shiver Ally had given when I'd asked her about children. I'd taken it as distaste for the idea. But maybe it was something entirely different.

Yeah, that did sort of change everything.

Not only did Ally share an eerily similar motive to the one I'd ascribed to Nina, but her pain was a lot fresher—nor was the forced abortion her only motive. And Ally had been at the party, even if I couldn't remember her near the bar. Someone else might be able to place her there.

Following my own train of thought, I said, "Did Jones's autopsy turn up anything to indicate he was terminally ill?"

Jake looked surprised. "How'd you come up with that?"

"I overheard Jones's first wife at the funeral. She said something in passing that made me think he might not be a well man. I mean, before he was murdered, obviously."

"Obviously. Well, she was right. Jones had been recently diagnosed with pancreatic cancer."

"Wow." I met his eyes. "Poor bastard."

"Yeah. Not the way I'd want to go, for sure."

"Did his wife know?"

"Apparently."

"Then...why would she kill him?"

He said patiently, "Because he was planning to divorce her."

"But was he? Have you talked to his lawyer? We only have the PI's word for that."

And Paul's—and now I understood Paul's comment about Porter not standing for being cuckolded. It turned out he had been right about that, so maybe he was right about the other things. Why was I so resistant to that idea?

I said, "Maybe Jones changed his mind about a divorce. Why would he have insisted on an abortion—why would she have gone along with it—if they were splitting up?"

Jake was silent, considering this.

"I'm just sayin'."

"It's worth checking," he said grudgingly.

"The other thing is that apparently Porter yanked financing for a project near and dear to the hearts of Al January and Valarie Rose. I don't have anything more to go on than that, but they were both standing at the bar. So was Paul Kane, come to think of it." I added maliciously, "In fact, Kane had the best access to Porter's drink of anyone. Any reason he might want Porter out of the way?"

Jake gave me a level look. "Funny," he said. But then, proving he was still the hard-hearted bastard I'd known and—well, sort of known—he added, "Just the opposite. Most of the funding for these indie projects came from Porter—or were underwritten by Porter, anyway. And they'd been friends—good friends according to everyone I've talked to—a long time."

I was smiling into my drink, and Jake said, "I wouldn't compromise an investigation because of my feelings for the people involved. You should remember that."

He wouldn't knowingly compromise an investigation, *that* I believed. But didn't he see that his feelings might blind him to certain possibilities? In the interests of impartial justice, shouldn't he really excuse himself from any involvement in this case? But he hadn't. And he wouldn't—because his personal connection to Paul Kane was something he couldn't admit to. Wouldn't want made public.

Oh yeah, I remembered only too well how that went.

Studying me, Jake said, "You don't like Paul, do you?"

I hadn't thought about it before. "Not particularly."

He nodded like that didn't surprise him.

I drained my glass, looked at my watch. "I should get going."

"Yeah, me too."

We paid for our drinks and walked out together. As we strolled around the building to the parking in the back, I said, "I still think Nina's movements on Sunday would be worth looking into."

"We'll check into it," Jake said. "I'm not ruling anyone out yet, and she's a squirrelly broad, no question."

The car alarm chirped in welcome as he stopped beside the conspicuously innocuous vehicle—with the police lights in the back window.

I said, "Night," and pulled my keys out.

He said abruptly, "You know that Kate lost the baby?"

I said awkwardly—realizing I hadn't mentioned it before, "Yeah, I'm sorry." And I was. I didn't wish Kate or that kid any harm. In fact, I had almost called Jake when Chan told me about it, but I'd thought better of it. It might have looked like I believed the only obstacle to our own relationship was that baby; the truth was, it had merely been the final roadblock.

He said unemotionally, "Since we have a choice this time around, she's not sure if she's ready to start a family. She's at a place in her career where taking time off could set her back years. She's in line for promotion."

I didn't want to hear this. I didn't want to feel sorry for him—I didn't want to feel anything at all. But I couldn't decently walk away, so I asked reluctantly, "How do you feel about that?"

I could just make out his lopsided smile in the parking lot lights. "I want a family. But she's worked hard for this. It's her call."

I'd thought the whole point of the marriage was so that Jake could have a family and a "normal" life. Maybe it was a real marriage, despite the fun and games with Paul Kane. Maybe Jake did love Kate. It was to his credit that he seemed to place as much importance on her career as his own—or at least understand that she would.

But I had no idea what to say to him. Good luck with that? He was talking to the wrong person. But he was looking at me like he expected something—needed something.

I said gently, "Drive safely, Jake," and walked away.

CHAPTER THIRTEEN

I groaned when I saw Guy's Miata parked outside Cloak and Dagger. How the hell much of this was I supposed to deal with in one night?

Then it occurred to me that my lover coming safely home to me should not, technically, fall into the stressful-shit-I-had-to-deal-with category. Yet there it was: the old familiar feeling of not wanting to face this—and I knew there would be something to face. I'd known since Guy had proposed a romantic weekend in Mexico, and I'd felt nothing but dismay that there was something waiting for me to face.

I let myself into the store, walked upstairs, and opened the door. Guy stood at the window, staring down at the empty street below.

"I didn't know whether to expect you or not," I said, as he turned to face me.

"I spoke to Peter," he said. "We need to talk."

Well, the good news was he didn't apparently care where I'd been, so I didn't need to admit I'd been having drinks with my own ex-lover. I dropped down on the chair next to the sofa. All at once I was very tired. "Sure," I said. "We could start with you explaining why you're pen pals with a kid who tried to kill me."

He inhaled like I'd tackled him out of the blue. "Peter did not try to kill you, Adrien. He is not a murderer—and that's not merely my opinion. The jury agreed. He was swept along with something that got out of control, that's all. He's young, he was naive. He was every bit as manipulated as Angus. You've forgiven Angus, haven't you?"

Had I? Yeah, apparently I had. I replied, "Angus never tried to kill me."

"He involved you in something that could have got you killed. It's the same thing, nearly."

"No, Guy, actually it's not."

He didn't bother to argue; his expression said it all.

I said, "Even if we put that aside for a minute, if you can't see how far out of line his coming here was...I don't know what to tell you."

"You're completely overreacting."

Now that was almost funny, considering that I'd been thinking Guy had spent the last week overreacting about Jake. I said, "I disagree. I think most people would disagree."

"Most people." He shook his head like that was unworthy of me.

Maybe it was.

Reaching out, he absently picked up the crystal-encased gold doubloon he'd bought me early in our relationship. He frowned at it as though he'd suddenly spotted a flaw in the lustrous surface. He said, "I know Peter." He raised his eyes to meet mine. "I've known him longer than I've known you."

"Yes. I recall."

"He needs a friend right now. He needs help."

I had this sudden Ebenezer Scrooge moment. *Are there no prisons? Are there no workhouses?* Maybe Lisa was right. Maybe I had grown hard, bitter. In any case, I seemed fresh out of the milk of human kindness.

I said, "He showed up here deliberately, Guy. He was challenging me, letting me know he was back, staking his claim."

A look of distaste crossed Guy's face.

I said, "Yeah, it is very high school. I agree. And we're both too old for this shit."

"I think you may have misinterpreted—"

I laughed. Shook my head. "I didn't misinterpret anything. He wants you back, and he wanted me to know that. He believes you still have feelings for him—and I'm not so sure you don't."

"I told you at the start there was nothing...serious between Peter and me. That is to say, I'm fond of him, I consider him a friend, and I want to see to him through this...difficult time. He *needs* someone, Adrien."

I need someone, I thought. But what I said was, "And you need to be needed?"

"Everyone needs to be needed," Guy answered succinctly. "Even you." He replaced the pirate coin in its place on the bookshelf.

When I didn't respond, he asked quietly, "Are you asking me to choose between you?"

I'd been massaging my temples against what felt like a looming head-ache. Migraine. Brain cloud. I looked up. "Wow. I guess I didn't realize it would be that tough a choice. No, I'm not asking you to choose."

"What does that mean?"

I gave a helpless laugh. "Damned if I know. I think...we seem to have reached an impasse. I feel betrayed by your friendship with Verlane. I realize that's not logical. I realize that if I'd made the mistakes Verlane has made, I'd still want my friends to stand by me, hope that someone would help me when the time came. I just..."

"What?"

I met his eyes. "I just need to come first for someone, Guy."

He said, "Is it fair to ask for that when I don't come first for you?"

Fair question. I'm not sure why it felt like I had suddenly run out of highway. I replied, "Probably not."

Neither of us seemed to have anything to add.

At last he moved. "Maybe we both need some time."

"Yes," I said, and I rose, as though seeing a guest to the door.

We went out on the landing, I followed him down the stairs; saw him out the side door. He hesitated. I knew he was trying to decide if he should offer to give his key back. I didn't want him to, but I couldn't seem to make myself say anything.

He said, "I'll call you."

"I'll be here," I said.

And he smiled as though we both knew that wasn't true.

* * * * *

"Morning," I called as the glass door swung open with a cheerful jangle of bells.

"I will never understand men. Why can't they just *say* what they want?" Natalie deposited the large pink box of pastries on the counter with strudel-smooshing force.

I glanced up from the register. "What's that mean?"

"That!" She jabbed her finger at my nose. "That look. That's exactly what I mean. It's like you think it's a trick question."

"It *is* a trick question," I said, "because if we just tell you what we want, you won't like the answer. And then it will be loud and messy and take up a lot of time we don't have."

Her eyes narrowed. "Lisa asked you to talk to me about Warren, didn't she?"

"God, no." I opened the pastry box. "Is it somebody's birthday?" Hopefully not hers—or anyone else's I was now related to.

She said huffily, "I thought I would like a doughnut this morning."

I blinked. "There must be twenty-four doughnuts here."

"Twenty-eight. You get two free ones with each dozen. Have one. Anyway, they're not all doughnuts."

"I see that." There was quite a nice selection of baked goods. I took a chocolate doughnut with sprinkles. "I thought carbs were out this month?"

"I don't give a damn about carbs," Natalie said viciously, and I raised my eyebrows, before returning hastily to counting out the register.

We always do a brisk business on Saturdays, and that day was no exception. In between helping customers—which she did charmingly—Natalie brooded and somehow managed to eat four doughnuts, two cheese Danishes, a cinnamon pecan roll, and a bear claw.

"I'd offer to take you to lunch," I said when twelve o'clock rolled around, "but I'm afraid you'll explode."

"We can't close the store anyway," she said. She fastened me with a darkling eye—well, as darkling as a blue-eyed blonde who looks like a Ralph Lauren model can get. "This is why we need some help in here, especially since you're busy out sleuthing half the time."

"We're going to get some help," I promised. "And it's not like I'm going to continue sleuthing—"

"So you *are* on a case!" she said triumphantly. "I knew the minute I heard about that murder at Paul Kane's mansion. I *knew* it."

I'd been so busy brooding over Guy and the situation with Peter Verlane, I'd walked right into that one. I said, "You make it sound more organized than it is. I just agreed to ask a few people some questions, that's all."

"I'll tell you right now, the wife did it," Natalie said.

"That seems to be the consensus of opinion. Why do you think she did it?"

"Well, for starters, did you *see* him? He was old enough to be her father. And he looked like a frog."

"Yeah, but love is blind," I said.

"No, it's not!" she scoffed. "Not for girls like her."

Now this was interesting. The feminine perspective. "What do you mean, girls like her?"

She made an exasperated little clucking sound. "Adrien. She is a *total* bimbo."

"Hey, bimbos have feelings too," I said. "Look at Anna Nicole Smith."

She just shook her head.

"Okay," I said, "but Anna Nicole Smith didn't knock her elderly husband off. So why take that risk—especially when the wife is always the immediate suspect?"

"Maybe she couldn't wait."

"Why wouldn't she be able to wait?"

Natalie shrugged. I thought it was an interesting point, though. What if there was some time factor involved? Like...what if Ally's lover had given her some kind of ultimatum? Or what if she was pregnant again? Or what if Porter—as Paul Kane had hinted—was planning to change his will?

I said, "But why do it in such a public way? Why not just arrange a quiet little accident?"

"Maybe she didn't know how. Or maybe she thought someone else would be blamed."

I stared at her. She had something there, but I couldn't quite put my finger on what it was. Would Ally have any reason to believe someone else would be suspected before her in her husband's death?

Natalie said, "That detective in charge of the case: is he *your* Jake?"

My mouth dried. The words felt arid and dusty as I forced them out. "Who told you his name?" Like I had to ask.

"Lisa pointed him out on television the other night, and I recognized him as one of the cops who was in here the other day."

I opened my mouth, and then shut it. Jake had to know he was fighting a rearguard action. And I was through lying to my own friends and family. "Yeah," I said. "We used to be friends. A long time ago. He's married now."

"Bastard," she said.

I shook my head. "Not really. He never lied to me. I just didn't ask the questions I didn't want to know the answers to."

It wasn't like I hadn't always known this was the truth, but as I said it aloud, I absorbed that I was finally able to accept it without being angry at myself or Jake.

Natalie went to lunch, came back, and I spent my break surfing the Web, finding out what I could on Langley Hawthorne. It was mostly a tangent. I started out doing some more searching into Nina's background, but a couple of references to Hawthorne's accidental death diverted my attention.

There wasn't as much information as I would have expected. Despite his wealth and his interest in movies and moviemaking, Hawthorne had kept a low profile. His relationship with his daughter was apparently always a stormy one, but he had doted on her. When he died, she inherited the bulk of his fortune.

That wasn't particularly noteworthy; what caught my attention was the manner of his death. He'd fallen off his yacht and drowned off Catalina Island. Hawthorne and a handful of close friends had been drinking heavily that evening—which was apparently not unusual—and the Los Angeles Coroner's Office had ruled the death an accident.

Even more intriguing was the lineup of guests on that fateful night. In addition to Al January and Paul Kane, Porter Jones and the first Mrs. Jones had been present—as had Nina. This would have been after Nina's affair with

Porter had ended. Or, more exactly, after her father had insisted Porter break it off with her. To my way of thinking, at best that would have been one very awkward get-together.

I considered it for a bit, then I phoned Lisa.

After we got past the pleasantries and unpleasantries—*Darling, I didn't realize it was* still *a secret*—I said, "Lisa, at lunch the other day, you said something about hiring a caterer for this SPCA banquet. Have you already done that?"

"You mean at the lunch we *didn't* have the other day?"

"That's the one. Have you already hired a caterer?"

"We're moving the venue to the Bonaventure."

I said, "Would you do me a favor and see if you can set up an interview with Nina Hawthorne? She owns Truly Scrumptious Catering."

"But we don't need a caterer, Adrien. The hotel will take care of all that."

"I know, but could you pretend that you're still holding it wherever you talked about before?"

"I suppose so. Why?" She sounded mildly suspicious.

"I'd like to sit in on the interview."

Silence.

"Why?" she said, and it was her no-fooling voice.

"I'd like to see what she's like."

She said tentatively, "Are you thinking of hiring her for some event?"

Oh God. Did she think Guy and I were about to tie the knot?

I said, "Sort of. I'd just like to get a feel for her and her company."

"All right, darling," Lisa said, highly amused. "I'll set something up, and you can tell me what it's all about later."

I hung up, and Natalie tapped on my office door.

"Paul Kane called while you were on the phone."

I sighed. "Thanks."

I called Kane back and got his PA. After a brief wait, she put me through to Kane.

"I was beginning to wonder if you were ducking my calls," he greeted me in that mellifluous voice.

I remembered that he had called the previous afternoon, and I'd never got back to him. Granted, I'd been a little preoccupied with the detonation of my personal life, but it did seem a little blasé now that I thought about it—especially when I still believed it possible he was the intended victim of last weekend's poisoning. Was I unconsciously hoping someone would take Paul out?

"Sorry," I said. "I've been a little busy. In fact, there's something I wanted to discuss with you."

Amused, he said, "This sounds ominous."

I said, "Has it crossed your mind that you might have been the target last Sunday?"

It was so abruptly quiet, I wondered if we had lost the connection. He burst out laughing, and I had to hold the handset away from my ear.

"Bloody brilliant! You truly had me for half a mo."

"Yeah, but I'm not kidding," I persisted. "I've been doing some digging, and I couldn't help but notice Nina Hawthorne catered your party."

"Lose a lot of clients to poison, does she?" He was still finding it all terribly humorous, pip-pip.

"I don't suppose all her clients share the history with her you do," I said.

He stopped laughing. In fact, he was silent for a few seconds. He said, "I gather from your tone you're aware that Nina and I have had a somewhat tumultuous past."

"I know you had a child together, and that—"

"Yes," he broke in crisply. "Quite. Well, you are thorough. I give you credit for that."

"I'm sorry," I said. "I'm not trying to open old wounds, but it occurred to me that the drink you handed me for Porter might easily have been mistaken for your own."

After a moment he said, "She wasn't there. At least—"

"At least what?"

"No. It's ridiculous."

"What's ridiculous?"

"Nothing. I appreciate your concern. Truly. But…not necessary, I assure you." Before I could respond, he went on, "Look, the reason I'm giving you a tinkle is I'm having a little get-together at the marina tomorrow. Valarie will be there, and it would give you a chance to speak with her."

"Sundays are awkward," I said. "I'm supposed to occasionally give my assistant a day off."

But Paul persisted—charming and intractable as ever—and I finally agreed just to shut him up.

"Marvelous!" he exclaimed after giving me the details. "We'll see you then."

"All right," I said without enthusiasm.

He chuckled at my tone, then said with unexpected seriousness, "Adrien… thank you. I appreciate your concern. I do. But the loss of our child actually brought Nina and me together. Allowed us to be friends again."

"Of course," I said. "I didn't realize."

"How could you?" he said easily. "But I am genuinely grateful for your friendship."

"No problem," I said.

With friends like me, who needed enemies?

CHAPTER FOURTEEN

The faded marina sign was missing an uppercase *O*. But *Watch for posing Drivers!* seemed pretty good advice given the number of Mercedes driven by guys in yacht caps.

I parked and walked past the clubhouse and Olympic-sized swimming pool. Gaily colored pennants whipped overhead. Gulls mewed, swooping and diving over the bobbing pier. The smell of ocean and diesel permeated the air; sunlight glittered blindingly on the blue water.

It looked like a good day to be out on the high seas. Or the low seas. The harbor was already full of boats heading out toward the breakwater—and even the vessels still moored at the dock seemed to be crowded with mateys intent on enjoying the sunshine, salt air, and—in more than a few cases—the hair of the dog.

I found the slip number Kane had given me without trouble. His luxury yacht, *Pirate's Gambit*, was a sleek seventy-eight-footer with a black hull. A pirate flag flapped briskly on the bow.

"Avast ye!"

I looked up and Kane was leaning over the railing, a bottle of champagne—very expensive champagne at that—in one hand. He was smiling down at me. Not for the first time, I was struck by how really attractive he was. He had it all, really—well, all that Hollywood cared about: looks, charm, personal magnetism.

And he wasn't a bad actor, either. I wondered if his bold and unapologetic sexuality had anything to do with the fact that he wasn't a bigger star.

I walked up the boarding ramp and Kane came agilely down the ladder from the upper deck to greet me.

"Perfect timing," he said, lightly squeezing my shoulder as he moved past me. "Everyone's topside. Go say hello."

I climbed the ladder to the smaller open deck. "Everyone" turned out to be Valarie Rose and Al January comfortably ensconced in lounge chairs. They were drinking champagne and arguing amiably. Valarie wore an emerald green swimsuit, and January wore orange shorts and some kind of Aztec print sports shirt.

"Welcome aboard," Valarie called. "I hope you brought your swimsuit. I feel a little underdressed."

I sat down in a blue-and-white striped deck chair. "Sorry," I said. The breeze off the water was chilly, but the sun felt good. Not so good that I was tempted to take my clothes off, but pleasant.

"How's the investigation going?" January asked, pouring a glass of champagne and handing it to me.

I murmured thanks, took a sip, and set the glass next to the railing. "I don't think the police are ready to make an arrest," I said. "But it's not like they're keeping me up to date."

Although my Friday night meet with Jake had been surprisingly close to it.

"I can't imagine what the holdup is," Valarie said. She was attractive in a no-nonsense way: good figure, good bones, good teeth, good skin. "We all know who did it."

January gave her a tolerant look. "Then I guess the holdup is, the police don't have enough evidence to make their case yet."

I asked, "Are you so sure Ally is guilty?"

"There! You see, I didn't even need to say her name," Valarie said. "You know exactly who I mean. We all know she murdered Porter. It's not socially correct to say so, but we all know it." She leaned back in her lounge chair, tilting her face up. The sun glanced off her large green sunglasses.

January looked across at me and smiled ruefully.

"You don't think anyone else had a motive?" I asked Valarie.

She lifted her head. "To commit *murder?*" Behind the big shades, she looked amazed at the idea.

Beneath us, the ship's engines rumbled into life. Paul Kane climbed up to join us, taking a chair next to Valarie.

"What do you think?" he inquired of me, nodding to the cockpit.

"Beautiful," I said. "How many crew members?"

"Captain and one deckhand this afternoon. I take her out on my own when I'm in the mood." He grinned, his teeth very white. "I fly my own plane too."

"Paul's a full-service action hero," Valarie purred, and ran a possessive hand down Paul's tanned arm. He caught her hand and kissed it playfully.

Well, blow me down, me hearties. I'd sort of guessed—and if you browsed the headlines of the celebrity gossip rags in the supermarket checkout—or even gave in and read a few pages while waiting for the line to move—it was common knowledge that Kane was bisexual. Nor would it make any sense for him to sit home nights when Jake was playing *Make Room for Daddy* with Kate. I'm not sure why I thought he would keep secret the scandalous truth of his appetite for women.

Meeting my gaze, Paul smiled again and said, "Take your shirt off, Adrien. We've paid extra for the sunshine."

I glanced down at my white polo shirt. "Mother Superior warned me about boys like you," I said.

January laughed, and Paul licked his lips. "She didn't tell you the half of it."

That pretty much set the tone for the rest of our voyage. Kane—to the apparent amusement of my other two companions—flirted relentlessly with me during the three hours we cruised the open water. It was harmless, but I couldn't help wondering what lay behind it. I hadn't previously got the impression that Paul found me irresistible—and all the winks and little smiles and brushing of feet and hands—didn't alter my opinion. Paul was doing his considerable best to charm me, and I wasn't sure why. Did he think I was considering abandoning my part in the investigation? Could he have placed that much faith in my sleuthing skills?

There was more champagne at lunch, which consisted of Caesar salad, pasta shells stuffed with ricotta cheese and spinach, and chicken Vesuvio in garlic white sauce. It was a lot of food—rich food—and I was very glad I wasn't prone to seasickness.

Oddly, although it was ostensibly the reason for this get-together, we barely talked about Porter's death. Instead, the three of them discussed various ideas for filming *Murder Will Out*.

"I sense Jason has a dark past," Paul said of Jason Leland, the protagonist of the two mysteries I'd written about a gay Shakespearean actor and amateur sleuth. "I think his past casts a long shadow."

"A secret sorrow," Al January said—with a straight face, as far as I could tell.

"Uh, sure," I said. In all honesty, I thought Jason was suffering about as much secret sorrow as Jackie Holmes, the Man from C.A.M.P. But I already knew from talking to writer friends that no one was ever happy with the screen adaptation of their work. My main interest was getting money for the bookstore expansion. That's what I kept telling myself.

"I have some concerns with the London setting," Valarie said. "What would you think about moving it to The Oregon Shakespeare Festival?"

"Ashland's beautiful," Al agreed.

And on they went. After a time they stopped asking for my input, and I stretched out on one of the lounge chairs. I hadn't had much sleep lately, and the food and drink and flattery—the warmth of the sun and the lulling motion of the water—had a soporific effect.

The next time I opened my eyes, we were heading back into the harbor and the three of them were talking quietly about Porter.

"...but if Porter really was dying..." That was Valarie.

January said, "Porter trusted Marla."

"Why not?" Paul said. "Marla knew where the skeletons were buried." His voice changed. He said, "Hello, Sleeping Beauty."

I glanced over and the three of them were watching me. Their expressions were a curious mix. "Sorry," I said, sitting up. "Too much sun and champagne."

"Did you have more than a glass?" Paul commented, amused. "Not that I blame you for flaking out. We occasionally put ourselves to sleep."

After that there was very little conversation. Valarie went below deck and changed into white slacks and a sweater. January and Kane chatted desultorily. It was just after seven o'clock when we put in at the harbor and prepared to disembark.

Paul put a hand on my arm. "Stay for a bit, Adrien. I'd like a word in private."

January said good-bye to me, patted Paul's shoulder. Valarie kissed his cheek, murmuring, "Are you sure you can't cancel your plans for tonight?"

"I'm sure, my flower."

"Well, watch out for the crazies." She caught my glance, and said, "Oh, that wasn't directed at you—although I do think you're nuts to go along with this last brainstorm of Paul's. You know, what you two are doing could be dangerous. Someone tried to run Paul off the road on his way down here this morning."

I turned to Kane, who laughed at my expression. "*No one* is trying to kill me," he said.

Valarie gaped. "You mean someone has threatened to—? Paul!"

He was shaking his head, gently steering her toward the gangplank. "Bad driving isn't a crime. The perils of amateur sleuthing: Adrien sees murderers behind road signs."

He waved them off, then turned smiling lazily to me. "Alone at last! Let's go down to the salon."

I followed him below deck to a beautifully appointed lounge paneled in teakwood, with panoramic picture windows of the harbor and the sky flushed with sunset. The plush carpeting and rich furnishings were in burnished earth tones. I'd been in nice hotels that weren't as lavishly decorated.

"What's your poison?" Paul asked, going to the bar.

Funny guy.

"Nothing for me, thanks."

His mobile mouth quirked. He poured himself brandy and joined me over on one of the long L-shaped sofas.

"Jake tells me you have a thing for pirates."

As "things" go, my affection for swashbuckling films is pretty tame, but his tone—and the understanding that he and Jake had discussed and laughed at me—turned it into something else.

"Aye, aye, Captain," I drawled.

He chuckled, studying me with his bright, inquisitive gaze. He took a swallow of brandy, savoring it.

"Is Jake behaving himself?" he asked.

"As far as I know."

He smirked at the implications. "He's not scaring you off the case?"

What was going on here? There was something very odd in this casual, almost—but not quite—friendly inquisition.

"No."

"And you haven't changed your mind about pursuing this…investigation?"

"No. Should I?"

He shrugged. "The police are very close to making an arrest, you know. The evidence is stacking up against Ally."

His main concern had not been justice for Porter—it had been that Alonzo viewed *him* as a suspect. Not that I could fault him for that, since my concern had been that *I* was a suspect. I said, "Did you know Porter had cancer?"

"Yes." He looked momentarily grave. "I was one of the few people he confided in."

"I assume Ally knew?"

He opened his mouth to answer, but turned his head at the sound of footsteps coming down the winding stairs that led into the lounge.

Boots. Jeans encasing long legs and lean hips. Wide shoulders in a black leather jacket. Jake.

"There you are," Paul said lazily.

Jake stared at me. In some alternate universe that dumbstruck expression would have been funny. Not so much in this one.

"Oh, don't run off," Paul said as I rose. "We could make a threesome of it." He chuckled. "Dinner, that is."

"Another time," I said. "Dinner, that is."

I had to step past Jake to get to the doorway. He had recovered from his shock and watched me without expression.

"Adrien," he said quietly.

I nodded at him. "Good night," I told Paul. "Thanks for the boat ride."

I heard Paul laughing as I climbed topside.

The air was chill and smelled of brine and something dank. Overhead, the palm trees rustled eerily, black against the blaze of sunset. The hollow thud of my footsteps followed me down the pier as I walked toward the parking lot.

It wasn't a shock…exactly. It was more the realization that Paul Kane had deliberately kept me onboard so that I would see Jake arrive.

Or so that Jake would see me?

Either way it was puzzling. Maybe I wasn't exactly clear for whose benefit that little performance had been staged, but I was dead sure it hadn't been an accident. That little meeting had been directed as any scene in a play.

Why?

CHAPTER FIFTEEN

I knew the minute I was ushered into Dr. Cardigan's office on Monday morning that the news was not good.

Dr. Cardigan was seated at his desk, frowning over a file that I had a suspicion was mine. He rose, shook hands, invited me to sit. I sat and glanced at the many smiling photos of his children and grandchildren on the bookshelves lined with medical tomes.

"How are you feeling?" he asked, sitting down again.

His black-cherry gaze rested seriously on my face, and I figured this was not a rhetorical question. "Good," I said determinedly.

He nodded like everybody said that and we all knew it wasn't true. "Fatigue? Some difficulty catching your breath?"

"Fatigue—but nothing unusual."

"Are you finding your arrhythmia a little worse?"

I think he could see by my expression that struck home. "Well, we've got your test results back and there are some things we need to talk about."

I nodded automatically.

"I don't think this is going to come as a surprise." He was studying my charts again. "You've been largely asymptomatic for the past fifteen years, but your last ECG indicates changes in ejection fraction and enlargement of the left ventricle." He looked up inquiringly. Apparently I was supposed to ask an intelligent question around about then.

I said, "Okay. In layman's terms?"

"The pneumonia has aggravated your heart disease. Your heart is working harder with fewer results."

I nodded, trying to process.

He looked up, scanned my face. "We've discussed surgery in the past. It's now a matter of when, not if. I'm going to refer you to a cardiac surgeon—"

I missed a bit of the next part. Open heart surgery. Not my favorite thing.

I asked, "How soon would he have to operate?"

"Your surgeon will make the determination once he's examined you. Once symptoms present, it's best not to delay."

I sighed. Rubbed my jaw. I felt broadsided. I guess I should have seen it coming, but I really didn't feel that ill. Tired from the pneumonia, naturally. Stressed.

Dr. Cardigan said, "We want to perform surgery before the left ventricle is irreversibly weakened. Repairing the valve is preferable to replacing it, but that's often not possible when the damage has been caused by rheumatic fever."

I nodded. I'd done a fair bit of reading on valve replacement the first time the subject came up. Repairing the valve not only increased my odds of both short-and- long-term survival but lessened the risk of stroke and worsening my heart failure.

Studying my face, Dr. Cardigan said, "I know this isn't the news you wanted, but it is not, by any means, a grim prognosis. It's not a routine procedure, I'll grant you, but there are over a hundred thousand heart valve surgeries performed annually in the United States alone. Most patients experience marked improvement in health and spirits."

"Great," I said.

"The recuperation process is a slow one, but there's every likelihood that you'll make a complete recovery. Your overall health is good. In fact, with surgery you may discover you no longer suffer from the arrhythmia at all."

So, really, everything was fucking terrific! Why did I have the ridiculous desire to cry?

* * * * *

"See! He likes you," Natalie said triumphantly.

I stared down at the scrawny scrap of fur cautiously sniffing my hand.

"He doesn't like me. He thinks I'm going to feed him."

"Now who's being a cynic? Anyway, every bookstore should have a cat."

The cat—assuming it was a cat and not some beige bug-eyed refugee from outer space—slunk uneasily down the counter, and flinched at the flutter of *Mystery Scene* pages as a gust of warm air blew in from the street.

It was Monday afternoon, and I was not in a great mood after my trip to Huntington Hospital. After leaving the med center, I'd stopped off for some lunch I wasn't able to eat, then spent an hour or two wandering around the Paseo. I'd stopped in at Apostrophe Books and bought a copy of Paul Kane's unauthorized biography, and then finally steeled myself to go home.

The sight of a flea-bitten alley cat—okay, alley kitten—on the antique mahogany desk that served as my sales counter did not improve my precarious mood.

"Nat," I said, "I don't want a cat."

"But he'd be good for you, Adrien. There are all kinds of studies about how pets help people live longer—just petting a cat can lower your blood pressure. And he would be company for you."

"My blood pressure is okay," I snapped. "At least it was a minute ago. And I don't want a *cat* for company."

The cat cringed at my raised voice, and slither-ran down the counter, sending papers flying before he leaped to the back of a nearby chair and balanced there, sinking his little claws into the leather.

"Now you've scared him!" she exclaimed, scurrying to retrieve the scattered flyers and receipts. "He's just a baby!"

"A baby *what*? He looks like a cross between a lemur and Gollum."

"He's starving."

"Then feed him and put him back in the alley where you found him."

"I didn't find him," she said indignantly. "He came in on his own." She gave me an expectant look. Like, what? This was supposed to be the universal sign that I and this feral cat were Meant To Be?

"He's filthy," I said, and to prove my point, the little beast balanced on three legs and proceeded to scratch itself briskly behind its torn ear with the fourth. "He's got fleas. He's probably disease-ridden."

"You sound like Lisa," Natalie said, quite unforgivably.

I gave her a long look. "I do not want this cat," I said. "No, Nat. Not in a hat. Not in my flat. Not in the store, not any more, just out the door—if you please."

I thought that was pretty good for off-the-cuff, but she was unimpressed. "He'll die out there!"

"Or you'll die in here. Take your pick." At her expression, I sighed. "Honest to God, Natalie. I don't—I can't take on the responsibility for a pet right now. And if I was in the market for a pet, it would be a dog."

A big dog. That ate cats for lunch.

Apparently Natalie's case of selective deafness had grown worse while I'd been out. As though I hadn't said a word, she said, "And I'll watch him during the day while you're working this case."

"I'm not—" I amended, "I don't know that I'm going to do any more sleuthing. It's taking up a lot of time I don't have." I hoped that wasn't as portentous as it sounded.

Even before Dr. Cardigan had advised me to take things easy for the next week or so before my surgery, I'd decided that it wouldn't be a good idea for me to keep poking around in Porter Jones's death. Not because it was dangerous—it hadn't been so far—and certainly not because of Jake. No, it was after leaving Paul Kane's boat the evening before. It bothered me the way Kane had manipulated me—and Jake—for his own amusement. At least, I couldn't see any other reason for his behavior the evening before. And it made me uneasy. I already didn't like him, and now I didn't trust him.

True, that left me still squarely in Detective Alonzo's sights as a murder suspect, but it sounded to me like Jake was guiding the investigation toward Ally Beaton-Jones.

Natalie was eyeing me curiously. I said lamely, "Besides, Guy is allergic to cats."

She didn't say it, but I could see what she was thinking: that Guy—at least as far as she knew—hadn't been around since last Thursday. Hadn't even called.

I missed Guy. I missed him a lot right now.

"Feed him a can of tuna and put him outside," I said. "He's an alley cat. He'll survive."

"He might not! He's just a few months old!" She was getting angry now, and—oddly enough—I was getting angry too.

"Then *you* take him home."

"You know Lisa won't allow animals in the house."

What the hell was a healthy, twenty-something-year-old woman still doing living with her parents anyway?

"Then call the pound. I don't care. It's not my cat, and this is not my problem."

She stared at me like I'd morphed into something that belonged in a Playstation. Even the cat seemed to be staring at me with those E.T. eyes.

I tried to bring it down a notch. "Natalie," I said placatingly, "Have a heart. I can't deal with this right now. You can understand that, can't you?"

She was still not speaking to me when I left to take Emma to her riding lessons.

*****

While I was watching Emma go through her paces, Jake called and left a message on my cell phone. I didn't discover it until I was back at the bookstore.

His recorded voice sounded terse and self-conscious.

"It's possible you're onto something with Nina Hawthorne. It turns out she was at Paul's the morning of the party. There's still no indication of how she might have introduced poison into the cocktail mixture, but it might be worth talking to her."

Why tell me? He was the police. It was his job to check this stuff out. If I didn't know better, I'd say he was using this development with Nina as an excuse for contacting me. Was he—like Paul—worried I might pull out of the investigation? He didn't agree with any of my theories so far, so why the hell would he care? Wouldn't it be easier, really?

Or was I the only one struggling with old feelings?

I listened to the message again, started to dial Jake, and then stopped myself. There was nothing to discuss. Not really. If I called him, it would be because I wanted to talk to him, and that way lay madness.

I opened a can of Wolfgang Puck's tortilla soup and made myself eat it, browsing through a stack of books that had arrived that morning from publishers. I'd been looking forward to Richard Stevenson's new one for months. There were enticing offerings from favorites P.A. Brown, Neil Plakcy, and Anthony Bidulka—and a promising first book by new author Scott Sherman (although if I had to read one more mystery about a hustler turning detective, I was going to shoot myself). I flipped pages and listened absently to the sounds of the street settling down for the evening outside my window.

Rising, I went to turn on the stereo and listened to the opening notes of Snow Patrol's "You're All I Have" from *Eyes Open*.

I tried not to think. I especially tried not to think about Guy.

I could call him, of course. If I called him and said I was ill and needed him, he'd be here in a minute.

But that would be the wrong reason to call. And the wrong reason for him to come back.

I remembered that I had bought Paul Kane's biography, and I went downstairs to retrieve it. For a moment I stood in the silent gloom of the store, staring through the plastic dividing wall.

Nothing to see but ladders and scaffolding. A couple of drop cloths. A generator sat to one side beside a pile of broken plaster. There were coils of wire, cans of paint. Nothing sinister lurked there. I was just getting jumpy in my old age.

I retrieved my book and returned upstairs.

The book was called *Glorious Thing*, a nod to Paul Kane's role as the pirate king in the fantasy flick *The Last Corsair*. This was the film that had made Paul Kane a star—maybe a minor star as Hollywood galaxies went, but a star nonetheless. I'd seen the film a couple of times, and I had very much appreciated Kane's acting—along with other things. Well, what was there to object to in watching a beautiful male animal run around half-naked for two and a half hours? Even if the dialog did consist of creaking lines like, "I swear by all that is holy, I will have my revenge!" and "What kind of demon are you?" (That last was supposed to be a rhetorical question, but had anyone asked me, I'd have been happy to explain that there was, in fact, a fairly complex demon hierarchy.)

I wasn't far into the book before I sussed that the author, Bonnie Kirkland, was not a member of Paul Kane's fan club. It was hard to put my finger on what it was. For the most part she seemed to be sticking to facts—everything seemed properly attributed and footnoted. And, if anything, Kane's background was one that should have generated sympathy. Born Humphrey Horfield in Bristol, England, he was orphaned at an early age and placed in institutional care. He ran away when he was fifteen to become an actor. He changed his name and supported himself as a rent boy on the streets of London. Talent, his extraordinary good looks, and luck won him a number of small roles in theater productions, but his big break came in 1980 when he won something called the SWET Award for Best Newcomer for his role as Phineas in *A Separate Peace*.

He played the role again in a film version, and then moved to the States where he landed a number of increasingly large parts in movies—some bad, some good, but all seeming to move his career forward. But the most significant thing during that period was the friendship he formed with wealthy entrepreneur Langley Hawthorne, who had recently put together his own film production company, Associated Talent.

Hawthorne thought Kane was going to be this generation's Cary Grant, and he had invested in him considerably. But it was more than a business investment. Hawthorne had befriended Kane—practically made him one of the family. Without actually saying so, Bonnie Kirkland managed to convey that she thought this was a mistake on Hawthorne's part, and that Kane was a charming and manipulative user.

As far as I could tell that opinion was based on two things: Kane's affair with Nina Hawthorne—Kirkland's sympathies clearly lay with Nina—and the fact that Hawthorne's death had left Paul Kane rich and in control of Associated Talent.

Not exactly conclusive proof. I flipped through the extensive photo section—picture after picture of Paul Kane in glowing health—and little else—selected from film and stage roles, as well as a number of candid shots. Fortune had favored him, no doubt about it. But it hadn't all been luck. He had worked his English arse off to get where he was, and there was plenty to admire in that.

After Hawthorne's death and the disastrous relationship with Nina, Kane grew less and less discreet about his sexuality—and I thought I began to better understand where Kirkland's disapproval stemmed from. As she elegantly phrased it, "If it moved, Paul screwed it."

In a couple of magazine interviews Kane had admitted he was bisexual and hinted that he had a taste for the kinkier side of romance. When he was photographed at Cannes in a compromising position with a male companion, his career had taken its first serious hit in over a decade. The experts at *Entertainment Weekly* and *Variety* had openly speculated that his career was over, but then *The Last Corsair* was released, and Kane ended up a bigger star than ever before.

It was late when I finished *Glorious Thing*, and I wasn't sure if I really had a better understanding of Paul Kane. I wasn't sure if it mattered. I tossed the book aside. It landed a few feet from the bed, cover facing up with Paul Kane grinning that dashing pirate king smile at me. I turned out the bedside light, pounded the pillows into shape.

The tune to Gilbert and Sullivan's "Pirate King and Chorus" was running through my mind.

> *Oh, better far to live and die*
> *Under the brave black flag I fly,*
> *Than play a sanctimonious part,*
> *With a pirate head and a pirate heart.*
> *Away to the cheating world go you,*
> *Where pirates all are well-to-do;*
> *But I'll be true to the song I sing,*
> *And live and die a Pirate King.*

Somewhere in the alley below, a cat was yowling.

CHAPTER SIXTEEN

"**I** realize that duck confit never goes out of fashion," my mother said, discarding the elegant foldout brochure she had been browsing, "but I was hoping for something with a little more...verve."

Verve. Yes, because what's the point of eating food that just tastes good? Not that duck confit with pomegranate molasses on crispy rice paper exactly fell into my "just tastes good" category. I'd have gone with crab puffs if it had been left to me.

But apparently Lisa was speaking Nina Hawthorne's language. "Of course," Nina said, very businesslike. "I know the exact thing." She opened a binder stuffed with gorgeous photos of comestibles—I mean, you couldn't call that stuff anything as plebeian as *food.* "Grilled New Zealand lamb lollipops with a blueberry port wine sauce."

"Oh my," Lisa murmured, gazing at the sumptuous photograph. She glanced sideways at me. "Adrien?"

Yep, she was enjoying this *way* too much.

"Lamb for an SPCA banquet?" I said doubtfully.

Lisa made a little exasperated sound. Another woman would have smacked her forehead. "He does have a point," she said regretfully.

Nina took it with good grace. She had taken everything with good grace, and that can't have been easy given Lisa's peculiarly playful mood. I studied Paul Kane's former paramour unobtrusively. It was strange to meet someone I had been studying as though she were on my final exam. Like meeting someone in history. Like Betsy Ross, but with fewer stars and more stripes.

She was a bit younger than Kane, but her odometer showed the wear and tear of those years of booze and pills and one-night stands. She was very pale—almost dry-looking—and her face was very lined. Her hair was still in the crew cut she had adopted a decade earlier, but she had let it go prematurely silver. The result was striking. She was small and fine-boned—and with that papery, delicate skin, she reminded me of origami.

"What about crispy swordfish bites with a wasabi dipping sauce?" she suggested, reaching for another binder.

Apparently she really wanted this SPCA gig.

"Your firm catered that party at Paul Kane's, didn't you?" I said, having decided we'd had enough preliminaries to get her relaxed. "I recognize the salmon canapés."

Nina stared at me. Her eyes reminded me of Jake's: that tawny color that looks almost amber in certain light. Lynx eyes, I thought.

"Yes," she said briefly, dampeningly, and offered another binder to Lisa.

And, astonishingly, Lisa leaped to the rescue, taking the binder and exclaiming, "Oh, I saw that on the news! How *dreadful* for you! The man was *poisoned.*"

"It was not the food," Nina said quickly.

"No, they think it must have been something in his drink," I said.

Her eyes flicked to mine again. "Yes. I heard that also."

"I was sitting right next to him when he collapsed," I confided.

Lisa turned and gave me a long look—which I ignored.

"That must have been terrible," Nina said politely. Hard to believe she had once been in love with Porter—but then she had been in love a lot back then.

"He was a big Hollywood producer," I said. "Maybe you even catered one of his parties."

"Porter didn't give parties," Nina said. Meeting my gaze, she said, "I knew him, yes. He was a friend of my family's."

"Was he the kind of person who gets murdered?" Lisa asked innocently.

Nina turned the lynx gaze on her. I could see various unkind comments going through her mind, but what she said was, "No. I can't imagine anyone wanting to kill Porter. He was..." She shrugged. "He was an inoffensive old sot, really."

I said, "Maybe the intent was to kill someone else and they poisoned Porter Jones by mistake?"

Her laugh was jarring. "That would make more sense. I imagine half the people at that party had reason to want Paul dead."

"I don't really know him that well," I said. "His production company optioned one of my books."

"Congratulations," she said politely. "Just watch the fine print on anything he asks you to sign."

"You sound like you're speaking from experience."

"Bitter experience," she agreed. To Lisa she said, "Might I suggest our cornmeal-crusted calamari with a hot cherry pepper aioli?"

"Oh, *yummy*," Lisa murmured.

I left them to it, concurring when requested, watching Nina while they pored over the books. I didn't place much significance on her curtness. I'd have been pretty curt too if someone had treated the death of someone I knew as a tourist attraction. She didn't seem particularly guilty, not that I would necessarily recognize guilt. I might mistake it for offense or wariness. But one thing did stand out: regardless of what Paul Kane thought, Nina Hawthorne still hated his guts.

* * * * *

After Nina gathered up her binders and departed, Lisa and I had lunch.

"You didn't want to observe her in action for any event," Lisa said, serving me a slice of spinach quiche warm from the oven—Marie Callender's oven, that is.

"Er...no," I admitted.

"You're investigating that man's murder, aren't you?"

"I wouldn't really use the word *investigating*," I said, avoiding her eye. I picked up my fork. "I'm asking a few questions at the request of Paul Kane, that's all."

"This is the case that Jake is working on." It was not a question.

I answered, "He's a police lieutenant. I think he keeps tabs on a lot of cases."

Lisa sighed.

I waited for her to say more, but to my relief she actually let it go. I smiled at her. "Thanks, by the way. You were great with her."

She preened a little. "I was, wasn't I?"

We finished lunch and I split for the bookstore so Natalie could have the rest of the day off.

"The cat was in here again," she informed me accusingly, as I glanced through the morning's receipts.

"Was he? Did you recommend Lilian Jackson Braun? She should be right up his alley." I glanced up. "No pun intended."

She was not amused. Glaring at me, she said, "I cannot *believe* how hard-hearted you are."

"Believe it," I said. I checked my watch. "Aren't you supposed to be meeting Warren in twenty minutes?"

She went.

I spent the rest of the afternoon refreshing my knowledge of what book-sellers actually did—sleuthing turned out not to be part of the job description—and trying to decide if it was worth calling Jake over anything I'd discovered talking to Nina Hawthorne.

Since I'd already decided I wasn't going to pursue the investigation, it shouldn't have been much of a decision, but reading the biography on Paul Kane the night before had unwillingly revived my interest in the case.

Or maybe I was just grasping for something—anything—to take my mind off my own problems.

Guy had still not called. I wondered just how much support from his friends Peter Verlane required? But I knew—or at least, I thought I knew—that Guy's withdrawal probably had more to do with me than Verlane.

Luckily the afternoon was busy, and I hadn't time to brood. By the time I pulled the ornate security gate closed and locked the front door, I was beat. I'd have liked nothing more than to get takeout from someplace and watch one of my favorite flicks from my collection of pirate movies, but I remembered that Partners in Crime was meeting that night.

I went back downstairs and assembled the chairs in a circle, set up the coffee machine, and hunted up extra red pencils. I finished off the orange-pine-apple juice while I glanced through the newspaper.

Porter Jones's murder was already off the front page, which probably said more about his noncelebrity status than the effort LAPD was making to solve the case. There didn't appear to be much headway in the investigation since Jake and I had last spoken on Friday night.

Friday night. It seemed like a lifetime ago.

* * * * *

Detective Paul Chan, Jake's former partner in homicide investigation, was the first of the Partners in Crime group to arrive.

Chan was middle-aged and putting on weight. He smelled of cigarettes as he set down a couple of packages of Oreo cookies on the counter, and I deduced his latest effort to quit smoking had crashed and burned.

"I'm thinking of self-publishing," he informed me.

Two packages of Oreos? What was Chan thinking? Golden Oreos did not count as a second selection. I could hear the womenfolk bitching now. And he hadn't brought any cream or milk. I'd have to supply that again—along with the sugar and paper plates and cups and napkins. Did these people think I was made of money?

I said, "Ah. Did you hear back from—?"

"I've heard back from everyone in New York publishing," he said. "What it gets down to is nobody's interested in a book about what real police work is like."

Well, no. Because it was apparently dull as ditchwater. At least the way Chan wrote it. I said, "Well, self-publishing is one option. Or you could try rewriting—"

But he was already on another track. "I saw Jake the other day." His brown eyes met mine. "He said he'd talked to you."

I didn't quite understand his intent expression. "Yeah," I said vaguely.

"He said you were on the scene when that Laurel Canyon homicide went down."

"I'm lucky that way," I said.

"So are you two square again?"

I halted, mid-ripping open the cookies, and stared at him. "Well, he's pretty square," I said. "I'm just a rectangular guy." With latent triangular tendencies.

Chan said painstakingly, "I mean...are you two okay again?" Adding quickly and uncomfortably, "Friends?"

For an instant I didn't have an answer. My mind was totally blown by the news that Jake had apparently confided—no, that couldn't be right. Jake had apparently been bothered enough by our falling-out that he'd let Chan see it. And Chan must have deduced...or Jake must have said...

Chan must have noticed and maybe drawn some weird conclusion.

Because...

Because anything else was...not even in the realm of possibility, right?

So why was I standing there feeling sort of warm and...utterly idiotic? Because Jake had apparently been sorry enough to lose my friendship that he'd let his partner know? Pathetic was what this was.

But I said gruffly, "Yeah, we're okay."

"That's good," Chan said, more uncomfortable by the minute. "So what do you think of Alonzo?"

"I think he's a freaking moron."

"He's not a moron," Chan said soberly. "He's a little rough around the edges, but he's got good instincts."

"I don't know about that. He was sizing me up for a pair of bracelets not too long ago. I may still be high on his hit parade for all I know."

Chan said easily, "He probably just sensed you were hiding something."

I stared at him, but he didn't seem to realize what he'd just admitted to knowing.

"Anyway," he said, flipping through the copies of his story, "Jake's staying involved on this one. You don't have anything to worry about."

I said slowly, "Do you think Jake would try to influence the outcome of an investigation to protect a friend?"

Chan stared at me. "You mean if the friend was guilty?"

"I'm just talking theoretical."

"You know better than that," he said scornfully, and went back to sorting through his papers.

I wanted to ask him if he had any ideas about the case, but Jean and Ted Finch arrived at that moment.

Jean was jubilant. "We did it! We've got an agent!" she crowed, waving a copy of an e-mail.

"We haven't signed yet," Ted corrected quickly, "but we've got an offer for representation."

"You're *kidding*," I said.

Jean and Ted had been writing and rewriting their ghastly first novel *Murder, He Mimed* for as long as I'd been hosting the group. There were many things I loathed about *Murder, He Mimed*, but my number one objection was that their main character, a gay gossip columnist by the name of Avery Oxford, bore an unsettling resemblance to me.

I seemed to be the only person who saw it, though. The one time I'd suggested it to the group, everyone had burst out laughing. The fact that Avery was thirty-two, had black hair, blue eyes, a cop friend by the name of Jack O'Reilly, and a penchant for getting involved in murder investigations was apparently just a coincidence. For four years I'd lived in dread of the Finches finishing that damn book, and now not only had they finished it, they'd apparently tracked down the only literary agent on the planet demented enough to want to represent it.

Jean—reading my response correctly—glowered at me. "No, we are *not* kidding. It's a wonderful book, and now that we have an agent, I *know* we'll sell it to one of the big publishers!"

Ted beamed at her fondly. "What we're really hoping," he admitted, "is that maybe we'll have the same luck as you, Adrien, and someone will option our book for the movies!"

CHAPTER SEVENTEEN

On Wednesday morning, I gave Al January a call and asked if he had Marla Vicenza's phone number.

I sensed his surprise. I'm sure he wondered why I wasn't asking Paul Kane for Marla's contact info, and I mentioned casually that I'd tried Paul's number a couple of times that morning without success. That was a lie, but January seemed to accept it. He said, "He's probably at the studio today. I think he mentioned something about it on Sunday."

I was in luck. January was in a loquacious mood. We chatted casually about sailing and boats, and I managed to work my way around to Langley Hawthorne and Porter's affair with Nina.

I said—stretching the truth a little, "I read Bonnie Kirkland's bio on Paul. I hadn't realized he and Nina also had an affair."

Al made a sound of disgust. "That book is garbage. The woman is a homophobe."

"She sure seemed to take Nina's side in the breakup."

"There wasn't any reason to take sides," Al said. "They were both kids. It wasn't anyone's fault."

"Nina must have been on the rebound after Porter?" I suggested.

"I never did quite understand the thing with Porter," Al admitted. "Who can fathom the heart of an adolescent female?"

Even the ones not doing drugs. I made assenting noises like a few years of rubbing shoulders with *les femmes* in high school and university gave me Man of the World status.

January said, "After the affair with Porter broke off—after Langley insisted it end—Nina got involved with Paul. They were both very young and...very stupid. I think in a way Paul was swept off his feet. He came from a poor working class background. Nina was beautiful, young, and the daughter of southern aristocratic privilege. For a kid from a slum in Bristol, it was like American Dream 101."

"And Hawthorne disapproved of that relationship as well?"

"No."

"No?"

I could hear the smile in his voice at my obvious surprise. "Not at all. Langley was very fond of Paul. Paul was his discovery, his protégé, and he admired the way he worked his way up from nothing. He thought the future was full of great things for Paul. He thought he was going to be the Cary Grant of our generation."

"Was Kane's sexuality under wraps back then?" Considering how voracious he seemed these days, I wondered how successful he would have been at concealing his cosmopolitan tastes.

"Jaded, aren't you?" He chuckled. "Yeah, Paul was pretty much in the closet back then. Conventional wisdom held—still holds really—that coming out as openly gay is the kiss of death in Hollywood as far as marketing to mainstream audiences. Back then we didn't have anything like *Logo* or *HereTV* And even if we had, being relegated to the boob tube was considered a fate worse than death."

Paul didn't strike me as someone who was overly serious about his art, but I could understand that he had probably wanted more for himself than guest appearances on *ALF* or *Moonlighting*.

January said, "Anyway, I think Langley was hugely relieved that Nina was involved with someone her own age. Someone unmarried. Someone he thought highly of."

"So what happened?" I suspected what had happened was Nina discovered the games Paul liked to play—I assumed he played those games back then.

"Unfortunately, Langley drowned. Nina went off the rails and her relationship with Paul ended. Not amiably."

"That seemed to be the gist of the Kirkland book." This was the tricky part. I asked, "Do you think part of Nina's problem might have been the way her father died?"

"Not sure what you mean." There was a cautious note in January's voice.

"Well, it was sudden. An accident, right?"

"Oh, right. Yes, I suppose part of Nina's problem was the shock of Langley's death." He still sounded guarded. Which wasn't unexpected, since he had been on the yacht that night along with Nina, Paul, Porter, and Porter's first wife, Marla.

I said, "Was there any suggestion that Hawthorne's death might not have been an accident?"

There was an abrupt pause.

"There was a full police investigation at the time," January said. "Which was only to be expected. Langley was very wealthy, and his death was a stupid one."

"He got drunk and fell overboard, is that what I read?"

"That's about the size of it," January said.

I changed tack. "Was Hawthorne married?"

"Widowed."

"That would have made it harder on Nina, I guess."

"It didn't help."

"Was Hawthorne a heavy drinker?" I asked.

"We were all heavy drinkers back then," January said.

There were a number of questions I'd have liked to ask, but if I asked them, January would be contacting Paul Kane—he might give Kane a ring as it stood now—and I preferred to fly under the radar for as long as possible.

I said, "I've met Nina. She seems…like an interesting personality."

"She's all that," January said, "but no way did Nina push Langley off that boat."

"That's what Paul said." I added, "I guess I've been writing mysteries for too long."

"Could be," he said. "Might want to watch that." Despite January's easy tone, I had a feeling he meant it.

* * * * *

It took some doing, but I finally got hold of Marla Vicenza and managed to set up a meeting with her for the following day. After that, my sleuthing had to be placed on hold. It was Natalie's day off and customers kept me jumping while they amused themselves pulling books off shelves and leaving them stacked around the store, abandoning their empty Starbucks cups on shelves, and informing me they'd changed their minds about books we'd special ordered for them.

Natalie was right about needing help. The way it stood now, any time she had a day off or I was out gallivanting, we were in trouble. Bathroom breaks, stockroom searches, even lengthy phone calls meant no one was available to help customers. And offsite lunches meant closing the shop for an hour or so. When I'd first opened Cloak and Dagger, that wasn't a problem, but now we were busy enough that closing for an hour irritated customers and cost us in sales.

I resolved to write Angus in Mexico and find out if he was serious about coming home, and then I locked the place long enough to get myself a frozen yogurt from down the street. It was too hot to eat, even if I'd been hungry, but the boysenberry yogurt was something to tide me over.

Checking my messages, I saw there was one from Jake. I listened.

He said in that careful flat voice, "There's been a development. It turns out that Nina Hawthorne has some kind of heart ailment for which she takes digitoxin." He hesitated, then added curtly, "Give me a call if you feel like talking."

It occurred to me that I hadn't seen or spoken to him since I'd walked off the *Pirate's Gambit*. I thought about what Chan had said—the fact that it mattered to Jake whether we stayed friends or not. I wanted to think that I was mature enough, sophisticated enough, to stay friends with him—I told myself I didn't blame him for making the choices he had made, that I saw him as a victim and a prisoner of his internalized homophobia—and yet...

The truth was, even if I could put aside the past, he was too close to Paul Kane for me to confide in.

When I got back from taking Emma to her riding lessons on Wednesday evening, I found Natalie's four-footed pal waiting for me beside the side door. The cat scampered away when I got out of the Forester, but then slunk back as I stood there unlocking the door.

It stood just out of range.

"Do I look like a cat person to you?" I asked it.

It meowed, showing all its little sharp teeth. It really was an unprepossessing creature. Its head was too big for its body—sure, partly that was because it was so damned skinny—its color a dirty dun.

"I don't know what she sees in you," I told it. "It must be your winning personality."

He ignored me, waiting for the door to open. I used my foot to block him, and slipped inside, closing the door firmly behind me.

The shop was quiet and warm. I went upstairs to my flat, let myself in. It was too warm up there as well. And too quiet.

There were no messages on the answering machine.

I changed into a soft, gray T-shirt and faded, comfortable Levi's and tried to figure out what to eat. I knew I needed to eat something, but I couldn't think of anything that sounded appetizing. I wasn't sure there was anything in the cupboards; I'd got into the habit of relying on Guy to bring home takeout.

I opened doors, examined shelves, but I just couldn't work up enthusiasm for ramen or oatmeal—and the cornflakes were stale. I could run out and get something, but I didn't have energy for that either.

Giving it up, I went into the front room and poured a brandy. I sat down in one of the comfortable overstuffed chairs and…suddenly I couldn't think of anything I wanted to do.

Ever again.

I closed my eyes. Everything seemed like too much effort. The silence seemed complete and final. I could just about hear the dust settling around me. What did I used to do before Guy?

Sit around wishing Jake would call?

No. Because it was Wednesday, and Mondays and Wednesdays had been "our" nights together. Work and his straight life permitting, Jake had turned up like clockwork on my doorstep and in my bed. In fact, by the end he was turning up more and more frequently and less scheduled, and, ironically, I had thought that was a good sign, that we were moving closer to each other.

What the hell was the matter with me? Sitting here feeling sorry for myself, drinking brandy—which was definitely a no-no for now. I'd been fine. For two years I'd been perfectly fine. This was silly. This was sad.

I got up and spilled the brandy down the kitchen sink, opened a can of salmon, and dumped it on a plate.

I took a couple of bites. There had to be something creative you could do with salmon, but I decided the most creative thing I could do was feed my neighbor in the alley. I carried the plate downstairs, set it outside the door.

"Yo, Top Cat," I called.

With an alacrity that indicated Natalie was probably feeding him on a regular basis, the thing slunk out of the nest of cardboard boxes against the cinder block wall. He trotted across the alley, keeping a wary eye on me, and delicately sniffed the plate.

"Yep, you should be worried about poison," I told it. "And cars. And rats bigger than you—which would be any rat in town."

He took little bites of the salmon, giving his flea-bitten head a tiny shake every so often.

Ear mites…fleas…bubonic plague. I shuddered and closed the door on him.

The phone was ringing as I reached the top landing. I paused in the doorway, stared at it, then crossed to pick it up.

Dial tone.

Well, I could always spend my evening doing what I used to do when I didn't have anyone, and kill way too much time poking into other people's lives.

I had a niggling feeling about that fatal accident of Langley Hawthorne's. Maybe he hadn't had a problem with his daughter's relationship with Paul Kane—there had still been an awful lot of money at stake. And that was an awfully convenient accident—not that it couldn't happen. Alcohol and boating were a bad mix. Everyone knew that.

A knock on the door to the flat sent me jumping out of my skin. Had I locked the side door? But yeah, I had. So that brisk tattoo could only be Guy—and he was feeling uncomfortable enough to knock rather than use his key, which was probably not a good sign.

But it was a relief that he was back. Right?

I opened the door and halted.

Jake stood on the landing.

For the life of me I couldn't think of anything to say.

"Can I come in?" he asked.

"Uh...sure."

I backed up and he walked inside the flat.

"You kept your key," I observed brilliantly. Either that or we were experiencing some kind of space-time shift. What year was this?

He stared down as though wondering how that key had got on his ring. Then he raised his light gaze to mine and said tersely, "You should have changed the locks."

I folded my arms, leaned against the entryway wall. "Yeah, I guess I should have."

He didn't say anything and even a moment of silence was more than I could take right then.

"But if you can't trust a cop, who can you trust?" My heart was thudding hard—too hard probably—but I didn't feel angry as much as excited. Like someone had reset a breaker and dormant systems were suddenly coming back to life, lights blinking on, transmitters pulsing, receivers crackling in anticipation. I added, "Anyway, I was pretty sure I didn't have to worry about you walking in on me unannounced—and here you are, trumpets blaring."

It was like we had both newly completed one of those Berlitz foreign language courses. Every comment was followed by a pause for translation. It shouldn't have been that hard because we'd been talking to each other fine for about a week now.

"I...didn't want to drag you downstairs to answer the door," he said. "You looked like hell the other night."

And suddenly it was easy again.

"Still the same silver-tongued devil I remember so well," I said. "What happens next, we relive our greatest moments and you throw me across the room?"

The flush in his face died away. He said quietly, "If you think I'm not ashamed of that, you really don't know me."

"That's a safe assumption." I turned and headed for the kitchen. "You want a beer?" I sure as hell did.

He didn't answer. I glanced back and he was just standing there staring down the hallway as though he expected to see me still lying on the floor, as though he could still hear the echo of smashing glass and our furious voices.

I kept walking toward the kitchen. I didn't want to relive one minute of that memory. Or any of them, if I was wise.

"I..." I couldn't catch the rest of it. His voice was unexpectedly husky.

I cut across in falsetto, "Love means never having to say you're sorry."

Something in his silence made me wish I'd shut up.

"Nice to know all the defense mechanisms still work," he said mildly at last.

"Better late than never."

Another loaded silence.

I stopped and faced him. "*Shit.* Sorry."

I didn't want to hear it. What was the point? What could he tell me that I didn't actually know?

But I waited. He didn't say anything. And then just as my self-control gave out and I was about to speak, he said flatly, "You're going to find this funny. I had no idea how much I would miss you."

I swallowed hard. "Funny. Yeah."

"I wanted to do the right thing. I wanted to have a real marriage. I knew things would have to change between us. I just...didn't expect to lose everything. I didn't intend to lose your friendship. Maybe that seems pretty dense."

On a scale of one to ten with ten being solid bone from the eyes up? Yep, a ten.

I said, "You know what I think? I think you needed—wanted—to make a complete break." I was able to say it without emotion maybe because I'd said it to him so many times in my imagination. "You hated yourself for being queer. I think you probably hate me too. Or did—when I was part of what you hated about *you*."

He was shaking his head. "You don't know what you're talking about. You were the only part of it that ever made it seem…okay. Sane."

It. *It?*

"Which tells you how crazy we both were. And even if you had wanted to stay friends—which you didn't, whatever you tell yourself now—how the hell long do you think we would have lasted as platonic pals? How the hell long did it take you to dig out the whips and chains? Or did you ever put 'em away? Maybe I don't understand your idea of real marriage."

He said angrily, "You're such an expert on commitment?"

"What the hell is that supposed to mean?" My heart tripped and started that goddamned staggering three-legged run. I ignored it.

"What we had together was about a lot more than fucking. We had a friendship. For chrissake, you were the only person in the world I could be honest with."

"You weren't any more honest with me than you were with anyone else." I had no idea what we were actually arguing about at this point, but I was still hoping to draw blood.

"Bullshit," Jake snarled. "You're the one trying to pretend it was nothing more than sex—"

"You've been telling lies to other people for so long that you've started telling them to yourself—" I had to stop to catch my breath.

The anger went from him just like that. "Are you okay?" he asked.

"Fucking A. Jake, there's no point…" I had to stop again. "Let's stick to talking murder." I turned, rested my hand briefly on the wall. "Get a beer. I need to use the john."

In the bathroom I got my pills out of the cabinet, scooped them down with a handful of water from the sink. Not a problem, I told myself. I was a little late taking my meds and I shouldn't have had the brandy. I shouldn't have let myself get so mad. I splashed more water on my face. Sat down on the side of the tub and gave myself a few moments. Pneumonia takes a while to get over. That's all. I wasn't seventeen anymore.

Jake was in the kitchen staring out the window over the sink. Two bottles of beer sat on the counter. He turned at the sound of my footsteps.

"Are you okay?" he asked again, scanning my face.

"I'm fine. Why do people keep asking me that?"

He said dryly, "Maybe they need reassurance."

"Maybe they should mind their own business."

He raised his brows, watching in silence as I got a tumbler out of the cupboard, poured myself a glass of water, and sat down at the table.

"I came to tell you the DA has given us the go-ahead to arrest Nina Hawthorne."

I swallowed a mouthful of water. "That seems premature. Do you have enough to make it stick?" I asked.

"She had means, motive, and opportunity."

"What motive did she have?"

"You should know that."

Revenge for a dead child. It seemed kind of melodramatic this afternoon.

"Have you figured out how she got the poison into Porter's glass?"

"Not yet."

I studied his face. "And you're not convinced she's guilty."

"I don't know that she's not guilty."

That sounded as convoluted as the French justice system. "So why—?"

He sighed. "Because the mayor's office is demanding an arrest, and the DA thinks we've got enough to move forward."

"And arrest the wrong woman?"

"One of those two is up to her neck in it. It was either the Hawthorne woman or Ally Beaton-Jones, and we haven't been able to connect Jones's wife to digitoxin."

"But it doesn't make sense to rush into this, does it? Especially if your gut instinct is telling you something else."

"I can't take my gut instinct to the DA," he said. "Anyway, it's not my job to convict them. That's why we have the courts. If Hawthorne isn't guilty—" He must have read my expression correctly, because he grimaced and admitted, "And because it's Alonzo's case and I've already roadblocked his first two lines of investigation."

Me and Paul Kane.

"Ah." I said. "And you don't want him looking too closely at why."

His mouth tightened. "I didn't want him wasting time and taxpayer dollars, no."

I smiled. "Right. And you didn't want him looking too closely at why you were so sure Paul Kane—or I—hadn't committed murder."

He gave me that long, dark look I remembered so well and then turned his profile to me, staring out the window.

I tilted my head, considering him. "Do you honest to God not see the compromises you're having to make?"

"Adult life is a series of compromises, Adrien."

"Yeah, only you're negotiating with the Devil."

Still not looking at me, he growled, "Oh, go to hell."

I raised my water in a toast. "Sure. I'll follow the trail of bread crumbs you're scattering."

He turned to face me again, and shook his head like he could not understand why he was making the effort. Which made two of us.

"You came to me, Jake. And I'm still wondering why. You didn't have to drop by in person to tell me Nina was going to be arrested. It's not like I'm really a colleague."

Or a friend.

And weirdly, as though he had read my mind, he said, "I would like us to be friends again."

"Well, I knew that was coming," I said, although I hadn't.

He said stubbornly, as though arguing with me—or maybe himself, "I miss you. I miss talking with you. I miss—laughing with you."

"I am pretty damned adorable," I said, "but as I recall we weren't doing a lot of talking, let alone laughing, at the end there."

He said, "You know that I didn't—that I never wanted to hurt you. You know—"

I cut in flippantly, "Kill me, yes. Hurt me, no."

"Adrien."

And it was my turn to have trouble meeting his eyes. I said—and it wasn't easy—"I don't think I can, Jake. I don't think it's even fair to ask."

Silence.

He said finally, without inflection, "All right."

And the funny thing was, that terse acceptance, the lack of any emotion, was somehow harder to take than if he'd begged or bullied.

He drained his beer, set the bottle beside the untouched one on the counter, and said without looking at me, "I guess I ought to get going."

I nodded. I didn't think I could get a word out if my life had depended on it.

He walked out of the kitchen, and I rose and followed him to the door. He took my key off his ring and handed it to me. "I'll let you know when Nina is formally arraigned."

I nodded. I felt the warm brush of his fingers pushing the key into mine all the way to my heart. I focused on the key because if I looked up, I'd see what he was feeling. Worse, he'd see what I was feeling—in a minute what I was feeling was going to be spilling out of me, and it didn't make any sense. It had been over long ago; we had just finally got around to saying good-bye, that was all.

Neither of us said a word. Neither of us moved a muscle.

Finally Jake said, huskily, "I lied. I didn't come here to tell you about Nina Hawthorne, and I didn't come here to ask you to be friends again."

I raised my eyes. "I know," I said.

CHAPTER EIGHTEEN

His face stilled—except for his eyes. Something blazed back into life there, and I recognized it because I'd felt it when he'd walked back into this room after a two-year absence.

I reached for him, and he wrapped his arms around me, and for a minute it could have been a hug good-bye...or maybe hello...because then his hands smoothed their way down my back, pulling me closer, closing on my hips, drawing me against him, unashamed of his arousal. Naked honesty right there, stretching the soft fabric of his jeans, poking against my groin.

And for once I had nothing to say. Jake's mouth found mine, his lips molding hot and soft to my own. His tongue tentatively tested the seal of my lips; I parted them and he pushed inside. It was startlingly sweet and achingly familiar, like finding harbor. Like I had been waiting decades for this, traveling leagues, Odysseus sailing at long last into the blue crystal waters of Ithaca—and never considering the trouble ahead.

I lifted my lashes and met Jake's tawny stare. Another switch flipped, and with something like shock I felt my cock rising as I finally turned back on. My breath caught on a half sob; relief made me a little giddy, and I leaned against him, making fun of us both like his kisses were making me swoon.

But I didn't fool him. His arms wrapped around me and he said softly, against my ear, "Okay?"

"Oh yeah," I said, nodding into his shoulder. "You don't know." I craned my head, seeking his mouth again, and he was right there, opening to my kiss, welcoming me home.

He tasted dark and bittersweet, like my memories—only more intense. My heart pounded hard, blood drumming away in my ears, like spring's freshet after the ice began to break. I kissed him with all the hardness and hunger in me—let him feel it all: my anger and grief and frustration. When we finally broke apart Jake didn't look shocked; he looked...predatory. Hot. Ravenous. Forty days in the wilderness and—well, not paradise at the end of it—maybe steak dinner with all the trimmings. His eyes glittered.

"Oh, baby," he muttered, and I laughed unsteadily as his hands slid beneath my T-shirt, shoving the thin cotton up to find bare skin. And it felt wonderful, those big, hard, callused hands moving over me, stroking and petting, relearning...

His dick was hard, rock hard through the Levi's—he had to be in pain—and I pressed closer, rubbing against him. Briefly, I wondered how much of this was me wanting the past back, the remembrance of all that heat and power—tempered with the occasional tenderness—because there were safer and saner ways to relive old times. We weren't either of us the same people, and this...was...madness.

And yet we were kissing again. We were locked onto each other as though we had just discovered this incredible thing you could do with two mouths pressing close and moist against each other. And the taste of him... the flavor of him... Horrifyingly, unbearably sweet—sweet in the way crack must feel hitting the bloodstream of an addict after years of staying clean.

As our kiss deepened, one of his big hands slid down and palmed my ass, and I groaned, desperate for that closeness—why the hell were we wearing so many clothes on a hot summer night? I wrapped my arms around him, and he moved right into them. He felt harder, leaner, fiercer than I remembered—all taut muscle and energy. He was smiling against my mouth, liking my hunger, my demand.

Fleetingly I wondered what Paul Kane was like with him. What Kate—his wife—was like. But I shunted those thoughts away, because I wasn't going to stop. Air raid sirens couldn't have stopped me.

"Yeah," he muttered. "Oh, yeah." Agreeing with everything I wasn't saying. Huge mistake this, and we both had to know it—and I'd've killed anyone who tried to get between us. His fingers fumbled with the top rivet of my jeans, worked it free as my shaking hands fastened on his waistband, yanked at his belt buckle. He made a furious, desperate sound in the back of his throat, bit the curve of my neck and shoulder.

I sucked in a sharp breath, grabbed at his shirt while he bent to jerk my Levi's down. A couple of his shirt buttons popped off and flew across the room. My laugh didn't sound like me, although I thought the idea of him eventually staggering out of my place with his clothes in tatters was pretty damned funny, and he yanked my boxers down, freeing my cock—which immediately began to wave with Pick Me! Pick Me! enthusiasm. Some body parts never learn.

Shrugging out of the damaged shirt, Jake said roughly, "I still dream about you."

"I have nightmares about you." I dragged my T-shirt over my head, threw it aside.

He gave another of those choked laughs as he stepped out of his trousers and briefs, his cock bobbing up, looking red and somehow disheveled. And for a strangely polite moment our dicks bowed and scraped to each other in formal greeting—like the first act of *The Mikado* or something, and then his cock kissed me hello, and mine nuzzled him back. Our attitude queer and quaint, all right.

Jake pulled me back against him, like any space between us was too much, and his dick pressed painfully into my naked belly. I wound my arms around his neck again as he picked me up, backing me against the wall—hard.

"Ow," I muttered, wriggling into better position as he hefted me higher. I hooked my legs around his hips. I'd forgotten how strong he was.

"Sorry..." His hands smoothed the small of my back as he cradled me close, his face resting in the curve of my shoulder for a moment. "So sorry," he said, and his voice sounded choked. But maybe it just sounded that way smothered against my skin because when he raised his head, his eyes were dry—shadowy in this light—and there was nothing to read in his face. His breath warmed my face, a hint of beer but mostly just himself.

The blond hair on his chest teased my nipples; his dick was poking rudely up along my crack. I pushed back instinctively, but he shifted so our cocks were rubbing against each other instead. It felt good. Very good. Just that. Friction. It's not always a bad thing.

"Hey," he said.

"Hey," I replied ruefully.

He rested one hand against my face, cupping my jaw. I tried to look away, but he leaned in, licking my mouth and then nipping my lower lip, a delicate sting. I closed my eyes and he rubbed his face against mine, the rough velvet of his jaw rasping against my mouth and nose and eyelids.

"I missed you," he whispered against my face, and he kissed me again.

A shiver rippled through me, and then another, and I was disgusted to find myself trembling—adrenaline overload, that's all that was. I lowered my brow to his shoulder, still humping against him. He humped back and we began to pick up the pace.

Ramming against him, breathing him in, I drew back enough to look down between our bodies and I could see Jake's cock, wet-tipped and huge and flushed, driving against my own. It was fascinating watching us scraping and parrying with each other, hips rocking, slipping right into that old rhythm.

Not a dream. This was Jake. Jake and me. It was for real. Painfully, exquisitely real.

He hitched me more comfortably against the wall, I threw my head back, banging it, hardly noticing as the two Edward Borein etchings of Spanish missions swung gently back and forth against the plaster. Tightening my thighs around him, I arched my spine. He thrust against me, and I bucked right back. We rubbed and ground against each other in what felt like an increasingly desperate race for release.

The buzz started in the root of my cock, like sparks shooting up—flaring along my nerves like wildfire, racing out of control. My balls tightened, and I jerked my hips in confined, fierce movements. The pictures on the wall rattled.

Jake groaned deep from within, thrusting back hard, and then the past and present seemed to fuse in a white-hot tangle like a magnetic storm dancing across the sun's surface. I slammed into him, hanging on for dear life, and Jake clutched me back like I was his life preserver in a lake of fire.

"Jesus *Christ!*" he cried out.

And that fountain of sorrow splashed up between us, baptizing belly and chest and chin. I yelled, and somewhere across the universe heard Jake yelling back.

Echo and answer, and it went on and on in lovely aftershocks, rippling out into infinity until at last it faded away.

And then I sagged forward, utterly spent, emptied...light as air. I felt like I could have floated up and out...slipping through the open window and drifting away across the rooftops and satellite dishes and telephone wires... sailing away into the faintly smiling stars.

He was breathing harshly against my ear. And beyond that sound I could hear the building creaking as though in the wake of a storm.

After a bit, Jake regained his breath and gathered me up, and I locked arms and legs around him, letting him carry me into the bedroom.

And I remembered Guy.

Guy.

The man who so often shared this room with me. Who wanted to share my life. My lover.

Who was still writing his ex-lover—who might be with his ex-lover this very moment.

Or who might not.

"You okay?" Jake asked, lowering me to the bed. "Did I hurt you?"

"Not this time," I said, rolling onto my belly and resting my face in my folded arms.

I had shared this room with Jake before I ever knew Guy.

Not that it made it right. It just...made it what it was.

The mattress springs groaned as Jake collapsed half on top of me, and his hands moved over me, warm, callused hands smoothing over my back and butt, stroking, quieting.

It felt so good to be touched again. Except—I was touched all the time, caressed and petted by Guy, so why did I feel like no one had touched me in years?

Jake continued to rub my back in that soothing way and I stopped thinking—I was getting pretty good at that—and eventually his hand slowed, and stopped. I heard the quiet, even tenor of his breathing as he slept, and I let myself fall after him into the blue-edged darkness of the summer night.

* * * * *

I came awake to someone nuzzling me beneath my ear, and even half-asleep I knew the difference, recognized the pleasurable rasp behind my ear. I rolled over, opened my eyes, smiling, memory moving more slowly than physical reaction.

Jake leaned on his elbow over me, gently trailing his fingers down my chest. His hand rested lightly for a moment on my breastbone. I looked down at his hand. His wedding band was simple: yellow gold, an interlocking braid. I could see the gleam in the light from the streetlamps through the lace curtains.

He asked, "How are you feeling?"

I stretched, arched my back, considering the question. Considered why it had never provoked me when Jake asked. Hell, he'd bossed me around more than anyone ever had. One of life's little mysteries. And despite the fact that tonight I'd broken a couple of my cardinal rules, I felt relaxed, warm—better than I'd felt in a long time.

"I'm okay," I said. "I'm good."

"Yeah?"

My mouth tugged into a smile. "Yeah."

He tickled my ribs lightly, and I drew my knees up, rolling away from him.

"Nah, come back," he said, and tugged me over. "I'll stop."

I flopped back over and stared up at him. "How are *you* feeling?" I asked.

His mouth contorted briefly. I touched the little frown line between his brows, smoothing it away.

"I figured," I said. "What's she like? Kate."

He seemed to consider the question for a moment, viewing her dispassionately. "Pretty, smart, aggressive." I saw the flash of white as he smiled faintly at some memory. "She's a tiger."

I nodded. She'd have to be, I guessed. I looked back across two years' worth of wondering, and questioned, "Do you still have that dog? What was his name?"

"Rufus?" He shook his head. "No. He died last year. He was pretty old for a shepherd."

I remembered once wondering if Rufus would cotton on to me. We'd never had a chance to meet, old Rufus and I. Not in a year of seeing Jake.

Had it only been a year? It had seemed much longer. Sometimes it had seemed like a lifetime. But maybe all lifetimes weren't measured in hours, days, and years.

"Are you still living at the same place?" I had only been to his little house in north Glendale once, waiting for Jake on our way somewhere—somewhere he had no doubt been terrified to be seen with me.

"Yeah." He rolled on his back and stared up at the ceiling fan's blur moving above us in the gloom. "We were going to move, but when we lost the baby we decided there was no hurry. It's big enough for two."

I wondered why I had started this line of conversation. Really not a good idea.

We listened to the fan whirring softly, spinning away. He asked, "So you're finally expanding the bookstore?"

I nodded.

He didn't ask anything else. Apparently I was still a lot more curious about him than he was about me. That reminded me of something, though.

I turned my head, studying his face in the dimness. "Guy said he saw you parked on the street in front of the bookstore a few times."

He closed his eyes, his mouth curving in an odd expression that was not truly a smile. "Twice. I thought he spotted me. I wanted to talk to you, and you weren't taking my phone calls." He opened his eyes. I could see their shine like something feral in the night. "By the second time it was obvious he was pretty much living here, and I wondered what the fuck I thought I was doing."

I had no answer to that. I wondered what the fuck we thought we were doing now. He moved suddenly, shifting around. He bent, rubbing his face against my cock, leisurely running his tongue down its length, tasting from base to tip.

I jumped and then sighed, settling more comfortably in the sheets, enjoying this, enjoying the care and attention from Jake's soft and warm mouth—hard to believe a man who could say such hard things could have such a sweet and soft mouth.

He took his time lapping at my skin, coaxing it back to sensation and reaction. I murmured my pleasure. Stretching out alongside me, his soft, sweet lips pressed my own and his hand closed on my hip, guiding me, the other hand linking fingers with me. That was nice. I didn't remember ever holding hands with him before.

"Something funny?"

"Well, yeah," I said.

He didn't ask what—maybe he knew it was better not to know. His mouth feathered over my skin, drifted to my shoulders, traced my collarbone. He'd shaved before coming over. For some reason I found that touching.

I half turned, humping against him and he stroked my flank, his mouth fastening on my nipple, and the sting of pleasure was surprising. Funny thing because I had never liked that from anyone but Jake. Somehow when it was Jake sucking that tight little nub, discreetly teething, it was different. I groaned and thrust up at him.

"Can I have you?" Jake asked.

"Uh, you can borrow me," I said shakily, and he said gravely, "Thank you. I promise to return you in working order."

My skin felt too tight for my body, too hot, my heart pounding too hard—and I thought that it would be nice to go out like this, check out in a kind of spontaneous combustion of sweat and sex and semen.

Serve him right to be stuck with the body.

He thrust back against me, still slow and easy, and I heard myself making a keening sound as he tongued and tugged my nipple.

"Oh, yeah," Jake said in a guttural whisper, "you do love that." His thumb tracked the wet slit of my cock, stroking, tracing. I could feel his own prick, engorged and beginning to push for attention, needy and neglected.

The nightstand drawer scraped open, and I heard him fishing around. I resented his notion that he would know where to find the things he needed, that I had changed so little—but the fact was, I hadn't changed in the little things. And maybe not as much as I wished in the big things.

Finding what he needed, he attended to himself with quick efficiency. I rolled over, stretched out, and he stroked a light, possessive hand down my spine. "You have no idea how often I've dreamed of this."

I shook my head—I'd had dreams too, but there was no point talking about this stuff. His finger tracked the crack of my ass, teasing as he found the sensitive places. I moaned, squirming into that touch, separating my legs, offering him access. The sheets felt cool on my belly and my half-hard cock.

His hand rested on my shoulder. "I want to watch your face."

"Closet romantic too, huh?" I said, but I let him guide me over onto my back, and I bit back the other things I could have said, pulling my knees up, opening for him.

Taking my cock in his big hand, he said, "You're the most beautiful guy I've ever had."

I snorted, thinking he probably said that to all the beautiful guys—assuming there was time for talk between the beatings.

Then his slick fingers circled my hole, pressed a fingertip inside, and withdrew.

I gulped.

Watching my face—though he couldn't have seen much in the soft darkness—he pressed in again, a little further, and I closed my eyes, wanting to focus on the feel and forget the emotions of it. A second finger followed, and then he flexed his hand, and I felt that knowing press on the spongy tissue of prostate—too knowing, but I focused on that sensation and shut out the rest of it, letting him stretch and stroke me as though it were my first time, giving into his strange pretense that I was fragile and terribly precious to him.

His cock entered me slowly, pushing with great care. I tried to rush him, tried to push back and capture his prick with my body—reduce it to basics: a fuck. But he wouldn't be hurried; he took his time, kissed my collarbone, the hollow of my throat, all the time shoving slowly past the ring of muscle, making it last and last, and then he was in, and we were sharing the same body, adjusting to the fit, trying on for size this being one. I wrapped my legs around him, pressed my mouth to his shoulder, bit him—paying him back for earlier. He grunted.

Pushing against him, I urged him to action, and we began the seesaw of push and pull, rock and roll, lock and load—physical sensation—and I didn't want to think more closely about it than that.

His hand wrapped around my dick—and astonishingly enough, he was right: I was getting hard. Weeks of nobody home and suddenly it was like I was sixteen again and my parents were gone for the weekend. And there was no need to say what I liked, a little tighter, a little faster—because he knew exactly what I liked—memory or just very good instincts. His hand slid up and down, squeezing with just the right amount of pressure, that smooth, knowing skid of skin on skin. It could have been my own hand, but it was so much better because it was Jake's.

He thrust into me, pumped me, we found the old rhythm, the pattern, the old steps, the way through the wood—and it moved beyond words or coherent thought, just skin and warmth and that hum of exquisite tension as it built and built, his hand jerking me off, his cock lancing past my gland, fast and faster—and a little frantic—

I felt him stiffen and then heard him shout.

He kissed me again.

We lay there for a while and then he slid out of me.

After a time he said, "I can't stay."

"I know."

He didn't move and then finally he sat up, wearily. He went into the hallway; the light came on, throwing a golden bar across the floor and bed. I listened to him dressing.

He came back in—a broad silhouette—and sat on the edge of the bed.

"Adrien…"

I smiled. "I know."

But I didn't, because what he said was, "I want you in my life—you can set the parameters."

"Oh my God." I pressed the heels of my hands over my eyes. "*Jake.*"

"What?"

"*What*? You know what. We can't pick up where we left off. And I can't be pals with you."

"Then what the hell was this?" The anger and hurt in his voice was painful to hear.

I sat up, forcing him to retreat. "You know what the hell this was, Jake. This was us saying good-bye properly.

CHAPTER NINETEEN

When I was sixteen I managed to catch rheumatic fever—no easy feat, by the way—and it left the valves of my heart damaged; the mitral valve in particular, which was the culprit in my current predicament. Lisa was convinced I'd never see eighteen, and I spent several months convalescing in bed like somebody in a 1920s novel, before I finally put my foot down—both physically and metaphorically.

But in addition to reading everything I could lay my hands on during that long enforced period of inactivity, I watched a lot of TV, so I was very familiar with Marla Vicenza's work—and "work" was probably the right word for it if running around like a maniac under the blazing Etruscan sun was anything to go by.

During the sixties, a very young Marla starred in a lot of those schlocky Italian historical dramas, and while I didn't find her escapades as Amazon or Arabian princess quite as entertaining as I did the glistening and muscle-bound adventures of Steve Reeves and his ilk, I did have a certain fondness for her cinematic ventures. She made a truly chilling Medea, as I recalled.

She still looked good for a woman in her sixties—much better than either Ally or Nina did—trim and fit. Despite those years filming in the sun, she had taken good care of her skin. Her hair was an unlikely brown, but it was skillfully done. She was surprisingly petite given how convincingly she had portrayed lady pirates and warrior queens.

"I have to say I'm a little vague on why you wanted to meet," she informed me, leading me through her spacious and lavishly decorated Santa Barbara hacienda. "You said you're working in connection with the police?"

"Er…yes," I said. And to cover that unconvincing "er"—and because I really wanted to know, I asked, "I've just realized—they used your real voice, didn't they, in those sword and sandal epics?"

"Sword and skivvies, don't you mean?" She was amused. "Yeah, they used my voice. I grew up in Little Italy. My grandparents were from Sicily. I spoke Italian like a native before I ever set foot in Europe."

"Did you meet Porter in Italy?"

"I did. Jonesy was interested in the historical epic market. In the end, he decided he preferred America and American film making—and I came back home with him."

We settled on the tiled patio beside the oblong pool. Marla's garden was filled with tropical flowers and fountains and small-scale classical statuary. "How long were you married?"

She gave me a quizzical look. "Over thirty years. Do you think I knocked Porter off because he dumped me for Ally Bally Beaton?" She poured pink lemonade from a pitcher on the table, and I noticed she wore wedding rings. As far as I knew, she'd never remarried.

"It's hard to believe you'd wait five years to do it."

"Well, you know what they say: revenge is a dish best served cold."

I had a sudden memory of her as Medea.

"True, I guess." I studied her. "But something tells me Porter's life with Ally would have supplied all the revenge you needed."

She burst out laughing. "Very good, sport! Yeah, that little bitch made poor old Jonesy's life a misery. Served him right." But her eyes were sparkling with humor. "So if you don't think I knocked my ex off, why exactly are you here?"

I said, "I got the impression that you and Porter stayed friends despite everything."

She inhaled slowly and let it out quietly. "This is true," she said.

"Did you know he was terminally ill?"

"Yeah. He came straight to me when he got the news."

"To you?"

She lifted a slender shoulder. "Like you said, we stayed close. Or, I guess, we grew close again."

"Who else knew that Porter was ill?"

"He didn't take an ad out in *Variety*, if that's what you're asking."

"Did Ally know?"

"Not at first. He told her after he decided to…" She didn't finish, lifting her lemonade to her lips. "He shared it with a few trusted friends."

"Was he going to divorce Ally?"

"In the end, no." Her smile was tight. "In the end, she convinced him that she did love him."

"That must have taken some doing."

"I always told him she was a better actress than he gave her credit for."

"But he knew about the affair, right?"

"With the health nut? He knew everything. He hired a private dick to follow her. But she broke off the relationship, and she was willing to k—" She swallowed hard.

"She had an abortion, I know. She got pregnant with Duncan Roe's child, and then terminated the pregnancy."

Marla looked at me, and I was dismayed to see the glistening in her eyes. "We didn't have children," she said. "I wanted them, but we weren't able to have them." Rather hastily, she retrieved her glass and sipped more lemonade. "Ally wanted to stay married. I give her points for resolve."

I tried my lemonade. Lots of ice and the pink was nice, but it tasted like the regular kind of lemonade as far as I could tell. "You were on the yacht the night Langley Hawthorne died, weren't you?" I asked.

Her sloe eyes flashed to mine. "Now there's an interesting leap of subject. Yeah, I was there. We were all there. The old crowd."

"What did you think about that accident of Hawthorne's?"

She stared at me for a long moment. "I thought it was very sad. He was a charming man, Langley. A real gentleman. And it was a tragedy for Nina. She was a very troubled young woman."

"How did it happen?"

She shook her head. "They were playing cards. Langley, Al, Paul, Jonesy. And drinking. We always drank too much when we got together for those weekends. All I know is Langley went on deck to get some air. He didn't come back, and when they found him, it was too late."

I'd read a bit about Langley's accident so I knew that he had apparently hit his head going over the side—although exactly where and how had never been determined. However, it was the single inconsistency in the case. Langley's blood alcohol content had been high enough to sink an armada.

"I think I read you were in your cabin asleep?"

"Yes, Nina and I had turned in earlier. It was just the boys being boys. I woke up when I heard the commotion on deck…when they were searching for him."

A butterfly swooped down to a feeder hanging from one of the silver dollar eucalyptus trees. I watched it for a moment, its fragile wings opening and closing languidly in the dappled sunlight.

I said, "Did you ever wonder whether Langley's death might not have been an accident?"

After a moment, she said, "That's another one of those odd leaps. What are you getting at, Mr. English?"

"I have a suspicious mind," I admitted. "Hawthorne's death left two people very wealthy. And it was the kind of accident that can be…something else."

"Those two people loved Hawthorne."

But the interesting thing was the way she said it—like it was something she had often puzzled over herself. She didn't reject the notion of Hawthorne being murdered—in fact, it was something she had considered.

I said slowly, "Did Porter ever mention anything about writing his memoirs?"

Marla was very still. Her gaze rested on the glass-smooth surface of the pool. The sunlight through the tree leaves speckled the water with snakeskin shadows.

She said at last, "Jonesy was always saying he was going to write his memoirs."

"But did he actually ever start them?"

She nodded. "He was working on them. He wanted to finish them before he..." She sipped her lemonade. "You know what you're suggesting?" she asked when she could.

"Yeah." I said, "Do you know what happened to those memoirs?"

She shrugged her shoulders—very Italian in that moment. "At home in Bel Air, I guess. If that little bitch didn't dump them with everything else of his."

"You don't think he would have taken some precaution to keep them safe?"

She stared at me. "It wouldn't occur to him. Jonesy wouldn't be thinking along those lines. He wouldn't consider..." She smiled, and I recognized that smile from many a candlelit cinematic moment. "Jonesy was no Machiavelli," she said.

We talked a little more, I finished my lemonade, and then I left her in her lush suburban paradise with the sound of the lawn birds and pool generator filling the silence.

* * * * *

When I got back to the bookstore it was after closing and Natalie was sitting inside with the security gate drawn and the lights off. She was crying.

"What happened?" I questioned, grabbing the box of tissues from beneath the counter. "Did something happen to the cat?"

"To the *cat*? I don't know. I haven't seen him. I'm crying because—" I lost the rest of it as she sobbed the words into the Kleenex.

"Sorry?"

She looked up with red, swollen eyes. "I said, I asked Warren if he wanted to move in together and he said no."

That was the best news I'd heard all day, but I said, "Oh. Well..."

"Well *what*?"

So many things I could have said, but none of them would be conducive to peace, love, and harmony. I said, groping, "Uh...did he give you a reason?"

"He said he wasn't ready."

"Well...that seems...reasonable."

"After three *months*?"

She was talking to the wrong person. I asked curiously, "Why do you want to move in with Warren?" I could just imagine what Warren's pad was like—what Warren was like in his own lair. What a shame parents couldn't send their wayward daughters off to the Continent anymore to get them over these disastrous misalliances.

"Why? Because *I love him*," she said very clearly. "And because I can't stand living in that house with Lisa."

I blinked at her. "Oh."

Her face crumpled and she sobbed into the tissue some more. Then she said, muffled, "It's nothing against Lisa. Really. I love her. But…it's her house now. I don't belong there anymore. And if Lauren moves home…"

"Why would Lauren move home?"

"She and Beavis are getting divorced."

Beavis? Oh. The Corporate Clone. When had all this happened? Where had I been?

I said, "Couldn't you just get a place on your own? Moving in with someone because you're not happy at home doesn't seem like the right—"

"I just told you, I *love* him. Don't you have any useful guy advice?" She glared at me—and with those red eyes, it was pretty scary. Medea could have learned a trick or two from my stepsis.

"Right. Okay. Well, here's my guy advice. Drop it, Natalie. Don't mention it to Warren again. Let him see that you're okay with it. I mean, if you still want to keep seeing him." Which I could not for the life of me imagine.

"That's *it*?"

I nodded.

"You don't think we need to talk about it?"

"Me and you?"

"Me and *Warren*!"

"God no, I don't think you need to talk about it. Leave it alone."

She picked up the box of tissues and blew her nose. "I'm supposed to ask you if you'll be at the house for dinner tonight," she said in subdued tones.

I'd totally forgotten, of course, but I said, "Yeah, I'm just going upstairs to change. I'll see you over there?"

She nodded and blew her nose again.

I left her mopping up, went upstairs, showered, and changed—and left a message on the snooty-sounding answering machine at Hitchcock and Gracen.

* * * * *

"Christmas in London!" Lisa announced.

"Whatever you'd like, my dear," Bill Dauten replied immediately, patting her hand. I had the impression he'd have said the exact same thing if she'd cried, *Off with their heads!*

The rest of us were noticeably silent. Even Emma wore a little frown. Maybe she feared Santa wouldn't be able to locate her across the sea.

"London is lovely for the holidays," Lisa insisted into that noncommittal silence. "Adrien and I spent the holidays there when he was ten. Do you remember, Adrien?"

"Not really," I said.

She looked a little hurt.

Someone—possibly even Dauten—distracted her with talk of the opera season, and the rest of us exchanged looks of silent relief.

Despite my complaints, I didn't really mind the occasional family get-togethers at the Dautens'. But I was distracted that evening with my thoughts of murders old and new. I was reminded of a quote by Camus: *...habit starts at the second crime. At the first one, something is ending.*

I was thinking about this, thinking about the likelihood of truth in it as regarded the death of Porter Jones, while we sat around chatting after dinner—and listened to Emma demonstrate the value of her much-hated piano lessons. She'd actually loved the piano before she started the lessons, which was probably a lesson in itself.

Bill skimmed the paper while Lauren and Natalie were in a huddle in the kitchen, apparently reviewing notes on their love lives, when Lisa alighted on the sofa next to me.

"Darling, are you feeling quite all right? You're *so* pale."

Now how the hell could she say that when I'd been out in the sun all day Sunday? My nose was still pink. I made some answer.

"Don't growl, Adrien." She gave me a disapproving look. "I think you should know I've had a long talk with Dr. Cardigan."

"You've had *what*?" I was too shocked to lower my voice. This was the very reason I'd changed doctors a few years ago. Doctor Reid had been too much the old family friend. He'd brought me into the world, ushered my father out, and was Lisa's sometime escort to a lot of society functions.

She ignored my astonished outrage. "Adrien, you must have that surgery. Why are you shilly-shallying? Do you realize—do you *want* to die?"

What the hell was the deal? Was she blackmailing these people?

"Of course I don't want to—" I interrupted myself. "This has got to stop, Lisa. You talked to my cardiologist?" I couldn't seem to get past that. Even the 'shilly-shallying' barely registered. "Do you know how unethical that is?"

She simply gazed at me with those wide blue eyes. "I'm your mother. There is no such thing as unethical behavior on a mother's part."

The scary thing was, she believed that. No, the scary thing was that in the parallel universe that she inhabited, everyone else seemed to believe it too.

"I didn't mean you, I meant my cardiologist." For once I didn't bother to hide my anger with her. "Look, Lisa, when the time is right, I'll have the surgery."

"That time is *now*."

"Really?" I glanced around the room where everyone was carefully paying no attention to us. "Well, I guess it will make a change from charades."

"Please be serious." That was her no-nonsense face and her no-nonsense voice. "Chronic MR complicated by A-fib is very serious, much more serious than they realized when you were growing up. *Thirty percent* of people who have A-fib wind up with CVAs."

Jesus. Lisa was speaking in acronyms. She must be terrified. She must have actually read up on the subject. I was touched. And ready to strangle her.

"And seventy percent don't."

"You can't take that chance. You don't have the right."

"*I* don't have the *right*?"

She said fiercely, "No, you don't. Does Guy know—?"

"That's it," I said, and I stood up. "I'm not going to discuss this with you or anyone else. And what goes on between Guy and me is nobody's damn business." I turned to the kitchen. Natalie and Lauren were gaping at me.

"I didn't say a word!" Natalie protested at whatever she read in my expression.

I didn't know if that was true or not, but the idea that my private life was being openly discussed—that Lisa was—had the gall—that she was daring to—and that my lawyer, my doctor, my *lover* for all I knew—

I could barely formulate the thoughts, let alone the sentences.

"Thanks for dinner," I said. "What I can't thank you for is interfering in my private life. I don't think I can even pretend to be polite right now, so I'm going."

"Adrien!" She looked *wounded.*

"Good night," I said, and the Dautens responded in various tones of discomfort as I walked out of the room.

* * * * *

I don't remember the drive back to Pasadena, but when I pulled up behind the bookstore, Guy's car was parked outside—and for a moment I considered driving away.

But in the end I turned off the engine, got out and unlocked the door to the bookstore, and went upstairs.

Guy was seated at the table in the kitchen drinking a beer. His long silver hair spilled over his shoulders, glinting in the overhead light. He wore a black T-shirt emblazoned with a pirate skull and crossbones. His eyes looked very green as they met mine.

"Can we talk?"

I nodded. Took the chair across from him. I felt very tired. Anger is exhausting, and I was out of practice.

"I want to explain about Peter."

I didn't bother telling him that I'd made a couple of phone calls and learned that he'd spoken favorably at Verlane's parole hearing. I knew he had done what he believed was the right thing. Talking to me first, hearing my feelings on the subject, wouldn't have changed his course of action.

I said, "I think I pretty much get it. You still have feelings for him."

"I do, yes. But they don't have anything to do with what I feel for you. I love you. I would like us to be together. Really together."

I nodded. "What about Peter?"

"Peter is a friend. He needs my help right now. But if you ask me to choose between the two of you, then I choose you."

"I'm not asking you to choose."

"Then what?"

I shook my head.

His silver brows knitted. "I don't understand what's going on with you."

"I don't either," I admitted. "I don't feel capable of making a commitment."

He thought it over. "Now or ever?"

"I...don't know."

"I see." I could feel him watching me. I stared at the knobs on the oven and wondered why the front left always stuck a little. "I suppose we could continue as we have been."

I sighed. "Yeah. I suppose so."

"Your enthusiasm is overwhelming."

"I'm sorry, Guy. I just—"

"Here's the thing about you, Adrien," he said. "You keep the walls up. I don't know if it's because of what's-his-name—your college boyfriend. Mel? Or if it's because of that asshole Riordan."

"D'you mind?" I said crisply.

He eyed me for a moment. Then he said evenly, "Or maybe you've always been like this. But there's this little distance between you and everyone else. And there's no bridging it. Because I've been trying for two years."

"Sure," I said, starting—against my best intentions—to get angry all over again. "But for the first nine months you were still sleeping with other people, partly for religious reasons and partly because—and I quote—'monogamy is not a realistic expectation of a healthy adult male.'"

"And I told you that if you would be willing to make a commitment, so would I. But you're not willing, are you?"

"Not on your timetable." I swallowed hard. "Let me ask you something. Did you have sex with Peter?"

His face went bleak.

"Uh-huh," I said.

"That has nothing to do with us."

"Really?"

"Really. It was comfort and affection, that's all. Peter has lost everything and everyone."

I said, "I let Jake Riordan fuck me last night. Do you think that has anything to do with us?"

He stared at me. He finally managed to say, "Does it?"

"To me it feels like it does."

"Call me when you're sure," he said.

CHAPTER TWENTY

"You know, they already arrested that caterer," Ally informed me, raising her head from the lounge chair beside the pool. She was clearly in mourning: a one-piece black swimsuit and Jackie O. sunglasses. "It was all a mistake. She was trying to kill Paul. Too bad she got it wrong."

Well, that seemed like the understatement of the year, although I'd already deduced Ally hadn't been much tempted to throw herself on Porter's funeral pyre.

"I heard that," I said. "I just wanted to ask you one or two questions."

She settled her head back on the blue cushion. The clouds overhead were reflected in her giant black lenses. "That's what you said the last time."

"Was Porter working on a book when he died?"

"A *book*?" Her tone implied that this was some avant-garde art form I was accusing her dead husband of experimenting with.

"Like his memoirs. Or an autobiography."

She pushed up on one elbow and pulled her sunglasses off. "Oh. Yeah," she said slowly. "He was working on that again."

"Do you know what happened to the manuscript? Is it with his papers?"

She drew her brows together. "No. I've been through all his stuff."

That I didn't doubt.

"Do you know if he'd finished it?"

She shook her head.

"Do you know if he had a publisher or an editor or a cowriter? Maybe a literary agent?"

"I don't *know*," Ally said and she sounded a little peevish now. "I think he showed it to someone. I mean, he was always trying to show it to people."

"But he had definitely resumed work on his memoirs?"

She replaced her sunglasses and lay flat again. "I guess so. I think he had some idea of finishing it before...The End." She said it casually, like people referred to the final credits of a movie. "I don't know if he'd bother to finish it, though, because who would want to read *that*?"

I asked, "Did Porter ever talk to you about the accident aboard the *Sea Gypsy*?"

"The what?" she murmured.

"The *Sea Gypsy*. It was a yacht belonging to a friend of Porter's named Langley Hawthorne. Langley drowned one night. Did Porter ever talk about that?"

She smothered a huge yawn. "I never listened to Porter when he started yakking about the old days. Just thinking about it makes me tired."

* * * * *

I'd faithfully phoned Jake before my visits to Marla and Ally. Each time I'd ended up leaving a message, and I hadn't heard back from him. In fact, I hadn't spoken to him since Wednesday night when I'd told him good-bye and locked the bookstore door after him.

Not that I was surprised at his silence. LAPD had gone forward with the arrest of Nina Hawthorne, and I figured Lieutenant Riordan had his hands full with the media—and with Hawthorne's lawyers who were claiming everything from harassment of a celebrity to police brutality.

It would have been nice to bounce some of my airier ideas off that hard head of his, but I realized that was unrealistic on my part. Jake's ego was smarting at my unwillingness to resume our old friendship, and that was pretty much what I had expected. If we could have really been platonic friends, then maybe I'd have made an effort, but I knew Jake wasn't going to respect the boundaries of—

Who was I kidding? I had no idea whether Jake was capable of maintaining a platonic friendship or not. And I didn't care. Because the bottom line—and no pun intended—was that *I* couldn't handle a platonic friendship with him. It was just too damn painful.

Maybe I could have handled it when I believed he was doing everything possible to have a real marriage with Kate Keegan, but the fact that he had fallen back into his old patterns, that he was seeing Paul Kane on what appeared to be a fairly active basis, that he wanted to have his cake and eat it too, made it impossible for me.

Not to mention the fact that once Jake figured out the direction my sleuthing was taking me, my popularity with him was once again going to nosedive. Apparently he'd forgotten just how truly annoying he'd found me in the past.

All the same, I called him to tell him I was going to visit Al January again, and as luck would have it, this time he picked up.

"Hey," he said neutrally.

"Hey," I returned—because sparkling repartee is my middle name.

He said, "I meant to call you earlier."

"It's okay," I said. "You've made your arrest. I'm just following up on a couple of things."

"That's not why I wanted to call you. About the other night—"

"There's nothing to say, Jake."

A little shortly he said, "You don't mind if I say it anyway, do you?"

Equally short, I said, "Go ahead."

But he said, after a pause, "Another time. What did you need?"

"Nothing. I'm just...following orders. I'm going to see Al January this afternoon."

"Why?"

"I told you. I'm following up on a couple of things."

"What things?"

"Apparently Porter Jones was writing his memoirs."

I could hear the crackle and static of empty air. He said slowly, "You're the one who thought Paul was the real target. That was your theory."

"I've been wrong before."

"Oh yeah, that's for damn sure." He was angry, but controlled. "Someone knocked Porter off because he was going to write a kiss and tell biography? That's the current theory?"

Kill and tell in this case. "Don't you think it's worth checking out?"

"No, I don't."

"Have you figured out how Nina got the poison into Porter's glass?"

He didn't answer.

I said, "Well, maybe Al can shed some light on that. He was standing right at the bar with me."

Still no answer.

It occurred to me—and it was not a happy thought—that perhaps his feelings ran deeper than I had allowed myself to believe. I was astonished to hear myself say, "Look, if you…ask…me not to go over there…I won't go."

"I…" He didn't finish it. Or I couldn't hear what he said over the heavy pounding of my heart. I felt like we were standing on the edge of some precipice—and I remembered two years ago and a vacation from hell when he'd kept me from taking a nosedive off a cliffside. So many close calls. So many near misses. I had relied on Jake to be my safety net then, and I was relying on him now. And I was willing to return the favor—if he needed it.

"Call me after you talk to him," he said abruptly and rang off.

* * * * *

"I was a little surprised to get your phone call," Al said, handing me a bottle of noni juice.

I set the bottle on the table. It was very hot today, the air still and heavy. Even the bees sounded hot and lazy. The wild grass rustled dryly on the burnished gold hillside.

"You were pretty definite the last time we talked that no way was Nina capable of murder."

"I didn't say that," Al said slowly, apparently thinking back to our last conversation. "I said, no way did she push her father over the side of that boat."

"But you think she's capable of trying to kill Paul Kane?"

One of the shar-pei dogs stood at alert, staring out across the gorge at the hillside. Al spoke quietly and the dog came back and sat down, panting, beside his chair. Al said, "I think Nina…at one time might have been capable of that. I find it hard to believe that she would wait this long to go after Paul. They've been…maybe not friendly, but…cordial for years now."

"Did Paul use her company a lot to cater his parties?"

"I don't really know." He frowned, thinking. "I think he might have used her once or twice. She's very good and very popular. I've used her a couple of times—back when I used to give parties." There was that little flash of bitterness again.

"So Nina's arrest took you by surprise?"

He sighed. "Yes. And no. It's the kind of thing I can imagine Nina doing—maybe not at this point in her life, but at another point, yes. She hated Paul very much at one time. Maybe she still does."

So much for that angle. I said, "Those cocktails Paul Kane makes. The Henley Skullfarquars. Was that an unusual thing?"

"The skull fuckers? No. Paul makes them at most of his parties—especially on the *Pirate's Gambit*. Liquid headache, that's what those are. Gin, grenadine, cider, Pimm's, Smirnoff...and we're usually drinking them in the sun on the boat." He shuddered.

I already knew the answer, but I wanted confirmation. "They're made by the glass or what?"

"By the jug. He mixes them up in an antique silver punch bowl."

I couldn't recall seeing a punch bowl anywhere, but I was pretty sure only Paul had been behind the bar that afternoon.

"That's interesting," I said, "because only Porter's drink was poisoned."

"Right. The punch bowl wasn't poisoned, just Porter's glass," agreed Al.

"Do a lot of people drink that punch?"

"Not more than once," Al said. "Like I said, it's a headache in a glass. Porter drank it. Porter would drink anything. Paul swears by the stuff. Paul can put the booze away."

I said, "I was standing right there at the bar—I handed Porter his glass—and for the life of me, I can't think how Nina would have got poison into it. She wasn't even there."

Al's eyes met mine. "That's for the police to work out, right? They must be pretty sure or they wouldn't have arrested her."

I used to think that way too a few murder investigations ago.

"You don't remember seeing anything?"

He was absently stroking the dog, which rested its big head on his thigh. "I'd have told the police if I'd seen anything." He glanced at the untouched bottle of juice. "Did you want some ice with that?"

"I've got to get going," I said. "Oh, did you know Porter had started working on his memoirs again?"

I was watching him, so I saw his hand freeze on the dog's broad head. He looked at me. He said slowly, "Yes."

I didn't say anything and neither did he. Then, finally, he said, "Why?"

"I wondered what happened to the manuscript."

"What do you mean?"

"Ally says it's not with Porter's papers. It's not anywhere."

"Marla—"

"Marla says no. She confirmed that he was working on the book again, but she didn't know what might have happened to it after his death."

"Maybe he lost interest," Al said. "Maybe he decided to let sleeping dogs lie."

"Maybe he did at that," I agreed.

* * * * *

I was not surprised that Jake didn't pick up when I called after leaving Al January's hillside home.

He rang me back while I was watching Emma riding around the paddock at the club that afternoon, but I didn't pick up. He knew what he needed to know: I was still alive and annoying people.

All I really had was a string of suppositions and my instinct. And I wasn't about to use the *I* word in Jake's presence. I needed more in the way of tangible proof, but I had no idea of how to make that happen. And if I tried to go to Jake with anything less than tangible proof, I knew he'd dismiss it—and I couldn't say I blamed him.

I was walking back to the parking lot with Emma when her riding lesson was finished, my thoughts a million miles away, when she said suddenly, very quietly, "Adrien, are you going to have that operation?"

Was it, like, a topic of dinner conversation around the Dauten household?

"Probably, kiddo."

She slipped her hand into mine.

* * * * *

When I got back home after dropping Em off, I found two police cars parked in the alley outside Cloak and Dagger.

One police car could mean anything, but two... Not that I have a guilty conscience or anything.

I parked next to the unmarked car and got out, making sure I kept my hands where everyone could see them; they were sweating—there's no way this could be anything but bad news; how bad was the only unknown—but I resisted the temptation to wipe them on my jeans.

The doors flew open on the black-and-white and two cops got out, holsters unbuttoned. The side door to the bookstore opened, and Detective Alonzo stood framed there. He was wearing that big, unpleasant smile of his.

"Mr. English! Where've you been all afternoon?"

The uniformed officers moved up on either side of me.

I said warily, "What part of the afternoon? I've been at the Paddock Riding Club down by Griffith Park for the last couple of hours."

"Yeah? I guess you can prove that?" Alonzo inquired, walking toward me. He had his handcuffs out. "And where were you before that?"

I said, "What the hell is going on?" I think I took an instinctive step backward.

One of the cops grabbed me and shoved me against the side of the Forester. Someone kicked my feet apart, yanked my arms behind my back. Someone else was patting me down with ruthless efficiency.

Alonzo announced cheerfully, "Adrien English, you're under arrest for the attempted murder of Al January."

CHAPTER TWENTY-ONE

The ground tilted sharply beneath me, and I rested my forehead on the Forester's warm paint, breathing in long and slowly. I thought just about anything would be preferable to passing out at the feet of that sonofabitch Alonzo.

Attempted murder. Now that I hadn't seen coming. Not at all.

After a few seconds the dizziness eased enough that I got a grip on myself. I turned my head to try to see Alonzo's face. No luck. "Al's alive?" I got out.

"That's right," Alonzo said behind me. "Disappointed?"

He snapped the handcuffs around my wrists—cold metal—and tighter than you'd expect—and peeled me off the side of the car.

I rasped, "Al said I tried to kill him?" I couldn't make sense of it. I felt dazed, as if someone had punched me hard where it counted.

"January's not saying anything," Alonzo said. "He's in a coma. The housekeeper—" He broke off as a silver sedan drew down the alley and rolled up beside us. I recognized Jake behind the wheel and—maybe illogically—I felt a surge of relief. I mean, for all I knew, he had ordered them to pick me up...

"Is that Riordan?" one of the uniforms said uneasily.

"Shit," Alonzo muttered.

Jake didn't even turn off his car engine. The door flew open, he unfolded, and there was no mistaking the fury on his face. He said, "What the fuck is going on here, Detective? I told you not to—"

Alonzo interrupted, "I have a right to pursue any avenue of investigation that I—"

And Jake roared, "Goddamn it, that wasn't a suggestion, I *ordered* you to back off. I *told* you I talked to English before and after the interview with January. I spoke to him at three o'clock. *I'm* his fucking alibi." His eyes—hard and flat—met mine for a fleeting instant. He jerked his head at one of the uniforms. "Cut him loose."

"Who the hell do you think you are?" Alonzo practically screamed. "This is *my* case. You've blocked me every fucking step of the way, trying to protect your rich faggot friends—"

Jake lunged forward; there was scuffling behind me and the uniforms let me go and tried to get between Jake and Alonzo.

"Lieutenant, Lieutenant!" one of the officers protested, sounding winded.

Jake had Alonzo backed up against the side of the building, massive fists bunching Alonzo's shirt as he pinned him. Alonzo fought to free himself, hand raised like he wanted to punch Jake, but one of the uniformed officers was hanging onto his arm—the other was shouldered between Jake and Alonzo, trying to keep his footing as the two men surged at each other. Then Jake stepped back, shrugging his shoulders, cranking his head side to side like one of the early Terminator models.

Alonzo was cursing—practically crying with rage. I couldn't make out what he was saying.

Jake jabbed his finger a centimeter from the detective's nose. "You think you got a problem with me? File a grievance, asshole."

"You think I won't? You think I'm the only one with a complaint? You think I'm the only cop who's noticed there's something hinky with you?"

"Alonzo, cool it, man," one of the officers warned.

Jake turned his back on Alonzo like he wasn't worth the time. He nodded at me. "Get the handcuffs off him," he told the other uniform, and the man moved to obey.

A moment later the handcuffs were off, and I was rubbing my wrists as Alonzo tore free and brushed by. He slammed into his car, screeched into reverse, and tore out of the alley, tires squealing.

The two uniforms hovered uneasily.

"Okay?" Jake asked me brusquely.

I nodded.

The message in his eyes was clear, so I turned and went inside the building.

I closed the door, leaned back against it. My heart was hopping and skipping like a rabbit that had unexpectedly been missed by a set of impending tires. I took a couple of long, slow breaths.

The phone jangled into life on the counter, and I pushed away from the door and picked it up.

"Adrien?" It was Natalie. "Is everything okay? Those cops kicked me out of the store! What's going on?"

"I don't know, but everything's okay. I'll call you in a little bit." I hung up on her protests. Since I couldn't see the alley from the bookstore, I went up to the flat and looked down. Jake was still there talking to the uniforms. He had turned his car engine off and everything looked calm. One of the officers was laughing, so it seemed like things were under control again.

The rush of adrenaline drained away, leaving me sick and shaky. I sat down on the sofa and rested my head in my hands. I needed to go downstairs and lock up the place, but for now I just didn't care—anyone who wanted to steal a book that bad was welcome to it. Hell, they were welcome to the cash register.

I tried to think. Al had been attacked. Was in a coma. It didn't have to be connected to Porter's death—to the questions I had been asking—but the timing was awfully coincidental.

According to Guy, there were no coincidences.

And Detective Alonzo probably agreed with him, which is why he was so eager to see me in stainless steel bracelets. I could sort of understand Alonzo's position. I remembered a saying by Grace Murray Hopper: *If you do something once, people will call it an accident. If you do it twice, they call it a coincidence. But do it a third time and you've just proven a natural law.*

Four murder investigations did seem like a lot for an average citizen.

After what seemed like a long time, the door opened behind me. Jake said, "I locked up for you downstairs. Are you okay?"

I glanced around. "Fine. Fabulous. What the hell was that about?"

He'd taken his tie off and unbuttoned his collar. He looked as tired as I felt. "January's ex-boyfriend dropped by and found January unconscious.

He'd been hit over the head with a pre-Columbian stone carving. According to the housekeeper, you were still with January when she left at two forty-five, which makes you the last person to be seen with January before he was attacked."

"That's probably true. I left a few minutes to three—and called you."

We hadn't talked, though, I'd left a message was all—and if anyone really investigated my "alibi" it was going to be immediately apparent that Jake had lied.

"We've got pretty good forensic evidence that January was probably attacked around five o'clock—not long before the ex-boyfriend showed up. In fact, the ex may have scared off January's attacker. You take the kid horseback riding around that time, right?"

I nodded.

"You've got more than enough witnesses to support your story, and January may pull through."

I said, "You've got him under guard, I hope?"

He preserved a straight face, but I could see he was amused. Grimly amused, but amused nonetheless. So okay, maybe I have read too many mystery novels, but January's assailant was ruthless and increasingly daring.

"Why the hell is Alonzo so eager to pin this on me? He's got his suspect in jail already."

Jake sat down across from me. "The case against Hawthorne isn't going to hold water. Her lawyer came up with a witness—one of Hawthorne's employees who swears Hawthorne was never anywhere near the bar the morning they went to Kane's to oversee the party arrangements. She's willing to testify that Hawthorne was never out of her sight. The DA is buying it. Hell, *I* buy it. This is a very credible witness."

"What possible motive would I have for attacking Al? Or Porter, for that matter."

Jake shook his head. "I don't think this is about you so much as me. Alonzo and I have history. He knows I don't want him coming after you—which is enough to make you...of interest to him."

"Great."

His mouth twitched at my tone. "Don't worry. I'll see he leaves you alone."

"My hero," I said glumly.

He gave me a funny look.

My thoughts moving in another direction, I said, "Al's got two good-sized watchdogs."

"The dogs were outside. That could mean January's attacker put them out—the dogs might have known him—or January might have let them out. There's every indication that he knew his attacker, or at least didn't feel threatened. He let his assailant into the house, and was in the process of pouring two drinks when he was hit from behind—twice."

"Is he going to make it?"

"They don't know yet."

I nodded, stared at my hands. I liked Al January. And if I was right in my speculations, I had brought this on him—inadvertently—but did that really absolve me? If I hadn't started poking around—if I hadn't insisted on continuing with the investigation even after I could see where it was headed—

And why? What was it to me? Nobody had asked—or wanted—me to keep digging after Nina Hawthorne was arrested. I had put myself back in Alonzo's sights and maybe got Al January murdered—and I still didn't have any proof as to who had really killed Porter. Nor did I have any idea of how to get it.

Jake said dryly, "Don't tell me you're actually second-guessing yourself, Mr. Holmes?"

"You think I never second-guess myself?"

He said a little wearily, "I think you're a chronic buttinsky."

I looked away from his hard gaze.

"Hell," he muttered. To my surprise, he rose from his chair, lowered himself to the sofa beside me, and put his arm around my shoulders. He pulled me over to him—and even more surprising—I let myself lean against him.

"It's not your fault," he said. "The only person who carries the blame for murder is the murderer. So don't put this on you."

I closed my eyes for a moment, willing it to be true. And more than that, allowing myself the pleasure of being in his arms for a moment, that unexpected mix of gentleness and strength—yeah, he was going to make some mixed-up kid a good father one of these days—the scent of his aftershave and the light tang of his sweat after his exertions with Alonzo. I listened to the quiet pound of his heart beneath my ear.

Jake added, "And we both know I sure as hell wouldn't say it if it wasn't true. I've never been in favor of sleuthing as a hobby—for anybody."

"I know," I said. "So why did you go along with this idea of Kane's? Because I just don't believe that you felt incapable of getting the truth out of a bunch of egomaniacal, pretentious Hollywood types without the help of a tactful amateur." I sat up, and I felt the reluctance with which he let me go.

"You know why," he said. His eyes met mine, and then he looked away. His mouth curled in something that might have been self-mockery. "One thing about you, when you make your mind up, it stays made."

The fact that I wanted what he seemed to be saying to be true was not a good sign. I said doubtfully, "You can't mean you wanted to work with me."

"I don't know if I'd put it quite like that," he admitted. "Although you do have a knack for setting things in motion. But, yeah, I wanted a reason to see you—to talk to you. To see if we could salvage a friendship. And I know a mystery to you is like catnip to a cat."

I said slowly, "But you didn't come up with the idea?"

"No."

"It was Paul Kane's idea."

He said softly, "Did I ever tell you that you talk too much?" And he leaned forward, his mouth covering mine in an expert and persuasive kiss. Warm lips and the funny little click of teeth as the kiss deepened into unpredictable hunger, and his tongue was insinuating its dark and secret way into my mouth, me opening to it, wanting it—my hand gripping his upper arm, fingers digging in, returning that kiss with single-minded hunger.

Strangely, my mind filled with the memory of our first real kiss—the first time Jake had really kissed a man.

Deep and slow, searching... His hand cradling the back of my head, drawing me closer, tasting me. Me tasting him back, breathing in gentle unison, filling each other's lungs with our quiet exhalations.

Except I hadn't been the first man he kissed. How could I have been? He'd been with Paul Kane for two years before he ever met me, right? And this was all...what? Besides serving to keep me distracted? And that kiss had only meant so much to me because I had kidded myself it meant so much to Jake—that he had trusted me with something precious. But the only precious things were my memories—and they were precious for the wrong reason.

I made myself let go, pushed him away, and got up from the sofa—none too gracefully.

"I don't even know who you are," I told him. "And I have trouble believing you were yearning for my company when you've spent the last five years fucking Paul Kane. Or, vice versa. We won't even bring your wife into it."

He stared at me with narrowed, tawny eyes. "I did what?"

"You and Paul Kane. He said you've been lovers for five years."

"*Lovers?*" He said the word like it was repellent.

There didn't seem to be much doubt about the genuineness of that response. Not that his distaste for the concept was exactly the stuff that dreams are made of, but I did feel a spark of relief that it hadn't *all* been lies or my imagination.

But then his face changed, and I saw I had once again been trying to convince myself of something when any fool could see what was true.

Jake stood up too—and he was watching me like I was the dangerous and incalculable one. "I've known Paul for five years," he said. "That's true. And I did keep seeing him for some of the time you and I were together."

"I must have blinked," I said. "I don't remember us ever being *together.*"

"Don't laugh about it," he said very quietly.

The expression on his face dried my derision. There was a time in my life I'd have given a couple of years to see that look on Jake's face.

He said, still quiet, still steady, "I have feelings for Paul, but you could not remotely describe the thing between me and Paul as love. Not the way someone like you uses the word."

Horrifyingly, I felt that burn in the back of my eyes. "And what way would that be?" I asked.

He said simply, "The same way as me."

I turned away. No way—no fucking way—was I ever shedding another tear over him. I walked to the window and stared down at the street below, distantly noting that it was emptied, that it was getting late, that streetlamps were coming on.

Jake walked up behind me. He didn't touch me but I could feel him all down the length of my body, feel his heat, his…urgency.

"I would give almost anything to get back what we had," he said. "And you know why."

Not really. Although we both certainly knew what the *almost anything* was that he wouldn't give up. But I closed my eyes, not resisting when his arms slipped around me.

CHAPTER TWENTY-TWO

We left the lights on, a seasoned brightness that allowed a few unthreatening shadows. It was strange and familiar. Sweet and bitter. Frightening—and, yes, reassuring. Because we knew each other, once past the talk, when we were down to the language of hands and mouths, we knew each other. Had always known each other. Our bodies fit together just right, and we rocked together gently at first, easy and slow, taking and giving comfort.

Jake groaned, rolled onto his back, taking me with him, settling me down the length of his own long, broad body—the press of my arousal caught between our tightly joined bodies as he thrust powerfully into me. It felt so good—hot and shivery and frantic. We twisted and writhed, circular pressings of belly on belly. He was all fierce muscle and sinew and bone. I put my hands on either side of his shoulders, raised myself on my palms, thrusting back, then pushing him deeper inside my body. His hands closed on my hips, urging me on.

So good.

So...*good*...

Jake came first, crying out, grabbing me tight, hips jerking against me, face buried in my chest. There was wetness on his cheeks. Beneath his lashes. Tears? The idea brought a grim smile to my own face. More likely perspiration. And I came a moment later, spurts of sticky moisture spilling between us, wetting our already damp bodies. I collapsed on top of him and his breath whooshed out unsteadily against my ear.

Little bright lights flashed behind my eyes and once again I had that sensation of flying...like I was floating through the air in a pirate galleon, sailing dizzily through the stars and clouds and swooping over the sparkling seas like the Peter Pan ride at Disneyland—flying away to Never Never Land.

And I probably never should have—I could hear the too-hard thump of my heart in my ears—too big for my chest—but it was done now and no regrets.

I smiled hazily into Jake's tiger eyes. He kissed me, a soft kiss, sweet as melting sugar, slid his arms around me, rolling me onto my side, spooning me, tender and all encompassing.

Second star to the right and straight on till morning…

* * * * *

We drowsed and woke and moved together again, but it was lazy and gentle, and the tightness in my chest, the flutter in my throat was emotion, nothing more. Something dangerously close to happiness, but…not. Because even quiescent and content, I knew this was the lull before the storm. But it was nice to pretend that it was old times, that Jake did not have a wife and another life to go home to in another hour or so. That it all might still work out between us. Nice to lie here and kiss and pet and explore each other as though we didn't know the contours of each other's body, the stroke of thumbs and fingers and flat of hand on satin-smooth skin.

The hand that had been leisurely rubbing my flank slowed. He said almost angrily, "Christ, you're thin. What's the matter with you, Adrien?"

I batted my lashes, playing Bacall to his Bogie. "Nothing you can't fix."

He gave a little snort of unwilling laugh, his exploring hand arrowing down to the swell of my ass. He pinched me, and I jumped, and then he smoothed away the hurt.

"Bastard," I said.

"Yeah," he said.

We rested there for a moment, and he was smoothing his hand over my ass. "Still beautiful, though," he murmured. "The most beautiful guy I've ever known."

I chuckled without much humor. Not more beautiful than Paul Kane—unless we were talking inner beauty. I was pretty sure I was more beautiful on the inside that Paul Kane. I hoped so anyway.

I turned my head on the pillow and he was watching me curiously. I said, "My heart's worse. I have to have surgery."

Jake's face stilled. "When?" he asked. His voice came out thick and unwilling.

I shook my head. "I haven't talked to the surgeon yet. It would be soon, I guess."

He had sucked in a sharp breath when I said I hadn't talked to the surgeon. He let it out carefully and said, "What the hell are you doing?"

I smiled, thinking how odd it was that he was the only person in the world I could say this to. "I'm scared."

He was staring at me. "No way. I've never known anyone with more guts than you."

"We're just not afraid of the same things," I told him.

His face tightened and he stared at the window. At the night beyond this room.

I brushed my knuckles against the rough velvet of his jaw. "Everybody takes chances, Jake. You take chances. You're taking a hell of a chance right now."

He didn't speak.

I stared up at the ceiling. Neither of us said anything for some time.

Then he bent over me and kissed my forehead, his mouth drifting down to the bridge of my nose...my mouth—lingering—my chin...the hollow beneath my ear...the pulse at the base of my throat...my breastbone. My heart beat quietly and steady beneath his touch. He kissed me. His lips were soft as rose petals, his breath warm on my skin. "Don't take a chance with this, Adrien," he whispered.

I didn't answer, stroking his head, feeling the short silk of his hair beneath my fingers. After a time my stillness must have communicated itself to him. He drew back, studying me.

"What?"

"You must know," I said finally. "Even if you weren't sure before, you must know now."

"I don't want to talk about that. This is what matters right now. You and me."

"You and I are together right now because of Paul Kane."

"No."

"Come on, Jake. How the hell are we supposed to ignore murder? He's manipulated us every step of the way."

He shook his head. "You're wrong." His eyes glinted. "About all of it."

"Nothing else makes sense. How would anyone else have got the poison in that glass? Having me hand the glass to Porter is exactly his sense of humor—so was bringing me in to ask a bunch of questions that any cop could have asked."

"Where would he get the digitoxin?" And I could tell by the ready question that he had been mulling this over—of course he had. He had an instinct for this kind of thing. The hunter's instinct.

I shrugged. "I don't know, but I know it's a lot more important to prove how the poison was introduced to Porter's glass than where the poison came from. The digitoxin could have been acquired a lot of different ways, but realistically only two people could have poisoned Porter's drink. Me and Paul. It wasn't me."

"It wasn't Paul."

I didn't say anything.

Jake said in a goaded voice, "And Paul's supposed to have killed Jones because of this autobiography Jones was writing. Is that it?"

"I'm almost positive it has to do with Langley Hawthorne's death."

"That is total, wild speculation on your part."

"Jake. Who else had a motive to get rid of Porter? The man was dying."

"If Jones knew a murder had been committed, why would he have covered it up all these years?"

"I don't know. Maybe he didn't know what it was that he knew. I mean, maybe he didn't realize there was something incriminating in what he remembered about the night Hawthorne died."

"You're *guessing,* for chrissake!"

"Yes, I am, but nothing else makes any sense. You either don't see it or…"

"Or what?" he asked evenly.

"You see it but you can't arrest him without outing yourself. And as far as you're concerned, that's as good as committing suicide."

He made an impatient sound.

I said, "You can't even afford to antagonize him because he's got you over a barrel. And he knows it—and gets off on it. It's just the kind of game he likes. He reminds me of my old friend Rob in that respect. Except he's got a cruel streak Rob never had."

Jake ignored the digression. "Are you suggesting Paul's blackmailing me?"

I met his eyes—he was very angry but I felt strangely unmoved by his anger. "I don't think he'd be clumsy enough to put anything into words, but you both know where you stand. He knows what you're willing to sacrifice—"

"You think I would let him get away with murder to keep him from outing me?"

"But you don't think he committed murder," I pointed out. "You won't even consider the possibility, right? So that solves that problem."

He rolled up and swung his legs over the side of the bed. "That's a great opinion of me you have. No wonder you wouldn't see me for two years."

I opened my mouth to refute this, but indirectly, he was right.

I said, "The real problem for you is what happens next. If he gets away with this, if January dies or can't remember what happened, and Paul gets away with murder—and you let him—basically you're handing him carte blanche over you. And who knows what favor he'll ask next. Maybe he'll ask you to get rid of me."

"Funny," he said thickly.

Not really.

"Even if I'm totally wrong about him killing Porter—even if that's completely unfair—you're in a dangerous position with him. I saw that—I think you did too—last Sunday when he staged that little tableau with the three of us. He likes yanking your chain."

"Bullshit." But he still wouldn't face me.

"He's arrogant and he's cruel." Of course, maybe that was the attraction. What did I know?

For a time neither of us spoke. At last Jake looked over his shoulder at me. "What's your suggestion?"

I sat up. "Come out. Remove his leverage over you."

"Come out?" His face tightened. "You have no idea what you're talking about."

"If you take away his leverage—"

He didn't let me finish. "Do you have any idea what it's like out there for a gay cop?"

Oh man, they were playing our song.

"Doesn't it depend on the cop?"

He was off the bed and across the room, dragging his clothes on. "Jesus, you're naive. It's hard enough to do this job without becoming an outcast with your fellow officers. Did you see that asshole Alonzo in action out there today? And he doesn't even know anything. He just *suspects.*"

"Okay, I'm naive," I said. "But I kind of thought that if you gave in to blackmail you became an accessory after the fact. Or an accomplice or something. You're not just contemplating compromising an investigation—you're contemplating letting a murderer go free."

"Paul is not a killer!"

Was my jealousy of Paul and Jake blinding me to reality? Warping my view of events? Was *I* the one who was just seeing what he wanted to see?

"You sure as hell know that he's a blackmailer."

He didn't respond.

Well, hell. We all put up with a little emotional blackmail now and then, right?

It was sort of funny that Jake, who ordinarily saw the world in black and white—in every possible sense—would suddenly develop night blindness on this. I understood his fear—I did—but I was disappointed all the same. And disgusted.

Swiftly buttoning his shirt—well in flight mode now—he jerked out, "It's not just the job. It's my family."

"There I can't help you." I thought of all the little compromises I had made through the years, the roster of eligible ladies I'd escorted to various functions for the sake of appearances—for the sake of my mother. But I had never tried to deny who I was—wouldn't have the strength or energy for the kind of deception he'd lived his entire life.

"My dad. My brothers. I'm *married,* for chrissake."

"Oh yeah," I said dryly. "I keep forgetting."

He stopped. "Okay," he said, meeting my look, "but what the hell did I go through these two years for, if I'm just going to flush it all down the toilet? If anybody ought to understand, you should."

I was still trying to work that out when he left.

CHAPTER TWENTY-THREE

"You're not drinking?" Paul inquired.

"Not at the moment," I said.

A private smile tugged the corner of his sensual mouth.

We were sitting at Café Del Rey at a table looking out over the marina. Yachts bobbed gently in the midnight blue water. A few forlorn stars blinked in the midnight blue sky. A young woman with a midwestern accent approached our table and asked for Paul's autograph. He signed the little brochure for Starline Tours she was carrying. "You see," he told her. "There *are* movie stars everywhere you look in California."

She laughed delightedly, and they chatted a few minutes more. He was infallibly gracious.

"I admit I was a little surprised to get your phone call," Paul said, turning back to me without missing a beat. "Not that it isn't always a pleasure." His eyes seemed bright with that inner mirth. I wondered yet again what Jake saw in him. I still thought he was beautiful, but it was such a strange, hazardous beauty. A little on the exotic side for Jake, I would have thought. But maybe I wanted to think that.

I hadn't heard from Jake since Friday evening when he'd fled my place like a creature of the night with a whole village of torch-wielding fanatics on his tail. I hadn't heard anything from anyone. No one had tried to arrest me or even interrogate me. It was Saturday evening now.

The last time I'd phoned the hospital was that afternoon. Al January's condition was reported critical but stable.

"Were you surprised?" I asked. "I can't imagine a lot surprises you."

"You," he said—and it was straight out of one of his films. "*You* were a surprise."

I sputtered into my water, and his fawn-colored eyebrows drew together. "I'm sorry?"

"No, *I'm* sorry," I said, although I clearly wasn't. "Actually, what I was sort of wondering was what you wanted me to do next."

The fawn-colored eyebrows drew together. "What I…?"

"Well, the case isn't over. What should my next move be?"

"Your next…?" He let that trail, adding thoughtfully, "I suppose the case *isn't* over. Interesting." He suddenly chuckled. "Well, I shall have to consult the stars." He winked. "The other stars. Did you know I had gypsy blood?"

"I did not know that."

"On my maternal grandmother's side." He held out his hand, palm up. "I'll read your fortune."

"Another time."

"Come on." He was amused by my reluctance.

"Shouldn't I cross your palm with silver?"

He shrugged. "We're friends. No charge." He took my hand in his, gently turning it heel up.

"Here's your lifeline." He traced a line with his thumbnail halfway down my palm and stopped. "Oh dear." He quirked his eyebrows and gave me a wry, commiserating look.

I tried to jerk my hand away, but he laughed.

"I'm teasing you, dear boy. You have a perfectly ordinary lifeline. Your loveline, on the other hand—" He shook his head, his eyes full of wicked amusement, and let my hand go.

I reached for my glass, the condensation chill on my palm—washing away the feel of his fingers, washing away whatever fate he pretended to see in the lines of my hand. I swallowed ice water, set the glass down.

"You know Nina's been released? They can't seem to figure out how she got the poison into Porter's glass."

"Yes, I'd heard," he said indifferently. He lifted his cocktail—something called an Admiral's Tea. He did like those sweet, flavored drinks. "I suppose it will be Ally next."

"You suppose what will be Ally?"

His eyes locked on mine. "I suppose the police are looking at her closely as a possible suspect."

"Oh!" I chuckled. "I thought you meant…well, people around you *have* been dropping at an alarming rate."

He stared at me.

I said gravely, "You know about the attack on Al January, of course."

"Of course." He continued to stare at me. "A tragedy."

"Hopefully not," I said. "Hopefully he'll pull through."

He licked his lips.

I smiled confidingly, "Granted, your original interest in this investigation was the same as mine. Mostly. We neither of us wanted to be suspects in a murder investigation—"

"And to that end, you succeeded beautifully," Paul assured me. "Neither of us are suspects any longer."

"Aren't we?" I arched my brows, mirroring his own elegant surprise. "But suppose the police don't arrest Ally? Suppose they look elsewhere? There's only you, me, and Valarie left. Al getting clobbered pretty much puts him out of the running."

"The attack on Al might not have anything to do with Porter's death. He told me once they have a great deal of crime in that neighborhood."

"Jake may successfully be redirecting that investigation, but I don't think there's much doubt that the attack on Al was connected to Porter's death."

He sipped his drink and said nothing.

"Jake's influence will only stretch so far," I said. "Someone is going to be arrested and eventually tried for Porter's murder. The LAPD take a very dim view of homicide—even among the rich and famous."

He gave me another of those long, bright looks.

"You're absolutely right," he said. "This isn't going to go away on its own. In fact…yes, this is rather perfect timing. I'm having a small get-together on the *Pirate's Gambit* tomorrow. Just a few friends from the party. Why don't you join us? You'll be able to do what you do so well. Snoop."

"Is that what I do so well?" I mocked. "I was sure Jake would give me higher marks for…well…other things."

His eyes locked on mine, and they were glacial blue. Then he smiled. "Tens all across the board, I assure you. I'm planning to seduce you myself."

"I'm planning to let you," I said. "But maybe tomorrow we can chat some more about getting this movie made from *Murder Will Out.*"

He said slowly, "You know, Adrien, that might not be so easy now. Porter was our financial backer and Al was writing the script…"

"Oh, I can write the script," I assured him blithely. "And I'm sure you'll come up with the money from somewhere." I raised my brows at the expression that fleeted across his face. "No?"

He smiled—and I blinked at the radiance of shining eyes and all those teeth.

"Oh, yes," Paul said. "I'll come up with whatever is necessary."

* * * * *

When I got back to Cloak and Dagger, I found the cat dying outside the side entrance.

I nearly stepped on him—it was dark and I was preoccupied with my own thoughts. Having arranged your own murder is not a comfortable feeling.

There was a feeble meow, and I saw the pale glimmer of his form right before I put down my boot.

I knelt and I could see in the wan security lights that its skinny frame was streaked with dark, its narrow flanks moving quickly up and down. It looked flat—like a cartoon cat after it's been run over.

I whispered, "What happened to you?"

Not that I was expecting an answer, but it gave another of those pained meows.

"You've got to be kidding me. Didn't I *tell* you?" I informed it. I rose, went inside, and ran upstairs. The timing could hardly be worse if the damned cat had planned it. I grabbed a towel from the cupboard, hurried back downstairs, and stopped behind the counter long enough to look up the address of the nearest emergency animal clinic.

There was a place on Colorado Boulevard that was supposed to be open from six in the evening to eight in the morning. I rang them; they were still in business and accepting customers. I thanked them and went outside to see whether the customer was still alive.

He was still breathing, which is always a good sign.

As gently as I could I picked him up, placed him on the towel, wrapped it around him, and put him in my car. I drove to the emergency clinic, the cat purring on the seat beside me.

"What's his name?" the young man at the front desk asked as my towel and cat were whisked to a back room.

"Uh…John Tomkins," I said.

"That's different," the receptionist said, writing it down.

"He was a pirate," I said. "I mean Tomkins. I don't know about the cat. Would you have any idea how long this might take?" I needed to call Jake before it got too late.

He shook his head, his expression politely sympathetic.

I sat down to wait, picking up a battered copy of *Cat Fancy*. Just the *name*… I was not—had never considered myself—a cat person. And I didn't plan on starting now. Yet here I was, watching the clock and reading an article on nutrition for young cats.

After about ten minutes, the vet came out. "It looks like a dog got hold of him."

I couldn't imagine where Tomkins found a dog to tangle with. "Is he… uh?"

He waited.

I gestured, which I guess was supposed to signify animation—or maybe what the hell was I supposed to do next.

"He's alive," the vet supplied—and I was astonished at the relief I felt. Mostly, I told myself, because I didn't want to hear what Natalie would have to say about the damned cat getting itself mauled.

The relief vanished in the wake of a nine hundred dollar bill for testing, X-rays, stitches, etc. The only good news was they were going to keep Mr. Tomkins overnight, so I wouldn't be tempted to strangle him.

I took my bloodstained towel and my bloodstained credit card back, bade them good night, and returned to Cloak and Dagger.

By then it was eleven thirty, which was way too late to be calling married friends at home, but I didn't have a choice.

I rang Jake up on his cell. It went straight to message.

I said, "Can you call me when you get this? It's…" A matter of life and death? I didn't want to be melodramatic, but it sort of was. And no sort of about it. "Urgent," I compromised.

I clicked off, went back downstairs to check the security gate and all the locks—jeering at my own unease. Why did I keep putting myself in these situations when they obviously scared the hell out of me?

As I returned upstairs the phone was ringing. I picked it up.

"What's wrong?" Jake asked. His voice was sleep-roughened, but he sounded alert.

"You're not going to like it."

"Tell me something I don't know."

"I've set myself up to go sailing with Paul Kane tomorrow. I'm pretty sure he's going to try to kill me."

There was a very long silence, and then Jake said, "He'll have to take a number."

"Look…" And then I couldn't think of what to say to him. I knew what I was asking—I'd known before I ever tried to set myself up as bait—and I knew it might just be too much to ask of anyone.

"You couldn't leave it alone, could you?" Jake said, and I could hear the fury, although he kept his voice low.

"Murder? No, I couldn't leave murder alone, Jake. And I'll tell you what: I don't know how safe it would have been for me to leave it alone, because your boyfriend has settled on murder as the quickest and easiest way to resolve his problems."

"Bullshit."

"Fine. If I'm wrong, I'll just go for a pleasant sail and come back slightly drunk and slightly sunburned. But if I'm right—"

"You think he's going to attack you in broad daylight? There's a crew on board, for chrissake."

"There was a house full of people at that party in Laurel Canyon. I don't think crowds intimidate him. And I don't think he's planning to shoot me. He's going to need it to look like another accident. He'll try to shove me overboard or push me down the stairs or something. Put something in my drink maybe."

Jake said in choked tones, "That's nearly as brilliant as your plan. What *is* your plan, by the way? Besides getting yourself killed?"

"It's the simplest thing in the world. You come too. And you stop him from killing me. And then you arrest him."

"On attempted murder? How the fuck does—" He abruptly lowered his voice. "Even if we get him on trying to take you out, how does that prove anything else?"

"Why would he try and kill me if it wasn't because—"

"I can think of a dozen reasons," Jake said.

"That hurts," I said after a pause. He was joking—sort of—and that had to be a good sign, right? I added, "Anyway, I plan to wear a wire. I bought some gear at Radio Shack—" I stopped. He was laughing.

It was one of those wheezy, near-silent Muttley laughs. When he managed to speak, he sounded slightly hysterical. "You're insane," he said. "How did I never notice this about you before?"

"I'm not insane. This is very simple, very straightforward. Provided he doesn't kill me, it's foolproof."

He said very quietly, "Listen to me carefully. Don't get on that fucking boat tomorrow. I am not going to back you up on this. I am not going to let you manipulate me any more than I am going to let Paul manipulate me. You think I don't know what you're trying to do here?"

Now that threw me. Talk about convoluted reasoning. "You think this is all about getting you to come out?"

"That's what you're asking of me. And you know—you *know*—I *cannot* do this. I *will not* do this."

"You'd rather that he got away with murder?"

"He didn't kill anyone!"

In the wake of that cry we were both silent.

I heard him cover the receiver and speak to someone, then he came back on the line. "I've got to go. We'll talk about this later. Don't—I repeat—*don't* get on that boat. Don't do anything stupid. Do you understand?"

And I did. And I believed him.

"Jake..." I wasn't sure how to say it. "I've set something in motion now that I can't stop. He's going to come after me, and it would be better if I could control the circumstances of it."

"You think a boat in the middle of the ocean is controlling the circumstances?" His voice shook both with anger and something not so easily identified. "You just told me your heart is worse, and you pull this stunt. Are you out of your goddamned *mind*?"

By now it was clearly a rhetorical question.

I said, trying for patience, "This way I know where and I know when he's going to try. I won't have that opportunity again. I won't have any control over it after tomorrow. And if I don't show up, he'll know that I know—"

He cut me off, and I almost didn't recognize that low voice as Jake's. "I know you're trying to do the right thing. I know this is partly my fault for letting Paul bring you into this. But I am asking you..." His voice dropped still lower. "I am begging you, Adrien. Don't do this. There isn't much I wouldn't do for you—but don't ask this. I can't help you this time."

"There isn't anyone else I can ask, Jake."

The click of the receiver was soft but definite against my ear.

CHAPTER TWENTY-FOUR

"Are you really intending not to drink or eat anything this entire trip?" Paul asked lazily.

It was just after nine o'clock in the morning, and we were sailing in open water. The fog was beginning to burn off. It was going to be a beautiful day, but it was still chilly, the ocean smelling of salt and rain and things down deep below the restless green water. Paul and I sat on the open deck of the *Pirate's Gambit*. A brunch tray sat on the table between us and it was enticingly arranged with plates. There was something called baked omelet roll—ham and cheese and mushroom—fresh fruit, muffins. I was more tempted by the pot of hot coffee.

"I'll probably have something later," I said.

He smiled. "I would have to be pretty stupid to poison you aboard my own boat."

"Yes, you would," I agreed, and he chuckled.

We were by ourselves. When I had arrived at the marina Paul told me he had canceled the party.

"You obviously have something on your mind," he'd said. "This way we can chat undisturbed."

But we hadn't chatted. We'd put out to sea—and I was not particularly reassured by the sight of Paul's captain taking the helm. I'd taken what precautions I could. I'd talked to Guy—and if possible he was even more disgusted and furious with me than Jake. I'd written down my detailed theory on why I believed Porter Jones had been killed—heck, I'd written down everything I could think of that might help prosecute Kane if things went wrong—and I'd mailed it off that morning to Mr. Gracen to be opened in the event of my death.

Of course just receiving a communication like that was liable to result in dear old Mr. Gracen popping off this earthly plane, but that couldn't be helped. If I wasn't successful, if Kane was stupid enough—desperate enough—to still try to kill me after I explained these precautions, then at least I wanted to know that LAPD would have sufficient cause to reinvestigate Langley Hawthorne's death. Not to mention my own.

But I was hoping it wouldn't come to that.

And certainly Paul had been easy and charming for the half hour or so we had been together, chatting pleasantly while he enjoyed his breakfast.

But at last he finished eating, brushed the muffin crumbs fastidiously from his hands, shoved the plate aside, and studied me with those bright, amused eyes.

"You know, I really don't believe that you're out here planning to try a spot of blackmail." His mouth twitched. "I have to say, though, you'd be quite good at acting. That bit in the café last night was brilliant." He mimicked, "*I can write my own screenplay!*" He shook his head. "What a turn for comedy you have."

I have to admit I wasn't quite expecting this relaxed frankness. I said cautiously, "If you don't think I'm trying to blackmail you, what do you think I'm doing out here?"

"Besides having seen one too many detective films? I think you want answers. I think you're insatiably curious. And I don't mind answering your questions. You won't be able to prove any of this. There is no proof. Now. And I like you, Adrien." He arched an elegant eyebrow. "I like you a good deal."

Oddly enough, that was the first scary thing he'd said. It was like finding a cobra curled up in the foot of your sleeping bag. I said, and it wasn't even a guess, "You destroyed Porter's memoirs."

"Yes." He said it promptly, like awarding points in a contest.

"But why kill him?"

"Because he knew why I destroyed the manuscript. That was a mistake on my part. I should have stalled longer."

"He knew you murdered Langley Hawthorne?"

"Just for the record"—he raised his eyebrows as though making sure we both understood this—"I didn't murder Langley. His death was an accident."

"Then why wasn't it reported as an accident?"

"Because we had been arguing, and I suppose I felt guilty. I knew I would be a suspect in his death. He had told me about his will—he was very set on Nina and me marrying. And of course neither Nina nor I had any desire to marry each other. We were young but we weren't stupid."

"So what happened?"

"We were rowing. Langley turned away and fell against the rail gate. He went into the water and he must have hit his head. By the time I got him out, he was dead. Porter came along as I was trying to resuscitate him. I was panicking—badly. It was Porter's idea to…put Langley back and recreate discovering the body. Then he provided me with an alibi for the time that Langley died."

He made it sound so simple, so plausible, it took me a moment to think of the obvious. "Why would he?"

Paul said irritably, "Because he was my friend and because he knew exactly how it would look to the authorities. He did it to help me—nothing could be done for poor old Langley. And it *was* an accident."

"And in these memoirs Porter described what had really happened?"

Paul nodded. "He wanted to set the record straight. Clear his conscience. Not that his conscience wasn't perfectly clear."

Maybe it was, maybe it wasn't. But I still thought the story of Langley Hawthorne falling through the rail gate and conveniently drowning before help could reach him was a little pat. How the hell long had it taken Kane to drag him out of the drink? Why hadn't he yelled immediately for help? Maybe Porter had begun to think Kane's story was a little pat too as he reexamined his past.

Paul said, "Porter couldn't—or refused to—understand that there was as much danger to me now as there ever had been should the truth of Langley's death come out."

I said, "So you poisoned the friend who had helped you when you needed it most—"

He interrupted, "Porter was dying. He had pancreatic cancer. Have you any idea of how painful a death that is?"

"*Oh,*" I said. "You did him a favor."

His eyes narrowed. "I did, actually. It was fast, relatively painless, and he had no idea it was coming. Not a bad death, frankly. Believe me, losing Porter as a friend and a business partner gained me nothing."

I could pretty well see the way this was going to play out. I just hoped Kane was speaking loudly enough for the tiny recording device taped beneath my shirt.

"So why drag me into it?" I asked. "Optioning my book—what was that about?"

He lowered his lashes and then suddenly opened his eyes and smiled at me. The beauty of that smile took me slightly aback. "I've always been curious about you: my unknown rival for Jake's affections." His smile was self-mocking. "But then he married and broke it off with you."

"But not with you?"

"Not for long." He watched my face. "After he married we grew closer. Much closer. One night he had a few drinks and he started talking about you. And I decided I would arrange a meeting with you by optioning your book. I do like the book, by the way, but I don't think it's particularly commercial."

The unkindest cut of all.

"So why the hell drag me into the murder investigation?"

"Didn't you enjoy it?"

I opened my mouth—and then closed it. He chuckled. "Of course you did. And I enjoyed watching you enormously—and watching Jake."

If I'd had any doubts before, that cleared them up. He could talk about accidents and panic and doing favors for old friends, but he was cold and calculating and cruel. A sociopath. No conscience, no remorse, no empathy. In fact, I thought it possible he might have drowned his own kid. I wondered if anyone had looked into that accident.

"And Al January?" I asked carefully.

"You can take responsibility for that one," he said. "Why the fuck you had to drag Al into it, I don't know. What did you think would happen when you started asking him about Langley and Porter's memoirs?"

He had me there. I hated thinking I might be responsible for Al's death. If I managed to get out of this alive, I was going to make damned sure I never got involved in another criminal investigation. I said, "So Al called you and told you I'd been asking questions about Porter's memoirs, which started him thinking—because the truth is, only one person could have easily poisoned Porter's drink, and that was you. That was a nice little touch having me hand Porter his glass."

"I thought so. I didn't plan it, though," he admitted. "It just happened. I thought you might drink it, actually. It stood beside your own glass for what felt like an eternity." He smiled. "But you were quite careful not to touch it, and I really couldn't afford to let Porter go on bitching about his lost masterpiece."

A chill went down my spine as I realized how close I'd been to dying that afternoon. It could have all ended right there—and Jake would have shown up and found me as his homicide case.

And Kane would have got away with it.

I said, "So you raced over to Al's, bashed him over the head—"

"Not hard enough apparently, but even if Al makes it, after traumatic head injuries the victim often doesn't remember the hours previous—he might lose the whole day."

"Well, we can only hope!" I said, unable to stop myself from copying his cheerful tone. His smile was odd.

"Any other questions? You're probably *dying* to know where I came up with the digitoxin, aren't you?"

"Nina left an old bottle around after the last party she catered for you?"

He looked pained. "Of course not. What a strange idea. No. A former lover left them. As a matter of fact, I hung onto those pills for nearly three years. I had a feeling they would come in useful at some point." And the look in his eyes sent another of those slithers down my spine. "Any other questions?" he asked gently.

"Just wondering where we go from here."

He drawled, "You mean you've no notion at all? Not a one? You're not wearing a wire under that sweater of yours? You're not carrying your grandmother's Webley tucked in the back band of your jeans?"

I didn't move a muscle.

High above us a gull swooped low, squawking. I thought that I would never forget the bright heat of the sun and the smell of salt in the air: so that was the sound and taste of betrayal.

Kane laughed. "Of course you are. Well, that narrows our options a bit. If you were willing to play…but you're not. You're bound and determined to see me brought to justice, aren't you? Regardless of the cost to…anyone. You included."

I don't think I could have moved if my life had depended on it—and it probably did.

"So let me tell you what *I* have planned for *you*. I'm going to settle one final curiosity, the curiosity of what the attraction is between men like myself and Jake. You've always wondered about that, haven't you?"

He raised his brows at my lack of response.

"Of course you are. Anyone would be. It's another mystery, and you love mysteries. You've wondered about this secret world, the world of exquisite pain shared between men who trust each other—trust each other beyond what any outsider can possibly understand. Men who share…everything."

"Including consecutive prison terms," I said.

He smiled and, oddly enough, that suave smile reminded me of the illustration of Foxy Loxy in my childhood copy of *Chicken Little*—and why the hell that thought was in my mind, beat me. I was probably in shock.

"Don't be so bloody ungrateful, Adrien. I'm offering to initiate you into such pleasures of the flesh as you can't possibly imagine. There's a room below deck." He glanced down at the teak deck beneath our feet. "A very special room for very special guests. We're going to spend hours down there, you and I, and I'll show you everything—teach you everything—or as much as your heart can stand."

"I'll pass," I said. It seemed like an unfortunate turn of phrase, once the words were out.

"You won't want to pass. Not when you learn who's waiting below deck for us."

I swallowed. "How many guesses do I get?" I asked. I was amazed at how calm I sounded. I didn't feel calm. I felt dead. I probably was dead—

even if I got off this boat alive. Something had died inside me the instant I realized Jake had told Paul Kane what I planned.

I thought of that painstaking letter I had written to my lawyer—doing my very best to keep Jake out of it as much as possible. That was actually kind of funny.

"Well, it was going to be a surprise," Paul said regretfully, "but I can see you're going to need a little persuasion."

He rose in a graceful, lithe movement and rang the ship's brass bell hanging behind us. There was motion above. I looked up. The captain appeared on the bridge above us. Paul waved him the all clear and he ducked away again.

I wondered idly how much Paul Kane paid him; how desperately did he want to keep his job?

There were footsteps behind us; the deck boards vibrated. I turned and watched Jake step onto the deck.

"I'm afraid the joke's on you," Paul said, watching my face. "Jake rang me last night after you called him with your wild scheme to entrap me. You do have a taste for the dramatic, Adrien. I give you credit."

I made myself look at Jake. His face was…harrowed. He glanced at me briefly, looked away. All his focus was on Paul Kane.

"I do have to say though, that although this kind of thing works in books or on the small screen, I'd never in reality have confided a single word to you if Jake and I hadn't worked it all out ahead of time. As it was, I admit, I did enjoy playing out this little scene. You were being *so* clever. It was sheer delight to watch you in action."

I said, "*My* scheme is unrealistic? You honest to God think you're going to sail into port with yet another victim of a fatal accide—"

"Shut up, Adrien," Jake said flatly.

"Fuck. You," I said.

"You're missing the point," Paul informed me. "We're going to fuck *you*. We're going to take turns over and over and over again. I think with a bit of cooperation from you we'll be able to present the authorities with a perfectly legitimate case of heart failure. It's going to be rather a scandal, but I like scandal." He winked at Jake. "And I have a friend on the force who'll help me navigate the legal waters, as it were."

My heart was pounding so hard I wasn't sure I could get the words out. I said, "If that's your plan, then you're a total lunatic. Did you ever hear of DNA? Did you ever hear of—" I broke off as Jake pulled out a pair of handcuffs. I stood up, rocking the battened-down table. "Jake," I said, and to my horror my voice shook. Not with fear—with grief, with disbelief. I was beyond anger. I think I felt something close to horror for what he had come to.

He never looked at me. He said in a dead, mechanical voice, "Paul Kane, you're under arrest for kidnapping, attempted rape, attempted murder—"

Paul laughed.

And something seemed to snap inside Jake. He said, "For Christ's sake, Paul! Did you honest to God think I would be okay with murder? I'm a *cop*. I've spent my entire adult life upholding and enforcing the law."

Into the silence that followed those anguished words, another gull swooped down, jeering.

"You're not serious." Paul looked...stricken. "James..."

"I didn't want to believe it," Jake said. "I couldn't believe it. But it's true. Every goddamn thing he accused you of is true."

"My darling—" Paul reached out a shaking hand. It was stagy and melo-dramatic—and yet I thought it was absolutely genuine. He had been struck to the heart. Or whatever he used for that organ.

Jake grabbed him, turned him, preparing to snap the cuffs on. "Don't say anything else, Paul. Wait for your lawyer."

Paul ducked away, sliding out from under Jake's hand. He turned and he was holding something small and metallic, glinting in the fitful sunshine. A gun. A little gun. A derringer.

He pointed it straight at me and fired.

And at the same moment Jake stepped in front of me. I felt him rock back as the bullet hit him, a tiny metal projectile burrowing into warm living flesh, heard the shot—like a clap of doom—and something kicked me hard in the left shoulder. My left arm went heavy and numb.

Fast. So fast. Bang and it was done.

Paul Kane stood there gaping at us, and the astonished horror on his face would have been comical in other circumstances. "James," he whispered.

"Jake!" I said. There was blood soaking his right shoulder. *"Jake?"*

He lunged forward, knocked the gun out of Paul's motionless hand. It skittered across the deck and fell with a clatter down the stairway. Jake shoved Paul back into one of the deck chairs. Paul collapsed without a struggle. Jake bent over him, handcuffed him. Stood up. There was blood staining the front of his shirt, spilling sluggishly from a singed hole in the fabric.

The deck tilted beneath my feet and I reached out for the gunwale. Jake reached for me.

"Take it easy," he said. He sounded very calm.

"He shot you," I said.

"It's okay. He shot you too."

I looked down and was amazed to see that there was blood welling out of a hole high in my shoulder, soaking the tweed of my sweater.

"Wow. He did."

Jake looked behind me, and I tried to look too. "Hold still." He felt gently over my back. "The bullet's still in your shoulder."

"Really?" The whole thing seemed unbelievable. I stared at his face, trying to understand. He seemed very calm. Grim, but calm. And calm was probably good, although I wouldn't have minded a little emotion from him about then.

He eased me down into one of the deck chairs, pulled his shirt off, wincing, and shoved it against my shoulder. Taking my right hand, he pressed it against the wadded cloth. "Keep the pressure on this."

There was blood on his hand—his own blood streaming from his wound. I couldn't tear my gaze away from his gory shoulder. "You're losing a lot of blood. How badly are you hit?" I asked faintly.

"I'll live." His eyes met mine. They looked black in his white face. "I'm okay."

I nodded.

"I told you this was a bad idea," he said.

"Please don't let your final words to me be *I told you so*," I said.

He said shortly, "You're not dying."

He left us then, going up to the bridge. He seemed to be gone a long time.

Paul said bitterly, "You did this. You brought this on."

I closed my eyes. I could hear the gulls and the waves and the rumble of the ship's engines. After a bit I thought we might be turning about.

I heard footsteps on the deck, but I was very tired.

Even without opening my eyes I felt the shadow fall across me. The scent of Le Male aftershave mingled with the smell of ocean and diesel. Warm fingers pressed against my throat.

"Listen to me. There's still a chance for us," Paul said urgently. "It's not too late to salvage this. If we stay together. Keep our heads."

No response.

"*Think* about what you're doing," Paul tried again. "This is a gift from the gods. To *both* of us."

"Shut up, Paul." Fingers brushed my cheek. I opened my eyes.

"Let him *die*," Paul said.

"He's not dying." Jake's gaze held mine. "You're not dying."

I shook my head, although I was afraid that I was.

"Help is on the way. All you have to do is hold on."

I said, "You wouldn't happen to have a warm rock, would you?"

"What?"

"If you wrap a warm rock in a piece of cloth and then press it against the wound, it's supposed to ease the pain."

"The only rocks I brought are the ones in my head. I should never have agreed to this."

"You didn't." I closed my eyes. My shoulder was starting to hurt. A lot. I tried to lessen the pain by analyzing it. Nausea, crushing pressure in my chest...maybe better to skip the analysis.

He crouched down beside me, gathering me against him. His hand covered mine, holding the bunched and wet shirt against my shoulder much harder than I was. I let him deal with it, rested my face in the curve of his neck. Breathed in the scent of sun warmed bare skin tinged with the sweat and gunpowder and the metallic tang of blood. His heart was pounding fast on an adrenaline rush.

I don't have to be strong, I thought. *I don't have to put a brave face on it. I'm dying. I'm entitled to a little weakness.* I hid my face in his chest, smothering the cry of pain that squeezed out of me.

It could be worse. I could be dying alone.

Or he could have hesitated. Even for a moment.

The pain eased up a little.

I could hear Paul still speaking urgently, still pleading for his own life in that stagy ultraplummy voice.

"Why can't you see what this means for both of us? This is a second chance—our last chance. This is fate. Why are you fighting what is clearly meant to happen?"

Jake said over my head, "Paul, one more word and I'll blow your fucking head off."

Paul gave a strangled laugh. "My God, you are a *fool.*"

Jake shifted, and I hoped he wasn't going to carry out his threat.

He tipped my head up.

"Okay?"

"Great." I'd decided to live long enough to see Paul Kane put away.

His laugh sounded funny.

The pain was getting worse again.

He bent his head and said against my ear. "Hold on."

I nodded and closed my eyes.

CHAPTER TWENTY-FIVE

Fuzzy...ceiling. There was something wrong with the light. Sort of eerie...

I unstuck my eyes. Blinked. I was in a hospital room and Lisa was sitting by my bedside.

She looked small and exhausted. She wore no makeup; her face was pinched and suddenly old.

My shoulder hurt. It seemed stiff, bulky with bandages. It hurt to move. My chest hurt. A lot. I became aware of tubes and wires and a soft mechanical swish and hiss. I was hooked up to a bank of machines with blinking lights— and I didn't seem to be breathing entirely on my own. Scary. Very.

I must have moved or made some sound because Lisa's gaze jerked to my face. She looked more scared than I felt.

"Adrien..." Her voice—little more than a whisper—shook badly.

I winked at her.

Her eyes filled with tears.

That pretty much felt like a full day's work. I closed my eyes.

* * * * *

The next time I opened my eyes there were cards and balloons. I recognized Emma's artwork on a large folded sheet of colored construction paper. I believe I recognized that jubilant stick figure with the spiky black hair, although it had been a long time since I'd felt like jumping for joy.

Everything still hurt but I was breathing on my own again. My mother sat beside my bed reading *Vogue*. She looked immaculately groomed as always, so all was apparently right with the universe once more.

I croaked, "I think Em should have her own horse."

Lisa looked up from the magazine. For a moment she seemed to struggle for composure, then she said, "Oh, Adrien! She'll just fall and break her neck." She wiped hastily at her eyes.

* * * * *

Bizarre though it may be, it took a while to remember that I'd been shot aboard Paul Kane's ship. I was so doped up that for a day or two I thought I was still in the hospital with pneumonia. My chest hurt like hell and breathing was painful in the extreme. Everything was an effort. Even thinking was exhausting. So I didn't. I hid out in a cocoon of painkillers and refused to let myself worry about how ill I was and what the future might be.

Apparently there was going to be a future, and that was the good news, but I'd suffered a couple of cardiac events. Everyone seemed a little vague about these "events." I gathered they were not cause for celebration—despite the cards and flowers and balloons that accumulated.

"Did someone pick my cat up?" I asked…well, I asked everyone.

"Darling, Natalie is taking care of that cre—your cat," Lisa assured me for the fourth time.

I closed my eyes…but I knew there was something I needed to remember. Something I had forgotten…

And that's when it came flooding back: my own personal voyage of the damned which had ended with Paul Kane shooting me. And I remembered Jake.

I opened my eyes again.

"Is Jake all right?"

Lisa's delicate jaw gritted against all the things she wanted to say. "As far as I know," she got out every bit as tersely as Jake.

"Can you find out?"

She huffed out a little sigh. "Yes. I'll find out." I watched her steel herself to ask, "Do you want to see him?"

It was a reasonable question but I felt a kind of internal flinch. I did want to see him. And I didn't. Not like this, looking like Emma's science project with wires and tubes and IVs and catheter and an oxygen tube up my nose.

Watching me, my mother said with that uncanny perspicuity, "Maybe when you're feeling a little more in control."

I assented, closed my eyes, drifted.

* * * * *

"What the hell *is* tapioca," I asked, studying it on my spoon. "Is it some kind of rice?"

"I don't know," Guy said, "but if you don't intend to spend the rest of your life on an IV, you'd better eat it."

"You usually don't get threatened for not eating dessert. Not that I really count this as dessert."

I took a spoonful.

Watching me, Guy said, "I've got some good news. That screenwriter, Al January, recovered consciousness. They think he's going to be all right."

The relief was like a weight off my chest. "Thank God. Thanks for telling me."

He opened his mouth but restrained himself from saying the things he had been longing to say since I regained consciousness—the things he had already said when I told him my plan to trap Paul Kane. He said instead, "When you're up to it, the police want to take your statement."

"Oh."

His smile was a little grim in response to my tone. "Lisa has been holding them at bay with the threat of court orders and injunctions and curses upon them and all their progeny."

"Does she think…what does she think?"

Guy raised one shoulder.

"What did Jake tell them?"

"I have no idea."

"But he *is* all right?"

Guy's black brows arched. "Is *Jake* okay? I never thought to ask." After a few beats he added reluctantly, "He was released from the hospital yesterday."

My heart did a little lurch, and it felt different. Weird. Although I couldn't have explained how; I wasn't even sure I didn't imagine it.

"Did he—what happened to Paul Kane?" In some of my drug-induced dreams Jake had shot Paul Kane to keep him quiet. In some of my dreams he had shot me.

"You mean the psychotic murdering bastard who shot you? He's currently in jail busy planning a lawsuit against the LAPD and claiming that you framed him."

I laughed, and Guy said, "I'm glad you think it's funny."

"Not funny, no." I grimaced. "I had all these grandiose ideas of bringing Kane to justice. Now I'm just grateful to be alive. Grateful Jake didn't..."

I didn't want to remember those long minutes when I had believed Jake had set me up, that his fear and paranoia had led him finally to murder.

"You mean because you were asking him to betray his lover?"

I shook my head. "I was asking him—insisting—that he come out. There was no way he could arrest Paul Kane that his relationship with him wouldn't be revealed. It didn't matter if I got Kane to confess or not. However Paul Kane went down, Jake was going down with him." I closed my eyes. "In a manner of speaking."

I was aware of Guy removing my meal tray, sitting back down next to the bed.

"How's Peter?" I asked after a bit, still resting my eyes.

"Young."

I smiled faintly. "He'll get over it." After a while I said, "Maybe I wasn't fair to Jake."

And Guy said dryly, "No?"

"I couldn't understand why..."

"He wanted to be friends if you weren't going to be together?"

That was the thing about Guy. He always seemed to know what I was thinking before I did myself. I nodded and moved my hand on the coverlet. His hand slipped under mine, fingers closing warmly about my own.

He said, "Maybe you weren't unfair. Maybe it was just harder for you to let go of your dreams." His thumb lightly traced the pulse beat in my wrist. He added softly, "Harder than it was for me."

I turned my hand over and laced my fingers in his.

The next time I opened my eyes Jake was there.

I smiled.

It must have been a lousy effort. He said, "I won't stay long."

He looked pale and tired. There were shadows like blue smudges under his eyes. His arm was in a sling. Yeah, I got life support and Jake got a dashing sling; that was pretty much par for the course.

"Not like I have to be somewhere," I told him.

"I think your mother is summoning security even as we speak."

They must have been taking their time because I had the impression he'd been sitting there awhile. Or maybe I'd dreamed someone was stroking my hair.

"How's the shoulder?" I asked.

"I won't be throwing out the first pitch at Dodger Stadium anytime soon."

"I thought you were going to sing the national anthem."

In fairness, it wasn't very funny. Clearing his throat, he said gruffly, "I wanted to...thank you."

My mouth tasted horrible, gluey. Like tapioca. I swallowed. "Sure." I offered him another flicker of a smile. "Likewise."

Not just for keeping Paul Kane from feeding me to the fishes. They'd told me my heart had stopped before we'd made it back to harbor. Jake had kept me alive long enough for the paramedics to do their bit—no doubt with Paul Kane reminding him of all the reasons he shouldn't bother.

He looked like he hadn't slept in days. The lines around his eyes had lines of their own.

"You okay, Jake?"

His smile seemed an effort. "I think that's my line. How are you?" His gaze moved to my bandaged chest and shoulder.

I started to shrug, remembered in time. "Pretty much stoned." I considered his question reluctantly. "I don't know. Everyone seems to tiptoe around that."

And it was freaking the hell out of me, although I didn't want to admit it. I turned my head, studied the monitors and medical equipment. I thought ungrateful thoughts.

"Hey." I looked back. Jake's gaze held mine. "You won't be leaping buildings in a single bound, but from what I gather you're expected to return to your pre-op condition."

His eyes never wavered and I relaxed a little. "Would that be before or after I was shot?"

He twitched a grin. "And being the thrifty guy you are, I know you'll appreciate the two for one special you got. Bullet hole patching and valve repair all for one low, low price."

I said, echoing him on a long-ago November day, "You shop around, you compare prices, you get the surgery right for you."

His smile didn't reach his eyes. I said belatedly, "I'm sorry about Paul. I know you cared about him."

He nodded.

"What's going to happen to him?"

"He's going to be tried for homicide and attempted murder." His eyes met mine and he said carefully, "They're not going to press the attempted rape and kidnapping unless you insist."

I appreciated that. Not a very dignified fate, the one Paul had planned for me.

"They've got plenty to nail him with," Jake said. "Even without the Langley Hawthorne homicide. They found the digitoxin onboard the *Pirate's Gambit.*"

Kane wasn't stupid, so it had to be arrogance. But then you expected arrogance from pirate kings. And ruthlessness. And daring. Kane had them all—along with a slew of other gifts from the gods.

Jake's smile faded. He took a deep breath and said, "I'm quitting the force."

That was a shocker. I didn't know what to say.

"It's the right thing to do," he said. "The honorable thing. The lies, the double life—you were right. I've compromised my position."

Still seeing things in black and white, regardless. No one judged himself more harshly than Jake. "What will you do?"

"I'm thinking of going into the private sector."

Again, I couldn't think of anything to say. I couldn't picture him as... what? Security guard in a bank? Armored car driver?

Into my silence he smiled sheepishly and said, "I was thinking of opening my own agency."

"You mean like a PI?"

"Yeah."

"Wow. Sam Spade."

It seemed unreal. I couldn't picture Jake as anything but a cop.

He was watching my expression. "I don't want to hit you with too much at once."

"There's more?" I smiled but I felt cold inside—like the hypothermic chill that hits you after major surgery.

"I don't know if this matters to you or not. I mean, matters in the same way it would have once."

I swallowed hard. Closed my eyes to keep him from seeing what I was feeling.

He said steadily, "I've asked Kate for a divorce. I told her the truth. All of it. Everything."

I gritted my jaw hard.

"I talked to my family. I told them that I'm homosexual."

My jaw ached but I still couldn't prevent moisture from leaking out beneath my lashes and itching its way down my face.

He said, "Does that still mean anything to you?"

I opened my eyes. Saw his expression through the prism of unshed tears, and took a deep, unsteady breath.

"Yeah," I said. "It means something."

ABOUT THE AUTHOR

Bestselling author of over sixty titles of classic Male/Male fiction featuring twisty mystery, kickass adventure, and unapologetic man-on-man romance, JOSH LANYON has been called "arguably the single most influential voice in m/m romance today."

Today Josh's work has been translated into nine languages. The FBI thriller Fair Game was the first Male/Male title to be published by Harlequin Mondadori, the largest romance publisher in Italy. The Adrien English series was awarded the All Time Favorite Couple by the Goodreads M/M Romance Group. Josh is an Eppie Award winner, a four-time Lambda Literary Award finalist (twice for Gay Mystery), and the first ever recipient of the Goodreads All Time Favorite M/M Author award.

Josh is married and lives in Southern California.

For more information, go to **www.joshlanyon.com**, or **f**ollow Josh on **Twitter**, **Facebook**, and **Goodreads**.

ALSO BY THE AUTHOR

NOVELS

The ADRIEN ENGLISH Series
Fatal Shadows

A Dangerous Thing

The Hell You Say

Death of a Pirate King

The Dark Tide

Stranger Things Have Happened

The HOLMES & MORIARITY Series
Somebody Killed His Editor

All She Wrote

The Boy with the Painful Tattoo

The ALL'S FAIR Series
Fair Game

Fair Play

The SHOT IN THE DARK Series
This Rough Magic

The ART OF MURDER Series
The Mermaid Murders

OTHER NOVELS

The Ghost Wore Yellow Socks

Mexican Heat (with Laura Baumbach)

Strange Fortune

Come Unto These Yellow Sands

Stranger on the Shore

Winter Kill

Jefferson Blythe, Esquire

Murder in Pastel

NOVELLAS

The DANGEROUS GROUND Series
Dangerous Ground

Old Poison

Blood Heat

Dead Run

Kick Start

The I SPY Series
I Spy Something Bloody

I Spy Something Wicked

I Spy Something Christmas

The IN A DARK WOOD Series
In a Dark Wood

The Parting Glass

The DARK HORSE Series
The Dark Horse

The White Knight

The DOYLE & SPAIN Series
Snowball in Hell

The HAUNTED HEART Series
Haunted Heart: Winter

The XOXO FILES Series
Mummy Dearest

OTHER NOVELLAS

Cards on the Table

The Dark Farewell

The Darkling Thrush

The Dickens with Love

Don't Look Back

A Ghost of a Chance

Lovers and Other Strangers

Out of the Blue

A Vintage Affair

Lone Star (in Men Under the Mistletoe)

Green Glass Beads (in Irregulars)

Blood Red Butterfly

Everything I Know

Baby, It's Cold (in Comfort and Joy)

A Case of Christmas

SHORT STORIES

A Limited Engagement

The French Have a Word for It

In Sunshine or In Shadow

Until We Meet Once More

Icecapade (in His for the Holidays)

Perfect Day

Heart Trouble

In Plain Sight

Wedding Favors

Wizard's Moon

Fade to Black

PETIT MORTS
(Sweet Spot Collection)

Other People's Weddings

Slings and Arrows

Sort of Stranger Than Fiction

Critic's Choice

Just Desserts

HOLIDAY CODAS

Merry Christmas, Darling

COLLECTIONS

The Adrien English Mysteries

Collected Novellas, Vol. 1

Collected Novellas, Vol. 2

Armed & Dangerous

In From the Cold: The I Spy Stories

In Sunshine or In Shadow

Sweet Spot

Male/Male Mystery & Suspence Box Set

NON-FICTION

Man, Oh Man! Writing Quality M/M Fiction

COLORING BOOK

Love is a Many-Colored Thing (with Johanna Ollila)

AN EXCERPT FROM

DARK TIDE

THE ADRIEN ENGLISH MYSTERIES
BOOK FIVE

JOSH LANYON

CHAPTER ONE

It began, as a lot of things do, in bed.

Or to be precise, on the living-room sofa where I was uncomfortably dozing.

Somewhere in the distance of a very weird dream about me and a certain ex-LAPD police lieutenant came a faint, persistent scratching. The scratching worked itself into my dream, and I deduced with the vague logic of the unconscious that the cat was sharpening his claws on the antique half-moon table in the hall. Again.

Except…that boneless ball of heat on my abdomen was the cat. And he was sound asleep…

I opened my eyes. It was dark, and it took me a second or two to place myself. Moonlight outlined the pirate bookends on the bookshelf. From where I lay, I could barely make out the motion of the draperies in the warm July breeze in the front room of the flat above Cloak and Dagger Books.

I was home.

There had been a time when I'd thought I would never see home again. But here I was. I had a furry heating pad on my belly, a crick in my neck, and — apparently — a midnight visitor.

My first thought was that Lisa had called Guy, my ex, to look in on me. That furtive scraping wasn't the sound of a key; it was more like someone trying to…well, pick the lock.

I rolled off the sofa, dislodging the sleeping cat, and staggered to my feet, fighting the dizziness that had dogged me since my heart surgery three weeks earlier. I'd been staying at my mother's home in the Chatsworth Hills, but I'd checked myself out of the lunatic asylum that afternoon.

If Guy had dropped by, he'd have turned on the light in the shop below. There was no band of light beneath the door. No, what there was, was the occasional flash of illumination as though someone was trying to balance a flashlight.

I wasn't dreaming. Someone was trying to break in.

I felt my way across the darkened room to the entrance hall. My heart was already beating way too hard and too fast, and I felt a spark of anxiety — the anxiety that was getting to be familiar since my surgery. Was my healing heart up to this kind of strain? Even as I was calculating whether I could get to the Webley in the bedroom closet and load it before the intruder got the door open or whether my best bet was to lock myself in the bedroom and phone the cops, the decision was made for me.

The lock mechanism turned over, the door handle rotated, and the door silently inched out of the frame.

I reacted instinctively, grabbing the rush-bottomed chair in the hall and throwing it with all my strength. *"Get the fuck out of here,"* I yelled over the racket of the chair clattering into the door and hitting the floor.

And — surprisingly — the intruder did get the fuck out.

Not a dream. Not a misreading of the situation. Someone had tried to break into my living quarters.

I heard the heavy *thud* of footsteps pounding down the staircase back to the shop, heard something crash below, heard another crash, and, as I tottered to the wall light switch, the slam of a distant door.

What door? Not the side entrance of the shop below, because I knew that particular bang very well, and certainly not the front door behind the security gate. No, it had to have been from the adjacent structure. The bookstore took up one half of a subdivided building that had originally, back in the thirties, housed a small hotel. The other half of the building had gone through a variety of commercial incarnations, none of which had survived more than a year or so, until I'd finally been in a position to buy it myself the previous spring. It was currently in the expensive and noisy process of being renovated, the two halves divided by a wall of thick plastic.

Not thick enough, clearly.

The contractor had assured me the perimeter doors were guarded by "construction locks," and that it was as safe as it had ever been. Obviously he wasn't familiar with my history, let alone the history of the building.

I leaned back against the wall, trying to catch my breath and listening. Somewhere down the street I heard an engine roaring into life. Not necessarily my intruder's getaway car fleeing the scene. This was a nonresidential part of Pasadena, and at night it was very quiet and surprisingly isolated.

There was a time when I'd have intrepidly, Mr. Boy Detective, gone downstairs to see what the damage was. That was four murder investigations, one shooting, and one heart surgery ago. Instead I got the gun from the bedroom closet, loaded it, returned to the front room, where the windows offered a better vantage point, and picked up the phone. The streetlamps cast leopard spots on the empty sidewalk, accentuated the deep shadows between the old buildings. Nothing moved. I recalled a line by Raymond Chandler: "The streets were dark with something more than night."

Reaction hit me, and I slid down the wall and dialed 911.

I was having trouble catching my breath as I waited — and waited — for the 911 operator, and I hoped to hell I wasn't having a heart attack. My heart had been damaged by rheumatic fever when I was sixteen. A recent bout of pneumonia had worsened my condition, and I'd been in line for surgery even before getting shot three weeks earlier. Everything was under control now, and according to my cardiologist, I was making terrific progress. The ironic thing about the surgery and the news that I was evidently going to make old bones after all was that I felt mortal in a way that I hadn't for the last nineteen years.

Tomkins pussyfooted up to delicately head-butt me.

"Hi," I said.

He blinked his wide, almond-shaped, green-gold eyes at me and *meowed*. He had a surprisingly quiet meow. Not as annoying as most cats. Not that I was an expert — nor did I plan on becoming one. I was only loaning a fellow bachelor my pad. The cat — kitten, really — was also convalescing. *He'd* been mauled by a dog three weeks ago. His bounce back was better than mine.

I stroked him absently as he wriggled around and tried to bite my fingers. I guessed there was truth to the wisdom about petting a cat to lower your blood pressure, because I could feel my heart rate slowing, calming — which was pretty good, considering how pissed off I was getting at being kept on hold in the middle of an emergency.

Granted, it wasn't much of an emergency at this point. My intruder was surely long gone.

I chewed my lip, listened once more to the message advising me to stay on the line and help would soon be with me. Assuming I'd still be alive to take that call.

I hung up and dialed another number. A number I had memorized long ago. A number that seemingly would require acid wash to remove from the memory cells of my brain.

As the phone rang on the other end, I glanced across at the clock on the bookshelf. Three oh three in the morning. Well, here was a test of true friendship.

"Riordan," Jake managed in a voice like raked gravel.

"Uh…hey."

"Hey." I could feel him making the effort to push through the fog of sleep. He rasped, "How are you?"

Pretty civil given the fact that I hadn't spoken to him for nearly two weeks and was choosing three in the morning to reopen the lines of communication.

I found myself instinctively straining to hear the silence behind him; was someone there with him? I couldn't hear over the rustle of bed linens.

"I'm okay. Something happened just now. I think someone tried to break in."

"You *think*?" And he was completely alert. I could hear the covers tossed back, the squeak of bedsprings.

"Someone did try to break in. He took off, but —"

"You're back at the bookstore?"

"Yeah. I got home late this afternoon."

"You're there alone?"

Thank God he didn't say it like everyone else had. *Alone?* As though it was out of the question. As though I was far too ill and helpless to be left to my own devices. Jake simply looked at it from a security perspective.

"Yeah."

"Did the security alarm go off?"

"No."

"Did you call it in?"

"I called 911. They put me on hold."

"At three o'clock in the morning?" He was definitely on his feet and moving, dressing, it sounded like, and I felt a wave of guilty relief. Regardless of how complicated our relationship was — and it was pretty complicated — there was no one I knew who was better at dealing with this kind of thing. Whatever this kind of thing was.

Which I guessed said more than I realized right there.

Jake's voice was crisp. "Hang up and call 911 again. Stay on the line with them. I'll be there in ten minutes."

I said gruffly, "Thanks, Jake."

Just like that. I had called, and he was coming to the rescue. Unexpectedly, a wave of emotion — reaction — hit me. One of the weird aftereffects of my surgery. I struggled with it as he said, "I'm on my way," and disconnected.

* * * * *

I went down to meet him, taking the stairs slowly, taking my time. From above, I had a bird's-eye view of the book floor. The register looked undisturbed. I could see where the bargain-book table had been toppled. Otherwise everything looked pretty much as normal: same comfortable leather club chairs, same wooden fake fireplace, same tall matching walnut bookshelves — strictly mystery and crime novels — same secretive smiles on the pale faces of the Kabuki masks on the back wall.

I unlocked the door, pushed open the security gate, which he'd knelt to examine. "You didn't have to come down. I'd have gone around to the s —" Jake broke off. He rose and said oddly, "Déjà vu."

I didn't get it for a second, and then I did. Echoes of the first time we'd met; although *met* was kind of a polite word for turning up as a suspect in someone's murder investigation.

Uncombed, unshaven, I was even dressed the same: jeans and bare feet. I'd thrown a leather jacket on partly because, despite the warmth of a July night, I felt chilled, and partly because I didn't want to treat him to the vision of the seam down the middle of my chest from open heart surgery. Not that Jake hadn't seen it when he visited me in the hospital, but it looked different out of context. The bullet hole in my shoulder was ugly enough; the incision from the base of my collarbone down through my breastbone was shocking. I found it shocking, anyway.

I said awkwardly, "Thanks again for coming."

He nodded.

We stared at each other. These last weeks couldn't have been easy on Jake, and not because I'd asked him to give me a little time, a little space before we tried to figure out where we stood. He'd resigned from LAPD, come out to his family, and asked his wife for a divorce. But he looked unchanged. Reassuringly unchanged. I think I'd feared… Well, I'm not sure. That he'd be harrowed by regret. For his entire adult life he'd fought to defend that closet he inhabited. Been willing to sacrifice almost everything to protect it. I couldn't help thinking he'd take to being out like a fish to desert sand.

He looked okay. No, be honest. He looked a lot better than okay. He looked…fine. *Fine*, as in get the Chiffons over here to sing a chorus. Big, blond, ruggedly handsome in a trial-by-fire way. He was very lean, all hard muscle and powerful bone. Maybe there was more silver at his temples, but there was a calm in his tawny eyes that I'd never seen before.

Under that light, steady gaze I felt unnervingly self-conscious. It was weird to think that for the first time in all the time I'd known him there was nothing to keep us from being together except the question of whether we both really wanted it.

He asked matter-of-factly, "Why didn't the alarm go off?"

"It wasn't set."

A quick drawing of his dark brows. He opened his mouth. I beat him to it. "We haven't been setting it while the construction has been going on next door."

"Tell me you're kidding."

He already knew I wasn't. "The city threatened to fine me because we had too many false alarms. The construction crew usually arrives before we open the shop, and they kept triggering it. So I thought...until the construction was completed..."

His silence said it all — good thing, because I was pretty sure if Jake got started, we'd be there all night.

"I think he must have come in from the side." I turned to lead the way.

He followed me across the front of the tall aisles. I pointed out where an endcap had been knocked over. "Only the emergency lights were on, and he crashed into that." I nodded to the fallen bargain table, the landslide of spilled books. "And there."

We reached the clear plastic wall dividing Cloak and Dagger Books from the gutted other half of the building. Staring from one side to the other was like peering through murky water. I could barely make out the ladders and scaffolds like the ribs of a mythological beast. I directed Jake's attention to the long five-foot slit through the plastic near the wall.

"Good call." He sounded grim.

I'd have happily been wrong. "The contractor told me that that side of the building would be secured with special locks. Construction locks."

He was already shaking his head. "Look at this." He stooped, pushing through the slit in the plastic, and I followed him into the darkened other side of the building. It smelled chilly and weird on that side. A mixture of fresh plaster, new wood, and dust. We picked our way through the hurdles of drop cloths and wooden horses and cement mixers to the door on the far wall. It swung open at his touch.

"Great," I said bitterly.

"Yep." He showed me the core in the center of the exterior handle. I discerned that it was painted, though I couldn't make out a color. "See that?"

I nodded.

"It's a construction core. That's a temporary lock used by contractors on construction sites. They're all combinated the same, or mostly the same, which means that if someone gets hold of a key, they've got a key to pretty much every construction core in the city."

"Better and better."

He shut the door and relocked it. "As security goes, this is one step above leaving the door standing wide open."

I swallowed. Nodded.

"Whoever broke in may have been watching the place and knew no one's been here at night."

I said, "It doesn't look like they touched the register."

"It might have been kids prowling around." Jake didn't sound convinced, and I knew why.

"Trying to break into my flat was —"

"Pretty aggressive," he agreed. "Again, I think that probably gets back to the mistaken belief that no one was home. No one has been staying here at night for three weeks, right? So it was a reasonable assumption."

I absorbed that. "This might not have been the first time he was prowling around in here."

"True."

"I don't know that Natalie would notice the slice in the plastic wall. Hell, if Warren were hanging around, I don't know if she'd notice the Tasmanian Devil bursting through."

Sort of unfair to Natalie; Jake snorted, grimly amused.

All at once I was exhausted. Mentally and physically and emotionally drained dry. I didn't seem to have much in the way of physical resources these days, and this break-in felt like way more than I could begin to handle.

Jake opened his mouth but stopped. Through the dirty glass of the bay window, we watched a squad car pull up, lights flashing, though there was no siren.

Better late than never, I guessed.

After a second or two, Jake looked at me. "You okay? You're shaking."

"Adrenaline."

"And heart surgery." He glanced back at the black-and-white. Drew a deep breath. "Why don't you head upstairs? I'll take care of this."

There it was again. That weird new emotionalism. The smallest things seemed to choke me up. Like this. Jake offering to talk to the cops for me.

Except this wasn't a small thing. Jake, who had hid his sexuality from his brother officers for nearly twenty years, who had been unwilling for people to even know we were friends, who had very nearly succumbed to blackmail and more to keep that secret, was offering to stand here in my place and talk to these cops — and let them think whatever they chose to about us and our relationship.

I'm not sure what was stranger: the fact that he was making the offer or that I was ready to start crying over it.

"I can handle it."

He met my gaze. "I know you can. I'd like to do this for you."

Hell. He did it again. It had to be that I was overtired and still shaken by the break-in. I worked to keep my face and voice from showing anything I was feeling, managing a brusque nod.

The cops, a man and a woman in uniform, were getting out of their car. I turned and started back through ladders and wooden horses and scaffolds.

* * * * *

I was sitting on the sofa sleeping with the cat on my lap when Jake let himself into the flat.

I must have been snoring, because the *snick* of the door shutting seemed to come like a clap of thunder in the wake of a windstorm. The cat sprang from my lap. I sat up, closed my mouth, wiped my eyes, and when I blearily opened them, Jake stood over me, looking unfairly alert for four in the morning.

"Was that a cat I saw running into your bedroom?"

I cleared my throat. "Was it?"

"It looked like it." He sat down on the sofa next to me — all that size and heat and energy — and every muscle in my body immediately clenched tight in nervous reaction. I didn't feel ready for...whatever this was liable to be.

I said lightly, "Maybe the building is haunted."

"Could be." He seemed to study my face with unusual attention. "Your burglary complaint is filed. Tomorrow, first thing, you need to tell that contractor to get real locks on those doors. In fact, I'd advise you to change all the locks on both sides of the building."

I nodded wearily. "I've been trying to think what he was after."

"The usual things."

"Then why not break into the cash register?"

"An empty cash register? Why?"

Good point. No point robbing the till after the day's bank drop had been made. I must be more tired than I thought. Maybe Jake had the same idea, because he said, "I thought you'd be in bed by now."

"I'm on my way. But I wanted to thank you…"

He said gravely, "Don't mention it. I'm glad you called me. I've been wondering how you're doing."

My gaze fell. "I'm all right." There was so much to say, and yet I couldn't seem to think of anything. "I'm getting there. The worst part is being tired all the time."

"Yeah." I could feel him watching me — seeing right through me.

"Jake…"

When I didn't continue, he said, "I know. I know it's a lot to ask. Probably too much, although I won't pretend I'm not hoping."

Forgiveness. That's what he was talking about. Forgiveness for any number of things, I guessed. I was talking about something completely different.

I shook my head. "It isn't — I don't know how to explain this. It's not you, though. It's me."

He waited with that new calm, that new certainty in his eyes. He was expecting me to drop the ax on him. I could see that. He had been expecting it since the last time we spoke in the hospital and I'd asked him to give me time. That's what he had expected when he answered my cry for help tonight — what he still expected — but he had come anyway.

Was that love or guilt or civic responsibility? He was the best friend I'd ever had — and the worst.

I said, "This isn't going to make sense to you, because it doesn't make sense to me. I know how lucky I am. I do. I know I'm getting a second chance, and even though I feel like utter *shit*, I know I'm getting well and I'm going to be okay. Better than okay. That's what my doctors keep telling me, and I know that I should be really happy and really relieved. But…I-I can't seem to feel anything right now."

Nothing from Jake. Not that I blamed him. What was he supposed to make of that speech?

I concluded lamely, "I don't know what's wrong with me."

"You feel what you feel. You're allowed."

It was getting harder to go on. I felt I had to be honest with him. "I was happy enough with Guy, but I don't want Guy. I don't want...anyone. Right now."

There was another pause after he heard me out. He said, "Okay."

It was that easy. I wasn't sure if what I felt was relief or disappointment. I heard myself say, awkwardly, "I felt like I should —"

"Got it." Was there an edge to his tone? He still looked calm. Actually, he looked concerned. He said, "Why don't you go to bed, Adrien? I've seen snowmen with more color in their faces. You need sleep. So do I. In fact, I'm going to spend what's left of the night on your couch."

I said, despite my instant relief, "You don't have to do that."

"I know, Greta. You vant to be alone. But unless your need for space prohibits a friend crashing on the sofa, that's what I'm doing."

I didn't have the energy to argue with him — or myself. I nodded, pushed off the sofa, and headed for the bedroom. "There are blankets in the linen cupboard."

"I remember."

A thought occurred to me. I paused in the doorway, turning back to him. "Jake?"

He was in the process of tugging off a boot. He glanced up. "Yeah?"

"Downstairs. With the cops. Was it okay?"

It seemed to take him a second to understand my concern. He smiled — the first real smile I'd seen from him in a very long time.

"Yes," he said. "It was okay."

Made in the USA
Columbia, SC
22 October 2017